"Black's books combine bold sexuality with terrific worldbuilding. When I'm in the mood for ultra hot romance, this is what I go for." - *Susan Sizemore, author of I Burn For You*

"The series as a whole is an intricate web of full, rich characters living in an outrageous, and sometimes shocking, world. Ms. Black has created a story that is full of lies, deceit, and horrors untold; but underneath she shows the hope, love and passion that these characters are able to find in their bleak and often frightening world. Ms. Black earns the title of Queen of Erotic Science Fiction and I look forward to the next installment." - *rated 5 stars by Amber Taylor of Just Erotic Romance Reviews*

Raw, suspense and action filled, hot enough to burn your fingers. This one will particularly appeal to female fantasies of being sexually dominated. Jaid Black in her finest hour." – *Pandora's Box on the Death Row serial*

Ellora's Cave Publishing, Inc.
1337 Commerce Dr. #13
Stow, OH 44224

ISBN # 1-84360-658-5

Edited by Martha Punches.
Cover art by Darrell King.

Warning: The following material contains strong sexual content meant for mature readers. *Death Row: The Trilogy* has been rated E, erotic, by a minimum of three independent reviewers. We strongly suggest storing this book in a place where young readers not meant to view it are unlikely to happen upon it. That said, enjoy...

DEATH ROW:
THE TRILOGY

THE FUGITIVE – *page 7*
THE HUNTER – *page 85*
THE AVENGER – *page 155*

JAID BLACK

THE FUGITIVE

"If the first woman God ever made was strong enough to turn the world upside down alone, these women together ought to be able to turn it back, and get it right side up again."

— Sojourner Truth

Prologue

My beloved Kerick,

How I grieve for you...for all that you have lost and for all that you will continue to lose as you grow into manhood. Why couldn't life have dealt us a better hand, my son?

But when all is said and done, it still comes down to this: There is no utility in wishing for a different life, nor is there any use in dreaming of a happy ending.

There is only the reality of our existence and the reality of our need to survive.

Tara Riley,
December 24, 2216

Chapter 1

Cell Block 29:
Death Row unit within the Kong Penal Colony.
40 miles outside the Mayan pyramidal ruins of Altun Ha in former Belize, The
United Americas of Earth, December 17, 2249 A.D.

"Prisoner, Riley. Remove your clothing."

Kerick Riley's dark head came up slowly, his cold gray eyes flicking dispassionately over the smirking face of the prison warden. Wiping mud from his eyes, he rose up to his feet from the pen of wet dirt and blood he'd been kicked into, simultaneously noting everything there was to see about the executioner. From the pristine white silk robe the warden wore, to the flash-stick in his hand that could ignite and thereby sizzle a man to death at mere contact, nothing escaped his notice.

For fifteen years, seven months, three weeks, and five days, Kerick had waited with an inhuman patience for the arrival of this moment. He'd never allowed his mental acumen or extreme physical strength to lessen from lack of use over the years, that both would be there to serve him when the hour of reckoning had at last come upon him.

It had worked — it *would* work.

Never once in all of those fifteen plus years had he allowed his thoughts to betray him. He knew when it was safe to think, and he knew as well when it was necessary to create a void in his mind to prohibit a detection scanner from probing what went on in his thoughts.

From a young age he had been taught the necessity of control, his mother having gone so far as to beat the lessons into him. She'd used such harsh tactics not because she had hated her son, but conversely because she had adored him, and more fundamentally, because she had wanted him to live.

The lessons in bodily and mental control passed down from Tara Riley had done more than help Kerick survive in the violent world of twenty-third century Earth; they had also made it possible for him to survive this day. Today. The dwindling hours of remaining daylight prior to his execution.

Kerick's sharp gray eyes continued to study the warden, but betrayed none of his emotions. They simply calculated and assessed with an almost robotic precision, doing the same as they'd always done these past fifteen years. He realized that the sadistic warden had always despised — and envied — his ability to think and behave as though he were a machine, for it made predicting his behavior impossible.

Warden Jallor tapped the flash-stick against his thigh, his eyebrows shooting up mockingly. He believed he'd won, Kerick knew, thought indeed that the prisoner was about to die...

But — no.

For nearly every waking moment of the past fifteen years, Kerick had calculated, assessed, plotted, and planned. He had noted the weaknesses of the 50-story structure surrounding him, had made certain that he'd learned all there was to know of the seemingly impenetrable fortress that was his prison. For the most part, he understood that Warden Jallor was correct — Kong was an impenetrable fortress. But Kerick also understood that there was no such thing as invincible, and he had spent fifteen years learning how to defeat the undefeatable Kong.

Officially entitled Correctional Sector 12, the penal colony of Kong had gotten its nickname from an old black-and-white movie none from Kerick's time had ever seen but all had heard tell of. It was said that in the old movie the god-like ape King Kong could escape from any prison, but not even the Mighty Kong could escape Sector 12. For most prisoners, that statement turned out to be chillingly true, but for Kerick Riley...

"Remove your clothes," Warden Jallor snapped, his patience nearing an end. His icy blue eyes flicked down to the innocuous bulge in the prisoner's pants. "Now."

He wanted to kill him. For year after bitter year, Kerick had comforted himself with thoughts of Jallor's death, with thoughts of avenging himself — and avenging his mother. But for the moment at least, such was not to be. He needed the warden alive. For now.

But when it was over, when all was said and done...

Kerick's stoic gaze never wavered from Jallor's as he slowly, methodically, removed first his prison-issued woolen tunic and finally his woolen pants. Both garments were a dirty, muted brown, filthy and greasy from having been worn for three solid years without a cleaning. In truth, removing the disgusting clothing was practically a relief. It would mean he was naked during the escape, but so be it.

When he was finished, Kerick stood before Warden Jallor in stone-faced silence, his heavily muscled six-foot five-inch frame completely divested of clothing, his brooding eyes that saw everything piercing the warden's.

Jallor's gaze wandered down to Kerick's penis, then back up to his face.

He was a stupid man, Kerick knew. Sadistic but stupid. Removing the prisoner from his chains would prove to be his downfall.

With the sensory chains on, Kerick never would have stood a chance at escaping. The moment he ventured outside the perimeter of the Kong penal colony, the sensors within the chains would have detonated and his skin would have gone up in flames, charring him to ashes within seconds.

But on the day of execution the chains were removed — the only day in a Death Row inmate's life where that was so.

Warden Jallor stepped towards him, careful to keep his distance, his smirk deepening. "Fifteen years ago you swore this day would never come to pass," he said in a mocking tone. "Indeed, how the mighty have fallen."

For the first time in fifteen years, Kerick smiled — a gesture that caused the warden to frown. "Yes," Kerick agreed, his deep rumble of a voice scratchy from a prolonged lack of use, "how the mighty have fallen."

Two guards appeared behind Jallor. The warden made a dismissive motion with his head, indicating it was time to retreat and step aside while the flash-stick was detonated. The warden barely had time to gasp before the flash-stick was snatched from his hand, rendering him completely defenseless from an assault.

"What are you doing?" Jallor snapped at one of the guards, his eyes promising retribution. "Hand the weapon over and take your place at the — "

The warden's words came to a halt when the "guard" holding the flash-stick peeled off his face armor. Jallor gulped as he looked up into the grim ebony face of Elijah Carter, a Death Row inmate who was scheduled to be executed next week.

Kerick walked slowly towards Jallor. His jaw tightened as he came to a stop before him, staring down at the wide-eyed warden. With a growl he picked Jallor up off of the ground by the neck, his grip tightening until the warden's throat began to elicit gurgling sounds.

"Don't kill him," Elijah warned. "Not yet." He glanced over to the secret panel in the execution pen that allowed for a magistrate of justice to escape should situations like this one ever arise. That panel would take them to the outermost perimeter of Kong. From there, Kerick,

Elijah, and Xavier would be on their own in the jungle. "The DNA scanner only responds to living flesh prints, amigo."

"You sure?" Kerick snarled.

"As sure as I can be."

Kerick grunted, but said nothing. He tightened his hold on the warden's neck fractionally, letting Jallor know he'd never allow him to live once they'd gotten from him the palm scan they sought.

"We need the bitch alive," Elijah reminded him.

Nostrils flaring, Kerick turned his head and stared hard at Elijah. Seeing his familiar face, and realizing as he did that Elijah would be executed next week if they were caught, he regained his sanity long enough to let loose of his hold on the sadistic warden.

Jallor gasped when Kerick released his throat. He panted for air as he fell to the ground and turned eyes filled with hatred on the prisoner-turned-executioner.

Kerick smiled slowly, his steel gray eyes locking with the warden's. "Indeed," he murmured, "How the mighty have fallen."

Chapter 2
Altun Ha, former Belize
December 19, 2249 A.D.

"Shit." A beleaguered Nellie Kan ran a hand through her sweat-drenched hair and sighed. She turned to the Spanish-speaking guard of Fathom Systems, Inc. and attempted to converse with him using what little of the language she'd managed to acquire while living and working in the Belizean sector these past two years.

Back when the sector had been its own nation the prominent tongue of the people living here had been English, but that had changed a few decades past when Belize had become federated within the United Americas of Earth colony. "Que le paso al sistema de ventilacción?" she asked in a thick accent. *What has happened to the ventilation system?*

Christ! she grumbled to herself for the thousandth time in two years, was it too much to ask of the mega-conglomerate company to provide air within the Altun Ha biosphere for its scientists and other workers? Apparently it was, for she had put the same question to the same guard at least three times a week for as long as she'd lived and worked within the synthetic black glass dome known officially as Biosphere 77.

She took a deep breath and blew it out. She really needed a vacation.

"Doctor Kan, voy a ver lo que pueda hacer antes de irme esta noche," Juan promised on a grin. *I'll go see what I can do before I leave for the night, Doctor Kan.* Juan was as accustomed to having this conversation as Nellie was. "Te digo buenas noches." *I bid you goodnight.*

Nellie smiled at the aging guard as he turned and walked away, the flash-stick in his hand absently thumping against his armor-encased thigh as he strolled from the sealed chamber whistling to himself. She watched him for a moment or two before turning back to the virtual reality display module she was currently working with, then settled back in her seat to resume her research.

Three more weeks, she thought excitedly, her heartbeat thumping against her chest as her fingers flicked over the keyboard. At the rate she was acquiring data, she would be able to produce a test serum from a randomly sampled control group of sub-humans within three weeks time.

She refused to consider the possibility that Boris Karli, her chief rival at Fathom Systems, might beat her to the punch and develop a serum first. She was aware of the fact that the lying, manipulative son-of-a-defective-droid had been thumbing through her notes on the sly, but she doubted that he had enough ingenuity to do anything with them.

If Boris defied expectations and developed a serum, well then, the more power to him. Nellie's goal was to ease the suffering of sub-humans. Dr. Karli's goal was and had always been fame and notoriety — preferably attained with as little work as possible.

Which was why Nellie doubted he'd figure out even the basics to a serum. He was one of those types of males who thought he knew everything, yet understood very little. The serum, she realized, was up to her.

And when it was done, when she had found the answers she was seeking, she would be careful, of course, to never break her word to the older, infected woman who had given her the dusty, worn-out diary that had proven to be a vital aide...and chillingly accurate.

Nellie would never tell anyone — *anyone* — that the basis of her entire research was derived from the journal of one Dr. Tara Riley. To do so would mean not only academic suicide, but it could also mean...

Well, she wouldn't think on that.

In life, the discredited Dr. Riley had been branded a heretic by her scientific peers. In death, she was still regarded as heretical, though there were those who whispered behind closed doors that perhaps — *perhaps*...

Perhaps Dr. Riley hadn't been as insane as the Hierarchy would lead people to believe she had been.

Her ideas had been...bizarre. And because of the oddity of them, because of the fact they had seemed too fantastical, too completely unbelievable, they had been systematically dismissed as the delusions of a paranoid schizophrenic. That schizophrenia had been cured and done away with decades ago...well, no scientist would have dared to bring *that* reminder up to her accusers in order to defend the outspoken heretic known as Dr. Tara Riley. Not if they had aspirations for waking up alive the next morning. That nobody had seemed to know exactly *who* the doctor's accusers were was proof positive it was a stone best left unturned.

Too hot and sweaty to concentrate on her work, Nellie sighed as her hands fell from the keyboard and she slumped further into the chair. She ran a hand through her dark red hair, absently reminding herself it was time to get a hair shearing. A low-maintenance female scientist, she preferred to keep her hair cropped short so she didn't have to mess with it. That she'd allowed it to grow so long was a sure sign of how immersed she'd been in her research as of late.

When the air in the laboratory grew too heavy and oppressive for her to remain inside, she took a deep breath to keep from passing out, then stood up. Parting the heavy woolen robe she was wearing into a wide vee, Nellie removed the thick article of body décor, allowing it to fall to the ground and cascade in a puddle around her feet. Naked, she padded across the lab chamber toward a storage closet, her goal to find a sheer robe or pantsuit she could don long enough to reach her domicile.

"Oh come on," she muttered to herself as she rummaged through the storage closet. She parted three woolen lab suits that had been slung haphazardly on cheap hangars to see if any sheerer body décors were hanging behind them. "There has to be — "

She stilled, the hair at the nape of her neck stirring. She swallowed nervously, recognizing the sensation she'd just experienced for what it was:

She was being watched. *Someone* was watching her.

Nellie closed her eyes briefly as she steeled herself to remain calm, realizing as she did just who that someone was. She could feel her heart rate betraying her, but she'd undergone enough detection scans in her life to realize when her mental and bodily reactions were being probed for answers and when they weren't. She felt no nausea, no cramping in her mind, so she knew she was safe. For now.

And now she also understood why the ventilation system was no longer working. She had, after all, been through this routine almost as many times as she'd been through the "what's happened to the ventilation system" conversation she frequently had with Juan. Difference was, she hadn't been expecting this tonight, for Henders hadn't come into the lab all day long.

Reminding herself it was best just to play along, she bent over into the closet, pretending obliviousness to her employer's voyeurism as she took her time searching for a sheer lab suit. She knew just how to angle her body into a lean, knew how far apart to keep her ankles, so that Vorice Henders would be given an arousingly close-up view of the folds of flesh between her legs.

Perversely, she felt her body respond to the knowledge it was being watched. She realized, however, that the tightening of her nipples and the saturation between her legs wasn't being caused by Vorice Henders the man — it was being caused by the idea of knowing a man, even a man like Henders, was watching her in this way. A big difference.

Nellie took her time locating a sheer lab coat, giving her voyeuristic boss plenty of time to bring himself to completion while watching her. In a world where men took women at will — and often times against the women's will — she supposed giving Henders jack-off material was a small price to pay for her independence. She was protected within the biosphere, an accomplished scientist allowed to work for pay rather than be bound to a male for free, and that's all that mattered. For now.

Still feigning obliviousness, she turned around and offered the sensory cameras a full view of the front of her nude body. She allowed a confused frown to mar her face as she pretended to glance around, searching out other places where a sheer lab coat might be located.

Just then the ventilation system came on full blast, inducing Nellie to gasp when the chilled air hit her square in the face. Her rosy nipples immediately hardened and elongated, which she realized was what Henders had been hoping would happen. His office was located on the other side of the concourse, but she almost felt as though she could hear him gasping and groaning while he yanked his disgusting self off into oblivion.

She took a deep breath and blew it out. She really needed a vacation.

Nellie debated within herself as to what she should do for as long as she felt she could get away with it without arousing suspicion that she was clued in as to Henders' activities. She could put on her body décor and retreat to her domicile — or she could finish this perverse little show, perhaps earning herself the right to be left alone for a month or more.

She decided on the latter.

Closing her eyes, she ran her hands over her breasts, her full lips parting slightly on a sigh as she began to massage her nipples. She used her thumbs and forefingers to latch onto the bases, gasping as she massaged upward to the tip of her nipples and back. She tried to pretend she was alone in her domicile and doing this for her own pleasure, for Henders was a vile, disgusting man, and it made her skin crawl to think about the fact that he was watching her do something so private and intimate.

It's best this way, Nellie, she reminded herself. *You need to finish that serum and Henders is your only protection from the others.*

Resolved, Nellie continued to massage her nipples as she hoisted herself up onto a nearby table and spread her thighs wide so her employer would get the best show possible. She was careful not to knock over any beakers as she settled atop the table, preparing to masturbate herself into orgasm.

She continued to toy with a plumped up nipple in one hand while her other hand began roaming downwards, over her lightly tanned belly, then lower still through the triangle of dark red curls pointing toward the flesh of her cunt. She could feel his eyes on her, devouring her, more intense than they'd ever watched her before...

Her fingers found the warm, wet flesh of her pussy. She moaned softly as she began running them through the sleek folds, spreading the puffy lips wide open for Henders' voyeuristic pleasure with the hand that had dropped from her breast. "Yes," she murmured, pretending she was alone, "yes."

Nellie gasped at the first touch of fingers to clit, the hedonistic sensations jolting through her not fabricated. She continued to pretend she was alone, then no longer cared if she was or wasn't when the pleasure grew in its intensity and she drew nearer to orgasm. "Oh god," she breathed out as her fingers briskly rubbed her clit in a circular motion. Her nipples jutted out as her head fell back and her eyes closed. "*Yes.*"

Panting heavily, she moaned as she masturbated herself faster, faster, and faster still. Her free hand came up and rubbed over her stiff nipples, then fell once more to her lap. On a groan she stuffed two fingers into her cunt, gasping and moaning as she finger-fucked herself with one hand and masturbated her clit with the other.

Blood rushed to her face to heat it. Blood coursed into her nipples, elongating them to the point of near pain. She could feel his eyes on her, the intensity of his stare more powerful than ever before...

"*Oh god.*" She stifled a loud moan as she broke, contenting herself with a softer one. Gasping, she fucked herself as hard as she could with two fingers as the orgasm ripped through her belly in a tidal wave of sensation.

When it was over, when she'd given Henders his show, she fell onto her back, exhausted. From the angle of the cameras, she knew he couldn't see her face. All he could see was her body laying spread out on the table like a submissive offering, her nipples stabbing up into the air, the flesh of her cunt ripe and swollen from a recent and powerful orgasm. She laid there for a couple of minutes like that, panting until her breathing resumed its normal gait.

Deciding she'd given the perverted Henders more than enough time to jack himself off once or twice, she sat up slowly, then looked around for her woolen lab coat. It was still laying where she'd first dropped it, puddled in a heap on the floor next to her chair at the virtual reality display.

She felt the sensory cameras turn off as she walked over to where her lab coat lay, and she breathed a sigh of relief at realizing that the show was well and truly over for tonight. Her nostrils flared at the injustice of it all as she snatched the woolen robe up off of the ground.

It wasn't right—the horrid price all women had to pay for freedom. And, she thought bitterly, was freedom at such a steep price truly freedom at all?

If the world had been a different place two hundred years ago, if males hadn't been so highly valued over females, then couples wouldn't have rushed off to genetic specialists to make certain the babies they birthed were all males. The result a couple of generations later had equaled disaster, for the planet was now overrun with men, making it so females of all races and nationalities were very rare—and very expensive.

Nellie couldn't recall how many times she'd been verbally slandered in her thirty-two years for petitioning to the Hierarchy for the right to practice a career over being auctioned off for marriage. But she'd never permitted the negativity of others to thwart her from her goals, for she'd always known she was born to be a scientist. Hypothesizing and finding answers came to her as easily as breathing. Researching and experimentation was as natural to her as violence was to sub-humans...

Sub-humans, she reminded herself as she finished donning the woolen lab coat—she was their best hope for help for few other scientists seemed to care if they lived or died. If she had to endure Henders and his voyeurism for a bit longer in order to finish that serum, then she would. She had lost her own mother to infection. She wanted to save other children from the same fate that had for all intent and purposes orphaned her at age fourteen.

Ten minutes later, Nellie flicked off the virtual display screen and padded over toward the sliding sensory door, ignoring the sound of rushing air as it whisked open. With the same rushing air sound it closed behind her, now sealed off against anyone not possessing either her, Henders, or the guard Juan's DNA genetic map.

Walking quickly toward the airbus railway that would take her to the other side of the biosphere where she lived, she didn't pay much attention to her surroundings. She gasped a moment later when she walked head first into a man, her face hitting a solid wall of muscle.

"I'm so sorry," she offered in the way of apology, her head coming up to find the man's face. "I wasn't paying attention to...to..."

She swallowed a bit nervously when her large green eyes found his steely gray ones. They were so intense—frighteningly intense—that for a moment she feared a sub-human had broken into the biosphere. But when she considered that his eyes were steel gray as opposed to that haunting blood-red color, she knew she was letting her overactive imagination rot her brain. "I wasn't paying attention to where I was going," she finished breathily.

The man said nothing, which made her more nervous. He simply stared at her from under the cowled hood of his black robe, his intense eyes flicking over her face, and over her body. He was a big man, much bigger than her five foot seven inch frame, and broader across the shoulders than any man she'd ever before seen.

Nellie backed up a step. He was handsome, yes, but he was far too intense. And eerily quiet. "I have to be going," she said dumbly, uncertain what to do or say. She backed up another step as her eyes flicked over his chiseled masculine face. The rest of his features were as intense as his eyes—brooding lips, a hawk-like nose, an expression akin to chilled stone...

She turned and walked away from him, no longer caring if she came across as rude or not. The man frightened her. And given her family history, it took a lot to frighten Dr. Nellie Kan.

She could feel his intense eyes following her movement, like a predator tracking prey. She realized that he was still watching her, not needing to turn around and see him to confirm it. She walked faster, and faster still, desperate to reach the main atrium off the corridor where she knew she could lose herself in the crowd...

Footsteps. Slow and heavy at first, then quick and paced closer together.

Shit, she thought uneasily, the man was following her.

Nellie picked up the edges of her woolen robe and sprinted at top speed toward the corridor. The footfalls matched her pace, the sound of them getting closer and closer and—

She pushed open the heavy doors with an oomph, and bodily thrust herself into the atrium. She breathed easier, understanding as she did that males—even *that* male if he possessed a modicum of intelligence—would be less likely to ignore her protected status and claim her when others were around to view the illegal activity.

The doors fell shut behind her. The footfalls came to an abrupt halt.

A group of ten females, chained and naked brides-to-be, were led in a procession in front of her, preparing to be taken to the bathing chamber before being auctioned off in marriage to the highest bidder. A group of young males were gathering around to watch, their moods light and festive as they playfully tweaked at the nipples of the females passing by.

"Can't wait til I have enough yen to buy one," a blond teenager with a hard-on announced.

"Shit, me neither," another one laughed as he ran his fingers through a frightened bride-to-be's thatch of nether hair. "Cummon, Auctioneer Morris," he said to the man holding the females' chains, "can't I fuck this one before you take her off to the auction block…"

Nellie expelled a deep breath as the normalcy of day-to-day living ensued around her, serving to calm her down. She was safe—for now. Her badge made it so she was safe in the atrium, her protected status clear to one and all.

If she thought it odd that the huge man with the intense steel eyes hadn't followed her into the atrium, that he apparently didn't want others to see him, she dismissed the peculiarity of the situation as she threaded her way through the crowd and walked quickly toward the airbus railway.

She sighed, her head shaking slightly. She really needed a vacation.

Chapter 3

"Mother?" she whispered.

Her teeth sank down into her bottom lip as she slowly backed away from the beautiful red-haired woman who lay naked on the bed, her entire body convulsing. A man stood at the foot of the bed smiling down at his victim, a dirty syringe-like mechanism in his hand, pleased with what he'd done.

Nellie's eyes filled with tears as she clutched her Daffy-dolly to her chest. Her mother began frothing at the mouth, her perfect body violently shuddering. "Mommy no! Please!"

The intruder was startled. His dark head shot up, and then twisted around.

Daffy-dolly fell to the ground, forgotten.

"Daddy?" Nellie whispered.

Nellie gasped as she bolted upright in bed, sweat plastering rogue waves of hair to her forehead. She panted heavily as she slowly assimilated the fact that she'd been dreaming.

Just a dream.

This time.

Sucking in a large tug of air, she threaded her fingers through her hair, grabbing handfuls by the root, and fell backward into the extravagant silk pillow-bed. She closed her eyes and expelled the breath slowly.

"End it, Nellie," she whispered. "You're the only one who can end it."

* * * * *

He gasped as his small frame hit the ground with a thud, the impact knocking the breath from him. Unable to move, his body still stunned by the blow, he could only lay there in defenseless horror as a low growling sound drew closer.

His head came up slowly, and his eyes filled with tears, as they clashed with a blood-red gaze.

"Please mommy," he whispered. "Please don't hurt me."

She stilled, her razor-sharp black claws retreating a bit. He saw the awareness come back into her eyes, knew the precise moment when she realized she'd just tried to murder her own son...

"Help me!" she cried, scratching at her own face with her retreating claws. Her eyes, gray again, looked frantic, desperate. "If there is a god," she sobbed, "I beg of you to help me!"

He backed away as his mother began to convulse, afraid she would turn again. He was young, but he'd seen enough infected humans to understand that one day soon his mother would be lost to him for good...

And she'd never again come back.

Kerick bolted upright within the concealed cave, sweat plastering rogue waves of hair to his forehead. He panted heavily as he slowly assimilated the fact that he'd been dreaming.

Just a dream.

This time.

Sucking in a large tug of air, he threaded his fingers through his hair, grabbing handfuls by the root, and fell backward onto the cold slab of stone and warm animal hides. He closed his eyes and expelled the breath slowly.

"End it, Riley," he whispered. "You're the only one who can end it."

Chapter 4

"This breaking news just in from the Hierarchy Security Command Centre:

Three Death Row inmates escaped from the Kong Penal Colony earlier this week, marking the first time in the history of Correctional Sector 12's existence that the maximum-security fortress was breached. The inmates left a gory trail of death in their wake, killing the warden and severely injuring five guards in the process of escaping…"

Freshly showered, Nellie stood within the dwelling chamber of her domicile, readying herself for a grueling workday before indulging in breakfast. Her gaze flicked up to the virtual wall console. She absently watched the news story unfold as she twisted her long hair into a tight bun atop her head.

"It is believed by the Hierarchy that the inmates have fled to the Dublin biosphere, where at least one of them was born and still holds strong Underground ties. The Altun Ha Hierarchy Command Centre has issued an official warning to the leaders of Biosphere 5, declaring the escapees armed and extremely dangerous."

She lost interest, not all that curious about news that was so far removed from her everyday life. Besides, she had a hell of a lot of work to finish today before the Fathom System's soiree tonight, she thought on a sigh.

Finished securing her hair into a neat bun, she strode toward the wall console, intent on turning it off as the first inmate's ebony face filled the virtual display screen.

"All three escaped prisoners are known enemies of federated Earth: Elijah "The Slayer" Carter, shown here after his conviction in the grisly murder of Hierarchy leader Maxim Malifé in 2238, Xavier "Romeo" O'Connor, convicted in 2239 on several accounts of rape against three wives of Hierarchy leaders, and finally, the infamous "Grim Reaper", who was convicted in 2234 and sentenced to die for the brutal murders of no less than five Hierarchy leaders in biospheres as far reaching as Dublin and Prague. The "Grim Reaper", also known as Ker – "

Rushed for time, Nellie flicked off the wall console. She padded into the auto-kitchen, found and peeled a banana, crammed a huge bite of the sweet fruit into her mouth, and schlepped toward the office in her domicile with Dr. Riley's journal in hand.

She sighed. She had a hell of a lot of work to do.

* * * * *

AND ALWAYS, NIGHT AND DAY, HE WAS IN THE
MOUNTAINS AND IN THE TOMBS, CRYING, AND CUTTING
HIMSELF WITH STONES...

Nellie ran a frustrated hand through her hair as she attempted for the thousandth plus time to figure out why Tara Riley, an avowed atheist, had referenced ancient Biblical passages within her worn diary. If the scientist had done so, there had been a reason. She just had to figure out what precisely that reason was.

"The airbus shuttle to the Fathom Systems party leaves in forty-five minutes," her personal droid chimed out in a monotone. "I have laid out your body décor and it awaits you in your sleeping chamber."

Nellie's dark red head bobbed up into the droid's line of vision. Her eyes flicked over its silver body, the appearance of the expensive piece of machinery resembling that of a naked woman with skin made of steel. The only part of the droid that could pass for human was her pussy. It looked, felt, and carried the scent of a real female vagina. In a world where women were rare and men sought pleasure wherever they could get it, she was hardly surprised that droids had been modeled in such a fashion. "Thank-you, Cyrus 12."

The droid nodded, a perfect human affectation. "I will await you in your sleeping chamber, Dr. Kan."

That quickly Cyrus 12 was forgotten. Nellie buried her face back into the journal, the next entry catching her attention.

AND JESUS SAID UNTO HIM, COME OUT OF THE MAN,
THOU UNCLEAN SPIRIT.

AND HE ASKED HIM, WHAT IS THY NAME? AND THE
DEMON ANSWERED, SAYING, MY NAME IS LEGION, FOR
WE ARE MANY.

"What are you trying to tell me, Dr. Riley?" Nellie murmured. She sighed, the diary dropping into her lap.

"Whatever it is, I'll figure it out," she promised, her hand running over the faded leather. "Just give me time," she whispered.

* * * * *

Twenty minutes later, Nellie stood in front of the image map in her bathing chamber, which presented to her how she looked in her body décor from all possible angles. She supposed she was pretty enough, but then again all females were. Scientists routinely engineered plainness in female fetuses out while the babies were still in vitro.

Her lips turned down into a frown when she considered the fact that the same engineering was never done on male fetuses. It was as common, if not more common, to see an unattractive man as it was to see a handsome one.

But women—women were a different story. Women were *always* a different story, she sighed. Even for something as simple as a corporate dinner party, like the one she would be attending tonight, Nellie was expected to show up half naked, while the male scientists in attendance would be permitted to wear any body décor of their choosing.

Her eyes flicked over the image map as she studied the body she'd been born into. Much of it had been engineered in the womb to one day give the man who purchased her as a wife the most pleasure possible, but some of it, like the color of her hair, was authentically her own. Geneticists were able to do many things, but they'd never figured out how to change the hair, skin, and eye color of fetuses—and have it stick. The colors always bounced back within the fifth year of life, proudly proclaiming themselves to be there.

And there was one other thing geneticists could no longer do, Nellie considered. They could no longer interfere with the gender of a human embryo.

When it had first become apparent that the females of the race were dying out, the male scientists had tried in desperation to stop any more would-be-mothers from breeding sons. But by then it had been too late, for the female reproduction system had evolved with its environment, rejecting embryos lacking a y chromosome, and for a solid thirty years not even one female birth had occurred. The three decades long famine of female offspring had transpired over eighty years ago, but the effect had turned out to be a profound and long-lasting one.

Nellie half-snorted as she thought back on a journal entry she'd read a few months ago in Tara Riley's diary:

MEN. FOR THE MOST PART THEY ARE STUPID, PATHETIC CREATURES. JUST WHAT DID THOSE SCIENTISTS THINK WOULD HAPPEN TO THE NATURAL ORDER OF LIFE WHEN THEY DECIDED TO BEHAVE IN THE ROLE OF GODS? GOOD CYRUS, BUT MY FIVE YEAR OLD SON SHOWS MORE INTELLIGENCE THAN THEY EVER DID AT FORTY AND FIVE!

Nellie grinned at the memory. She slipped into her skirt as she absently glanced at the image map.

BIOLOGICALLY SPEAKING, THE MALE IS LESS VALUABLE THAN THE FEMALE. I SAY THIS NOT OUT OF FANATICISM, AS MANY IF NOT ALL OF MY COLLEAGUES PERPETUALLY ACCUSE ME OF, BUT OUT OF TRUTH.

THINK ABOUT IT: IF YOU HAVE A THOUSAND MEN AND ONE WOMAN, ALL THOUSAND OF THOSE MALES CAN FUCK THAT ONE WOMAN UNTIL THEIR COCKS DRY UP AND THEIR BALLS QUIT MAKING SEED, AND YET WHAT IS THE RESULT IN NINE MONTHS TIME? THE RESULT IS ONE, OR IN EXTREME CASES TWO TO THREE, BABES.

NOW PUT ONE MALE IN A ROOM OF A THOUSAND WOMEN, SPILLING HIS SEED LEFT AND RIGHT, AND WHAT IS THE RESULT IN NINE MONTHS TIME? A THOUSAND BABES OR MORE.

AS I SAID, THE MALE IS BIOLOGICALLY MORE EXPENDABLE THAN THE FEMALE...

Nellie studied her body intently on the image map, her eyes flicking over her form. She had been engineered in the womb like all other females had been so that when she grew into womanhood she would be the walking, talking, breathing epitome of male aesthetic pleasure.

Her legs were long and lithe, with just a hint of padding around the thighs to make it comfortable for the male to ride her body for long periods of time. Her breasts were huge—veritable melons—firm and perky, yet lush and soft. Her areolas were large, round, and rosy, and her nipples were generally stiff.

Her face had been hand-sculpted by a genetics artist in the image of male-perceived female perfection. Full lips, cat-like eyes, a small slip of a nose that pointed a tad upward at the tip...

But the dark red hair was hers, inherited from her mother. The creamy tanned coloring was also hers, the combined genetic result of her mother's pearly white skin and her father's darkly tanned one. The green eyes she'd inherited from her father, which probably explained why she avoided looking into them while gazing at the image map.

Nellie's gaze flicked down to the body décor she was wearing. She frowned.

The male scientists at tonight's soiree would be fully attired, but the only body décor Nellie had been permitted to don was a pair of sparkling gold high heeled boots, a heavy gold chain with the Fathom Systems emblem dangling from her hips that declared her protected, and a tight white skirt that started at the ankles and inched all the way up to just underneath her breasts so that it lifted them up to make them appear even bigger and more swollen than usual.

Her breasts, of course, were to be left non-attired.

Chapter 5

He refused to be defeated by a damned female. Dr. Nellie Kan should be naked and in chains, preparing herself to be auctioned off to a husband. She should not be in *his* lab, or rather, she should not be in the lab that would have been his had he gotten that promotion instead of Nellie.

Dr. Boris Karli motioned to the male graduate student he'd taken with him on safari to follow his lead. He knew that young Miklos was frightened, terrified even, but then so was Boris.

Nobody, not even the right-hand hired arms of the Hierarchy leaders themselves, ever dared to venture to the Outside. Life outside of the biospheres was violent and ruthless, for the only sorts that dwelled within the jungles were outlaws and sub-humans. The first group would cut your throat without hesitation that they might dig the yen chip out of your brain and steal your assets, while the second group would cut your throat with nary a qualm that they might dine upon you at their leisure.

No—the Outside was no place any man ever wanted to go. But then this was an extreme circumstance, he doggedly reminded himself.

"I-I don't know about this, Dr. Karli," Miklos whispered in a thick Russian accent. A hybrid insect, which had the body of a beetle and the small but sharp talons of a predator buzzed over his head, causing him to gulp. If that thing stung him, he'd be dead in an hour. "Nyet," he breathed out in Russian. "No, I will go no further. We are barely twenty yards outside the perimeter of the Altun Ha biosphere and already—"

"Silence!" Boris whispered back in an irritated voice. "Do you wish for Nellie Kan to develop a serum before we do?"

Miklos shrugged, not particularly caring. He doubted Dr. Karli would give him any credit for his help anyway. He knew he'd end up doing all the work in terms of developing the serum, the basis of which had been stolen from Dr. Kan's notes to begin with, and then Dr. Karli would act as though he had done it all himself and give neither Nellie nor Miklos any credit. "What is important is that a serum be developed, Doctor. It is not important who actually develops it."

Boris rolled his eyes and laughed without humor. "It sounds to me as though you've been sneaking some of Old Man Henders' virtual memory chips again, boy." He laughed harder when Miklos' face burned red. "I don't blame you for wanting to see the bitch in all her naked glory stroking that cunt of hers, but that hardly means she is a good scientist."

Actually, Miklos thought to himself, she was probably the most intelligent scientist he had met since he'd become a protégée. And the only scientist he'd met who actually seemed more interested in helping her fellow humans rather than seizing glory for her own reward. But Miklos could see for himself that Dr. Karli was already angry, so he kept his thoughts to himself.

"We are *males*," Boris spat out, his teeth gritting. "Males whose rightful positions in life have been usurped by a mindless, dimwitted female whose greatest asset is her huge tits." His jaw clenched unforgivingly. "Now cease your prattle and do as you're told."

Miklos' nostrils flared. Enough was enough. He was not about to surrender his life to the Outside in the name of Boris Karli and his misplaced loathing of Dr. Kan. "I am returning to the biosphere," he said simply, but firmly.

Dr. Karli shook an enraged finger at him. "You will never," he hissed, "work in my lab or at Fathom Systems again."

Miklos shrugged. "I doubt you hold such a power as to have me removed from Fathom Systems, but if you do then so be it. Losing my position in life is much more desirable than losing my life altogether." He grinned when Boris' cheeks went up in angry flames for they both knew he held no true clout within the Hierarchy. "Perhaps I shall ask Dr. Kan if she desires a male protégée," he taunted. His blue eyes twinkled as he mockingly saluted the doctor, and then turned on his heel to leave the jungle. He felt better than he had since the day he'd first arrived at Fathom Systems. "I bid you good day, Doctor."

Boris' eyes narrowed at the protégée's retreating back. His hand shook with rage as he balled it into a tight fist. If he had to go into the jungle alone, then so be it. To those with guts went the glory.

He realized, of course, that he only had one real shot at usurping Nellie's place in Fathom System's good graces, and that shot depended upon his developing a serum before the bitch did. How else could he hope to compete against her? he thought. The slut was always taking off her clothes, giving Henders his own little perverted jack-off material.

Unfortunately, the dimwitted little idiot had apparently figured out that her notes had been rifled through, for she'd locked them up in a keystroke sequence he hadn't been able to decode. But it didn't matter.

He was Boris Karli—a *male*—and he would develop that damned serum before Nellie did if it was the last thing he ever accomplished.

Boris tightened his hold on the flash-stick, his senses on full alert. He ignored the frightening buzzing sounds of the hybrid insects hovering overhead and made his way deeper into the jungle.

He would find a nest of sub-humans. He would abstract a bit of DNA from them, and then he would develop that serum.

To those with guts went the glory.

Chapter 6

Nellie stood at the far end of the massive ballroom within the Fathom Systems corridor of the Altun Ha biosphere and stared unblinkingly at a star-carrier cruising by in the nighttime sky. As she stared out of the black glass, which was actually a misnomer for the "glass" was made of mass-produced black diamonds from a planet in a neighboring galaxy, she absently wondered where the star-carrier was headed to.

Perhaps the planet Kalast, she thought dreamily, her index finger swirling around the rim of the chalice of spirits she held. She'd always wanted to see Kalast, but had never had the opportunity. The planet was allegedly red-tinted and filled with lush mountainscapes…sort of like a habitable Mars. And, even better, Kalast was an oasis for females as the government was operated solely by women.

Nellie sighed, realizing as she did that there was no use in wishing to ever lay eyes on Kalast. Female Earthlings were forbidden by the Federation Charter of 2195 to venture off-planet without a male escort. And even then they had to be bound to him with sensory chains. No male would be fool enough to vacation on a planet where his woman would have an opportunity to flee from him without the security of sensory chains. The typical male Earthling had to save his yen for many, many years in order to purchase a wife; he certainly wouldn't chance losing one after paying such a steep price to own her.

"Dr. Kan, what a pleasure it is to see you again."

Nellie heard the familiar voice greet her at the precise moment she felt two large male hands wrap around her from behind and palm her non-attired breasts. She thought nothing of it when he began stroking her nipples, for it was the legal right of a male to caress an unmarried female in any way he chose to do so, so long as she was lower in the Hierarchy than he. She smiled, then turned on her boot heel to greet her former professor and mentor. She handed her chalice over to a passing by droid. "Dr. Lorin, I didn't expect to see you here tonight."

He smiled, his Cajun inherited brown eyes crinkling at the corners. "Good Cyrus, but it's been a long time, Nellie." He slowly ran two tanned hands over her swollen breasts, then began to softly massage her stiff nipples with the pads of his thumbs while he engaged her in conversation. "I don't believe we've had the delight of attending the same corporate party since you were under my tutelage."

"C'est vrai," she agreed in the native French tongue of his homeland biosphere. *That's true.*

Treymor Lorin had to be in his late fifties by now, yet he was still as handsome and distinguished looking as ever, if not more so, she thought. Nellie had always been grateful that when she'd taken the chance and petitioned to the Hierarchy for the right to forgo the marriage auction block in lieu of a career, it had been to a man as handsome and sophisticated as Dr. Lorin that she had been given.

She could have ended up anywhere and been given to anyone of the Hierarchy's choosing, but she had been fortunate that she'd been placed under the protection of a respectable man like the esteemed professor. Treymor Lorin was everything her current protector Vorice Henders was not — honorable, dedicated to his work, and loyal to those under his protection.

Nellie reflected on the five years she'd lived with and learned from Dr. Lorin as he proceeded to bring her up to date on all the new changes in his life and work. Apparently he now had another female protégée living with him, a young woman whom the Hierarchy had placed with him a few months back. She was pleased by such knowledge, and even more delighted to hear that the young female planned to gain employment at Fathom Systems when her years of tutelage were over, for it had long been Nellie's contention that the mega-conglomerate company needed more female scientists within its ranks.

"Is she taking to her studies well?" Nellie asked. Her eyes closed briefly when the beginnings of arousal stirred in her belly from the gentle nipple massage Dr. Lorin was giving to her.

He grinned, his thumbs working her stiff nipples into a pleasurous ache. "She's flourishing more quickly than the hybrid peoples of planet Rolfi can procreate."

She chuckled at that. "She must be quite intelligent then."

His look was thoughtful. "In most subjects, yes, but she's having a Kong of a time getting the gist of virtual display theory."

One dark red eyebrow shot up. "Good Cyrus, I seem to recall having trouble with that very subject once myself! But look at me now," she encouraged, "I know everything there is to know about it." She nodded definitively. "Your new protégée will learn, Dr. Lorin, I've no doubt."

He cocked his head, his eyes wandering over her face. He deepened the nipple massage as he studied her features, his fingers expertly remembering how she liked it best. "She reminds me of you," he admitted, "in that she enjoys having her beautiful breasts laved with attention." He grinned. "Though I daresay it's an activity I never minded indulging you in."

Highly aroused, Nellie stared at him through hooded eyes. "She's a lucky protégée," she murmured, trying to keep her thoughts on the topic at hand. But Dr. Lorin was correct when he'd stated that she enjoyed having her breasts massaged, so keeping her thoughts linear to the discussion was proving difficult.

Her former protector backed her up against the black glass wall, and then pressed his erection against her tummy. When he released her breasts in favor of grabbing at her skirt and hoisting it up to her waist, she felt a moment's shyness at having her intimate triangle of dark red curls exposed to the ever-greedy gaze of all the males in the ballroom.

And yet conversely she knew that there was no point in being shy, for it would be considered tactless and rude to refuse to satiate the lust of a former protector while she still had no permanent master. It was implicitly understood by all in attendance that should Dr. Lorin decide to fuck her right here and now for all to see, Nellie was expected to not only submit to his desire, but to show gratitude for the privilege of being wanted by a male so esteemed.

At eighteen, when Nellie had first been sent to Dr. Lorin's domicile, she had felt very grateful for the older man's protection and instruction. He had schooled her in all things scientific, and in exchange she had handed over to him the use of her body as it is required of a female protégée to do.

Dr. Lorin had never balked at the opportunity, but had reveled in it instead. He had been in his late forties and she just eighteen when she'd been sent to live with him, and he had delighted in her youth. She could still recall the way he had gritted his teeth every time he'd sank his cock into her young, tight pussy.

She could still remember lots of things — like how he'd always commanded her to sit on his lap and spread her thighs on the days when her grueling schoolwork had required lectures. The entire time he'd lectured her his fingers had played with her pussy, sometimes rubbing her clit, and sometimes merely contenting themselves with running through her soft nether hair. And inevitably when the day's lesson was finished, he would bend her over the desk and thrust into her from behind, pounding into her until he found completion.

At eighteen she hadn't minded turning over the use of her body to her protector, for she had understood it was his right as her temporary master to reap the benefits of having a rare human female under his tutelage. And yet as she stood here in the ballroom and felt him press his erection against her bared mons, she found that at thirty-two she did mind. She was no longer dwelling in his domicile and didn't feel as though she owed him reparation any longer. Indeed, she had given him all the sex he'd desired back when it had been required by the law for her to do so.

Dr. Lorin backed up slightly and replaced his erection with his hand. Nellie felt his gossamer white robe tickle her thigh when he took a step back. She immediately relaxed when he began running his fingers through her triangle, for she realized he wasn't about to fuck her in front of the entire chamber. If all he meant to do was stroke her into orgasm, well, that much she could deal with.

"I've missed your kitty-cat," Dr. Lorin said thickly as his fingers leisurely combed through the soft curls.

Nellie blushed, having forgotten that's what he'd always referred to her pussy as back when he'd been her protector. She hadn't minded him calling it a kitty-cat when she'd been eighteen, but again, she found that at thirty-two she did mind. She wasn't a child any longer. She was a woman—and a scientist. Naïve girl protégées had kitty-cats. Mature women scientists had pussies.

Her breath caught in the back of her throat when his index and middle fingers began rubbing her clit in a slow, circular motion. She moaned softly when the fingers of his other hand came back up to play with her nipples.

"Such a succulent cunt you have, Nellie," he murmured. "So wet and sweet, and so swollen."

She closed her eyes on a whimper, her body responding to his words and his touch. It had been so long since she'd been with a man—far too long.

"And these nipples..." he praised her, his hand running worshipfully over both breasts. He clucked his tongue. "I've never seen nipples quite this color before, Nellie. But then you already know that, chere."

She did know that. Dr. Lorin had always been quite taken with her nipples. Her aureoles were large and round, and a tad puffy. Her nipples were long and stiff, and colored a deep, rare rouge. Their coloring was so unique, in fact, that she knew her price on the auction block would be steep if ever she decided to allow such an event as marriage to transpire. It was the same with her hair. The rare dark red coloring of the pelt of curls between her thighs was highly sought after on auction blocks world over.

Nellie expelled a breathy moan as her former mentor toyed with her nipples and clit. Her eyes still closed, she tilted her head back and rested it on the black glass wall as her orgasm drew rapidly near. The sound of boisterous conversations ensuing around her was drowned out by the fast beat of her heart. The reverberations from the techno-opera musique the band was playing faded into the dim recesses of her mind.

Clearly, it had been far too long since a male had brought her to peak. She could think of nothing but the need for completion, the need for—

The hair at the nape of her neck began to stir, much as it had last evening in the lab when the ventilation system had been purposely shut off. That eerie sensation was back again, that feeling of being watched. Watched and…intensely coveted.

Nellie's cat-like green eyes flew open. As if she knew precisely where to look, as if it didn't matter that the party chamber she was standing in was three balconies high and a thousand feet across, her head came up slowly, her line of vision immediately honing in on the second balcony balustrade.

She sucked in her breath.

The man—*him*.

The giant looked much the same tonight as he had yesterday when she'd bumped into him in the corridor. He wore the same hooded black robe, the same grim features, and those eyes…

Those intense steel gray eyes never strayed from her the entire time Dr. Lorin continued to stroke her toward orgasm. She knew the man could see everything there was to see about her, for there was no body décor concealing her breasts and her skirt had been hoisted up to her waist.

Nellie's eyes clashed with the giant's and a chill of foreboding passed through her. He was angry—very angry—and somehow, though she didn't understand how she knew it, she realized that the man was angry with Dr. Lorin for touching her. And possibly with her as well.

The man's eyes strayed from her face and down to her breasts. He studied them intently, causing her already stiff nipples to unwittingly pucker further. She felt hands grab her breasts and pinch appreciatively at her nipples and it was only then that she realized Dr. Lorin had invited his colleagues over to help him make her come. But she couldn't concentrate on them. She could only stare up at the balcony...

The giant's nostrils flared as his eyes strayed down further, to the triangle of dark red curls. He gazed at her pussy so intensely, so possessively, that Nellie half-wondered if he'd managed to brand it without an auctioneer's branding tool to aid him.

"Such a lovely kitty-cat, Nellie," Dr. Lorin praised. "I want her to purr for me."

Another male laughed at that. "Losing your golden touch, Treymor?"

"Indeed," a third male chimed in as he pinched at one nipple, "she's yet to purr, Trey."

Her former protector grunted at the challenge. "I shall remedy that oversight immediately."

Nellie felt inexplicable panic bubble up inside of her as the trio of esteemed males stripped her of all body décor and carried her to a black glass table located right below the giant. He was only one balcony up from her and the three scientists had splayed her out before him, unknowingly giving him a private show.

She felt one pair of male lips latch around a plump nipple, and then a second pair latched around her other one. The males sucked on them like treats, bringing to mind boys tasting lollipops for the first time. When Dr. Lorin settled himself on a chair between her spread legs and began lapping at her pussy, her gaze flew up to the giant's.

Nellie's eyes widened at his look of promised retribution to come. Whether that retribution was to be dealt out to her, or to the males touching and kissing on her, she couldn't say. But the huge man's clenched jaw and flaring nostrils said it all: he thought that he owned her, believed that her former protector had no right to taste a cunt he clearly considered to belong to him.

She blinked at the incredulity of her thoughts, for they made no sense. She didn't know the giant, had never seen him before yesterday, so how on Earth could he possibly be feeling the emotions she was pinning on him?

"Purr for me," she heard Dr. Lorin growl against her clit.

Nellie gasped as her former protector thrust his tongue into her pussy, then groaned when he slurped her clit into his mouth and suckled it vigorously.

The male scientists licking and sucking her nipples increased the pressure of their mouths, driving her wild. She expelled a worried breath as her gaze flew back up to the balcony, realizing as she did that orgasm was inevitable. It was madness, of course, to worry over what the grim-looking stranger might do to punish her, but the feeling was still there.

Nellie's head fell back on a gasp and her eyes closed. She wanted to stop herself from coming, but —

"*Ooooh.*" She burst on a low moan, her splayed legs trembling from the violence of it. She felt her nipples stab upwards into the still suckling mouths of the males latched onto her there, and could hear Dr. Lorin's appreciative *mmmm* sounds as he lapped up all her pussy juice.

Her huge breasts heaved up and down from under the males' mouths, perspiration dotting her cleavage as she came down from the sensual high. Her senses coming back to her, and her memory along with it, her eyes flew open and up to the balcony.

Gone — the man was gone.

Nellie blinked, wondering if she hadn't imagined him to begin with. There was no way he could have gotten off the balcony without descending the staircase and that would have taken some time to do. More time than she'd had her eyes shut for at any rate.

Five minutes later, Nellie closed her eyes and sighed when it appeared that the males sucking on her nipples had no intention of letting them go any time soon. She knew human females were scarce, so this was no doubt a true treat for them. They brought to mind the image of suctioning fish whose mouths had latched around a lure and couldn't let go.

From between her splayed thighs she heard Dr. Lorin chuckling at his colleagues' infatuation with her breasts. As he ran his fingers through her drenched nether hair, she idly listened while he beckoned a young male of eighteen over to look at her puffed up pussy. She could tell from the sound of the boy's labored breathing that he'd never been this close to a real cunt before, had probably only seen them in virtual reality movies and four-dimensional magazines.

Nellie took a deep breath and expelled it. She really needed a vacation.

Chapter 7
December 21, 2249 A.D.

And I stood upon the sand of the sea, and saw a beast rise up out of the sea...And they worshipped the beast, saying, Who is like unto the beast? Who is able to make war with him?

And he causeth all, both small and great, rich and poor, free and bond, to receive a mark in their right hand, or in their foreheads: And that no man might buy or sell, save he that had the mark...

Here is wisdom. Let him that hath understanding count the number of the beast for it is the number of a man; and his number is six hundred, threescore, and six.

Wide-eyed, Nellie gently set the journal down on the desk she kept within her domicile. Her gaze flicked back to the last entry she'd read, a passage from the Book of Revelation that had been painstakingly scrawled out in Tara Riley's hand.

Here is wisdom. Let him that hath understanding count the number of the beast for it is the number of a man; and his number is six hundred, threescore, and six.

Nellie slowly rose to her feet. Pale as the moon, she turned on her heel and padded out of her office and into her bathing chamber. She stopped when she reached it, coming to a halt in front of the four-dimensional image map.

Staring unblinkingly at her image from all angles, she raised a trembling hand to her skull and ran a single finger over her chip-implanted forehead. The chip made it so she could buy and sell, so she could live within any biosphere of federated Earth...

She swallowed roughly. The chip had been manufactured by Fathom Systems. It had been the company's pet project for over fifty years until it had finally been perfected twenty and some odd years ago.

Nellie closed her eyes briefly, then opened them again and stared at the image map. In that moment she became chillingly aware of the fact that her life would never be the same again. What had started out as a quest to ease the suffering of sub-humans had grown into a search for a truth she couldn't even begin to comprehend. And, she feared, if she was successful, if she ever found out just what that truth was, it would probably get her killed. Or infected. Or...worse.

She bit down onto her bottom lip as her finger tracked the area where she knew the chip to be located behind the skin of her forehead. She stilled, her finger abruptly coming to a halt.

The chip, she uneasily considered, had a name. Officially termed the *Biological Enzyme And Skin-cell Tracker*, or simply the *BEAST* for short, it had taken the fusion of six natural gases, six strategically extrapolated brain cells, and six molecules of a liquid substance indigenous to planet Kalast known as Erodium to create a chip that could be hosted within the human body without dire consequences.

Six gases, six molecules, six brain cells...

666.

Nellie took a deep breath and expelled it. Why the Kong hadn't she taken that vacation?

* * * * *

An hour and three chalices of spirits later, Nellie sank down onto her lush pillow-bed feeling overwhelmed. She was also feeling drunk, and decided she might just stay that way.

Like the ill-fated heroine in a dramatically tragic virtual reality movie, her hand flew to her forehead and her eyes closed on a martyr's sigh. All she needed was for the famous and studly cyber-droid Cabel Modem to whisk into her domicile and steal her away to help him on a secret mission in galaxies hitherto unknown and the tragic heroine imagery would be complete.

She sighed, deciding that a fourth chalice of spirits could hardly do much damage to her already inebriated state. In fact, the world might seem a much better place a hallucination or two later.

Frowning, she stood up and padded out of the sleeping chamber and into the auto-kitchen. "Cyrus 12," she grumbled, "have you fixed the slave yet?"

Slave was the generic term for a machine hooked up within the kitchens of most domiciles. Slaves made it so all free citizens could receive any buyable item available in their sector with a mere verbal command stating what it was that they wanted. Body décor, spirits, hot meals—so long as you knew what you wanted, and so long as your chip had enough yen in its memory bank, the slave could fetch your heart's desire for you within seconds.

"Affirmative, Dr. Kan," the droid said in a monotone, "but it will take an hour or so before it's been recharged and has reached online status."

Nellie sighed. She'd gone and drank the last bit of spirits she'd had left about ten minutes ago. What a damned day. "Thanks anyway, Cyrus 12. I suppose I'll retire to my sleeping chamber."

"Do you require me to deactivate for the remainder of the evening, Dr. Kan?"

She shrugged her shoulders dismissively. Turning to walk back to her pillow-bed, she stepped out of her lab coat to get naked for sleeping. "Yes, go ahead and recharge, Cyrus 12." She could do without the droid's protection for a few scant hours. Besides, her domicile possessed all of Fathom System's latest and greatest security technology. She doubted even a god could breach the fortress should one be so inclined as to try. "I'm going to bed."

Chapter 8

Boris Karli cried out in pain as he stumbled toward the entrance to the cave he'd found. The bite dealt to him by the mutated insect was deep and required immediate attention. If he didn't shoot himself up with a drug that could counteract the poison immediately, he'd be dead outside of an hour.

In the throes of agony, he gritted his teeth against the pain as he fell to his knees at the mouth of the cave, unable to walk.

I need to be in some manner of shelter, he thought hysterically, the fear of impending death at last swamping him.

Using what little strength he had left, he came up on all fours and crawled into the cave, determined to get inside before he shot himself up. The pain of crawling was so intense, so sharp and shooting, he was unable to restrain himself from gasping at the agony of it.

But finally, as he'd known in all of his arrogance that he would, he made it inside the dimly lit cavern and scooted up against a wall. His hands violently shaking, he dropped his satchel to the earthen ground and fumbled through its contents until he located the proper syringe.

"You can do this, Karli," he ground out, perspiration soaking him. His hand trembling, he palmed the syringe, snatched it out of the medical satchel, and buried it deeply into his arm. He cried out as the drug lanced through him like fire, the feeling akin to acid shooting through his veins.

A minute later, when the pain began to subside and his heart rate began its descent to homeostasis, he chuckled aloud, pleased with himself. Nellie Kan might have a cunt and huge tits, but she was no Boris Karli. Information that had taken the bitch years to collect would all be his in the matter of days. As soon as he located a nest of sub-humans and gathered some DNA samples to take back to the lab, he would be able to develop a serum in the matter of a week or less.

And then, he thought arrogantly, Nellie Kan would cease to matter at Fathom Systems. A fait accompli.

A blood-chilling scream echoed throughout the cave, sending goosebumps down Boris' spine. His eyes wide, he swallowed nervously as he quietly stood up and tightened his hold on the flash-stick. A low, tortured moan followed by another scream pierced the air, causing the scientist to tremble.

If he was right, an outlaw had just been attacked by a sub-human. That meant to Boris that the sub-human's attention would be snagged by the dying carcass it was dining on, allowing him precious time to immobilize it.

He took a shaky breath and expelled it, then fumbled through his satchel for a vial of numbing spray. The spray would render the sub-human immobile long enough for him to collect a DNA sample, after which time Boris would simply kill the creature with the flash-stick.

Creeping slowly into the bowels of the cave, Boris made his way toward the innermost chamber of the cavern — the sub-human sanctuary where he heard the sounds coming from. As he drew nearer, the horrific noises grew more intense, inducing his stomach muscles to knot.

You must do this, Boris, he mentally reiterated. He swiped at his dripping brow with a forearm. *To those with guts go the glory...*

His body began to shake uncontrollably as he approached the inner chamber, knowing as he did that when he rounded the corner he would be faced with a nest of sub-humans. He had no idea how many of them there would be, or how hungry they would still be, which was the most frightening aspect of his impending showdown with fate.

When he quietly crept into the cave's inner sanctuary, when he at last laid eyes on the species he had spent days tracking, he was so shocked by what he saw that the hand holding the flash-stick fell to his side, forgotten.

There was no outlaw in here being dined upon, he realized, his stomach churning. He gazed surrealistically at the scene before him, vomit creeping up his throat and threatening expulsion. "The species is breeding," he murmured.

The Hierarchy did not know that sub-humans could breed amongst themselves. If they had known, Boris told himself, they would have taken the threat imposed by the Outside a lot more seriously than they did.

Boris watched in horror as the new mother finished birthing the last of her three monsters. When it was done, when all three fanged babies had come out from between her legs, she gathered them together and walked them toward the other side of the cavern where a sub-human male, the babies' apparent father, had been haphazardly thrown, his legs broken, unable to run away.

The sub-human male screamed in terror, realizing his fate. The female predator, showing no pity or remorse, placed her hungry young beside the body of their father, then sat back and watched while their serrated teeth tore chunks from his flesh.

Boris closed his eyes and whimpered, the sounds of pain and terror the male was eliciting overwhelming to him. It was horrid and blood-curdling...a literal nightmare.

He supposed that from a scientific standpoint he shouldn't be surprised, for sub-human females weren't the only species of predators that killed off the male either during the act of copulation or immediately following the birth of her babes. The female preying mantis ripped off the head of its mate during the act of copulation in order to get pregnant. The female black widow spider spun a sticky web so her mate couldn't escape her clutches, allowing him to live until her eggs hatched, after which time she fed him to her young. Even a species of mega-raptors back in the age of dinosaurs had used the same method; after the female's eggs had hatched, she lunged down upon her mighty thighs, whipped up into the air and spun around, and gutted her mate with one deadly slice dealt from her massive talon, spilling his innards for her newborn young to dine upon.

Boris knew that the killing off of the male was common enough amongst predators. But knowing it and watching it were two different things. The male was dying slowly, agonizingly, unable to move, unable to defend himself.

Closing his eyes briefly and willing himself to calm down, he took a deep breath and told himself to get out of there. *Now*. While the female's attention was snagged and he still had a chance.

Boris turned on his heel and ran as fast as he could, his heart thumping madly against his chest, his feet kicking up dirt and pebbles as he fled for his life. He ran out of the inner sanctuary and headed straight for a steep incline that he knew would spit him back out into the jungle.

A low growl sounded from behind him, getting closer and then closer still. He willed his legs to move faster, a small cry of terror erupting from him. He would never make it, he realized. She was closing in on him. She would —

Boris expelled a breath of relief when he remembered the flash-stick. Halting in his tracks, his nostrils flared in renewed arrogance as he spun around on his heel and aimed the sites of the flash-stick where the creature should have been standing.

But wasn't.

He gasped when the flash-stick was snatched from his hands, and then cried out in pain when he was violently thrown to the ground in an act that snapped the bones in his legs like frail branches. His jaw agape, his gaze shot upward.

He screamed.

The female was hovering above him, her mouth forming a sickly smile that still showed the bloodstains of her last kill. Bits of flesh were wedged in between her serrated teeth, a grotesque reminder of what was in store for him.

Boris gasped. "Please," he muttered, his hands coming up in a futile effort to shield himself. "Sweet Cyrus, please do not!"

As he heard the hissing sound she made, as he saw a set of black claws lash out at his belly and spill his innards on the cavern floor, he heard the scampering of tiny feet come up quickly behind him.

His last thought before dying was that the children had apparently finished dining on their father.

And, he thought as he surrealistically watched the three tiny creatures slurp up his intestines, they were still hungry.

Chapter 9

Groggy with sleep, Nellie's forehead wrinkled in confusion when, from somewhere in the far corners of her mind, it occurred to her that her domicile security system had just emitted a low frequency buzzing sound. The noise was familiar, she thought sleepily, but she was so tired that she couldn't quite place from where—

Her eyes flew open. Her breathing stilled. Wide-eyed, and now very awake, she immediately realized precisely what that low frequency buzzing sound meant.

The sector's security system had been breached. And, more importantly to her peace of mind, her own domicile's security system had been compromised.

Her heart rate soaring, her breathing labored, Nellie bolted upright in the pillow-bed and scrambled to her feet. Her gaze flew wildly about the sleeping chamber as she tried to find some manner of weapon. Swallowing roughly, and growing more terrified by the second, she quietly inched her way towards the adjoining bathing chamber, her instincts screaming to get out now.

One step. Two steps. Three...

A dull thudding sound came from her domicile's auto-kitchen, confirming the fact that someone had just broken in. The intruder had somehow managed to crawl through the sector's ventilation system, for it was through the auto-kitchen that all domiciles were hooked up to the public air.

Nellie's eyes flicked toward the bathing chamber. If the intruder had just entered the auto-kitchen, she thought with a spark of hope, then she still had time to sneak out through the hidden panel behind her image map...

Turning abruptly, she bolted toward the bathing chamber, her breath coming in pants. When she reached the closed sliding doors, she frantically pressed a palm to the DNA scanner, biting down onto her lip as she waited for the doors to slide open with a whoosh.

They never did.

"Please," Nellie cried out softly, afraid for her life. She had no idea who had just broken into her domicile but given the fact that she'd been studying Tara Riley's journal in secret she feared the worst—she feared it was a member of the Hierarchy who had managed to find out what she'd been up to and had thus come to silence her.

Throwing her palm back up against the DNA scanner, her body began to violently tremble with fear of impending death. Ice cold terror lanced through her, inducing her skin to goosebump and her nipples to harden as she broke out into a cold sweat. Sweet Cyrus, she thought, please don't let me die this way!

A whooshing sound filled the sleeping chamber a second later, only the noise hadn't come from the sliding doors of her bathing chamber. It had come from the other set of doors. The ones that led into the domicile proper. The ones, she thought on a soft cry, that someone would use to get to her if they'd just broken in through the auto-kitchen.

Nellie closed her eyes briefly as she placed her shaking palm one last time against the DNA scanner.

Nothing.

She laid her head against the doors, defeated. Her killer-to-be had managed to disengage the bathing chamber doors without disengaging the ones he needed to get to her.

Shaking, she lifted her head and slowly turned around, determined to face her executioner with dignity. She would not die a coward, she told herself with more staunch than she felt. She would look her murderer defiantly in the eye while—

"You can't escape, Nellie."

Her head flew up at the sound of the deep, rumbled voice. She squinted her eyes, trying in vain to make out the shape of the man who'd come to kill her. It was no use. Apparently the domicile's illumination system had been tampered with as well. All she could see was a large figure clad in what looked to be black.

"Just kill me and get it over with," she breathed out. Her breasts heaving, she backed up as far as she could against the bathing chamber doors.

"Now why would I want to do that?" the deep voice rumbled back. "After all the trouble I've gone through to have you for my own."

She knew he was getting closer to her. She couldn't see him, but she could hear him, feel him, smell him, sense him…

He took another step forward, and one half of his face was illuminated by a pale moonbeam.

A hooded black robe. A large, extremely muscular frame. Intense, steel gray eyes…

"Oh my god." Nellie's eyes widened when she realized who it was that had come to murder her. She should have figured out he'd been sent by the Hierarchy the day she'd first bumped into him. Only a hired assassin would be as big as this male; none but a hired assassin would have the occasion to acquire a musculature of that size.

She gasped when, in a lightning quick movement, the stranger's hand shot out and he wrapped a set of callused fingers around her neck. "Please," she whimpered, her earlier promise to herself to remain brave forgotten, "please make it quick and painless."

The callused hand worked its way downward, slowly running from her neck to her breasts. He used the palm of his hand to lightly graze the tips of her nipples, while his other hand found her pussy and threaded through the triangle there. "Painless—that's up to you," he murmured. "But quick...never."

Nellie gulped, wondering exactly what he'd meant by that enigmatic statement. Wondering too if they were talking about the same thing. "Who are you?" she whispered, her mind frantic. She wanted to cling to any shred of hope the giant might throw her way, wanted to believe he wasn't from the Hierarchy. But if he wasn't from the Hierarchy, what was it he wanted from her?

The feel of a long, thick erection poking against her belly caused Nellie's breathing to still. Her cat-green eyes widened in dawning comprehension. But—

No...

"Males don't chance imprisonment or worse just to illegally claim a woman," she shakily informed him, her breath coming out in a rush. Dismantling her security system would have required extinguishing the system throughout the entire sector. Such was madness. Sheer lunacy. He could have been caught at any stage of the game.

A callused finger stroked one of her nipples. His other hand remained at her pussy, playing in it. "All mine now," he murmured.

Her eyes rounded to the shape of full moons when it finally struck Nellie that the man had done just what she'd thought no man would ever be foolish enough, or bold enough, to do. As crazy as it sounded, as unbelievable as it was, the giant had brought the security system of an entire sector down to its knees just to fuck her. And, she thought on a nervous swallow, to own her.

Oh yes, she realized when his intense eyes hooded in lust, this male wanted more from her than a quick fuck. He meant to keep fucking her—he meant to master her.

The stranger was frighteningly cunning, yet she could practically see the direction his thoughts were going in as if they were being displayed before her in a virtual reality movie. He would simply make it look as though she'd left the perimeter of her protection, allowing him to claim her legally. Inferring that he had the right to take her, no male would interfere with his claim of ownership when he took the claim to the public arena.

And she would be at the mercy of a madman. Forever.

Terrified, trembling, and having no idea exactly what fate the stranger meant to relegate her to, Nellie opened her mouth to scream. She'd barely dragged air into her lungs to make a sound when her cry for help was abruptly cut off by a rough palm slapping over her mouth.

Sweet Cyrus, she thought hysterically, please don't let him take me! If he took her away he could do anything to her and nobody would be the wiser. He could pass her around to friends that they all might share of her body, he could...good Cyrus, he could do anything. And worse yet, her peers would think she was dead. Unless, of course, he went public with his claim of ownership.

In the throes of a violent panic, Nellie used all of her strength to shove away from the huge stranger, but a quick pinch to her neck thwarted any effort she might have made to escape.

She blinked, then stumbled into his arms. A second later, the world went black.

Chapter 10
December 22, 2249 A.D.

Nellie made a soft moaning sound as she slowly came-to. She blinked a few times in rapid succession while her eyes adjusted to the dim lighting. When she could see again, when she was able to make heads or tails of her surroundings, she attempted to sit up, only to realize that she couldn't.

Her eyes widened when it dawned on her that she was chained up. A shackle on either wrist and a shackle on either ankle, her arms were chained above her head to an iron pike jutting out from the dirt wall behind her. Her feet had been chained in such a way that her legs were spread wide open and bent at the knee, completely exposing her pussy. A single animal fur had been draped over her, but she was otherwise totally nude.

She closed her eyes briefly, trying to figure a way out of her predicament. Perhaps if she —

She sighed. Who was she kidding? She'd been shackled with sensory chains. If she did escape, she would never do it and live to tell about it. She could only wander as far as the chains had been preprogrammed to allow her. For all she knew the giant might have instructed the chains to detonate within a foot of her lying position.

The sound of approaching voices caused Nellie's heart to beat rapidly. Not knowing what else to do, she abruptly closed her eyes and feigned unconsciousness when the voices entered the chamber she'd been placed in.

"Shh, we've got to be quiet."

There was a pause, and then, "I don't know about this, Kieran. If Kerick finds out he'll kill us."

Nellie could surmise from their voices that the males were young. Seventeen, maybe eighteen at best. Their next words confirmed it, for they were obviously too young to have enough yen to visit a Pussy Parlour.

"Don't you wanna see what a real cunt looks like?"

"Well yeah but —"

"All we're gonna do is look. That's all. Just a quick look and we'll leave. My brother will never know."

Another short pause. "What if the female wakes up? What if she tells him?"

Kieran sighed. "There's no way she'll wake up. She ain't been down here long enough."

That seemed to appease the other boy. "Okay then." His voice squeaked. "Let's do it."

Nellie could sense their growing excitement, could have sworn she'd heard both of them swallow in anticipation as they made their way across the chamber. When they reached the slab of stone and animal hides she'd been chained on, she felt one of the boys put his hand on the scrap of animal fur that had been draped over her body to give warmth.

His hand stilled. "Are you ready to see this, Alasdair?" Kieran murmured.

"Fuck yeah," Alasdair whispered back. "Take it off her, amigo."

A tug later, Nellie felt the animal fur fall from her body. Her nipples instantly stiffened from the chill in the air, and she experienced a tremor of arousal when a puff of cold wind hit her clit.

"Sweet Cyrus," Kieran said thickly. He traced her pussy lips with his index finger, rubbing all over the sleek folds of flesh. Nellie willed herself to feel no arousal, for what good it did. Still, she didn't want to give away the fact that she was awake to the curious teenage boys.

"What does it feel like?" Alasdair asked a bit hoarsely.

"Soft. And wet."

Alasdair gulped. "I want to feel it."

A second hand found her pussy. Fingers ran through her nether hair, then fell lower. The first hand opened up her vaginal lips, stretching them.

"Look at this," Kieran whispered. A finger gently poked at her clit. "Shit, she's beautiful. Ripe as a berry."

"Looks even better than in the movies." The second hand left her pussy. "If you're gonna play with her cunt," Alasdair said quietly, "then I want to play with her tits for a while."

"Cyrus! They're big, ain't they?" Kieran thought things over for a second. "Okay, but let's trade places in five minutes, amigo. That way we both get to play with everything."

Nellie didn't know whether to laugh or cry when the teenagers began exploring her body in earnest. The arousal she experienced was made a thousand times more pronounced by the fact that she had to remain perfectly still lest she alert the boys to the fact that she was wide awake. No matter what they did, no matter how they touched her, she knew she had to will herself from coming.

For the next twenty minutes, Nellie was tortured in a way she'd never before thought of as painful. But then again, usually when her cunt and nipples were being poked and prodded, licked and sucked on, she was allowed release.

"You think you can talk your brother into letting us fuck her?" Alasdair's mouth unlatched from her erect nipple long enough to ask the question.

"I doubt it," Kieran grumbled.

And then Kieran did something Nellie had been praying the teenager wouldn't figure out to do. He lowered his face between her legs and greedily began sucking on her clit.

Beads of sweat broke out on her forehead.

"Mmmm, mmmm mmmmm," Kieran said dreamily from around her clit, half talking and half sucking on it, "she tastes so damn good."

Her stomach knotted. Desire shot hot and fast throughout her entire body.

"Her nipples are getting stiffer," Alasdair mumbled. He kissed the tip of one, then lowered his mouth to the other one and wrapped his lips around it.

Kieran's breathing grew increasingly labored. She could tell he wanted something from her, but was too unschooled to know exactly what. And then, his breathing frenzied, his face dove hard for her pussy and slurped up the clit. With a groan he sucked her hard, moaning against her cunt while he sucked, and sucked, and —

Nellie's body trembled violently inside as she burst. She didn't know how she managed it, would never know where the control came from, but she managed to keep from crying out, managed even to keep her breathing under control.

"Mmmmmm," Kieran said appreciatively. "If you suck on her cunt long enough it makes juice."

Alasdair's mouth unlatched from her stiff nipple with a popping sound. "No shit?" His head came up. "Lemme try."

Nellie mentally groaned when he did just that. For the next half hour she lay there, still as stone, while the boys repeatedly took turns sucking on her pussy until it made the juice they wanted to taste. They lapped it up like dogs, draining her over and over, again and again.

And then came the final bout. Kieran and Alasdair ate her out at the same time, one of them sucking on her clit and the other one sucking at her hole. She knew this was going to be it—the orgasm that was so violent she wouldn't be able to stifle her scream.

Oh damn, she thought. She'd managed to make it this far and...

Kieran's mouth unlatched from her clit. His head bobbed up. "Did you hear that?" he whispered.

Alasdair released her pussy. "Kerick's back!"

"Shit! Let's get out of here!"

Tears of mingled fear and frustration welled up in Nellie's eyes. Fear because Kerick was no doubt the name of the man who'd kidnapped her. Frustration because she'd been left on the brink of a violent orgasm and been offered no completion.

She could feel her swollen pussy throbbing, needing release. She felt as though she was being driven mad.

Nellie's eyes flicked open when the boys fled the chamber. She sighed. "What happens now?" she whispered. "What will be done to me?"

Chapter 11

It grew worse instead of better. The tingling between her thighs, the need for satiation—she was going insane, she thought on a low moan.

For the past hour Nellie had laid on the bed of stone and animal hides, her body naked and spread wide, the chill in the air grazing her already erect nipples and swollen clit. Several times she had tried closing her eyes and willing herself to orgasm, but it hadn't been enough. She needed direct stimulation. If only she could free one of her hands...

Footsteps approached, dull thuds on a stone and dirt floor. She swallowed nervously, for she had a fairly good idea who they belonged to. A minute later her suspicion was confirmed when the man she assumed to be named Kerick stormed into the chamber she'd been chained in. And, she thought warily, he looked angry.

"Did they fuck you?" he growled, his nostrils flaring. Three long strides brought him to the slab of stone she'd been stretched out onto. His jaw was tight, his gray eyes murderous. He spread open her cunt lips and checked the size of her hole for recent penetration. *"Did they?"*

Her eyes widened. "N-No," she stuttered.

"Are you lying?" he barked.

Nellie's nostrils did a little flaring of their own. Her gaze flicked down to the hands spreading apart her pussy for inspection, then over the black cloak he wore, then back up to his grim face. "Why would I lie about being raped?" she snapped. Her eyes narrowed at him. "If they'd raped me, I'd want revenge," she spat out meaningfully.

One black eyebrow shot up. He grunted, ignoring the double entendre. "Did they touch you?"

She hesitated. "Yes." She decided he'd know if she was lying.

"Where?" he ground out.

"Everywhere."

His nostrils flared further. "They will be punished," he promised on a low murmur.

As if remembering for the first time that she was lying there naked, stretched out for his use on a slab of stone, his eyelids grew heavy as he stared down at her splayed flesh. His fingers rubbed over her cunt lips, gently massaging them until her breath caught and she felt her nipples stiffen again. When her breasts began to heave up and down in arousal, he placed the pad of his thumb against her clit and applied agonizingly hedonistic pleasure in a circular motion. She gasped.

Sweet Cyrus, Nellie thought on a moan, she didn't want to orgasm for the very man who had kidnapped her. But those boys — they had worked her up into a fit of arousal, and then left her uncompleted. She'd been a step away from climaxing before her abductor had even entered the stone chamber. Now that he was here and stroking her clit...

"Please," she whimpered, her lower back arching.

His eyelids grew impossibly heavier. "Good girl," he said thickly. His intense steel gaze never once left her face as he watched her writhe and moan about on the slab of stone. He increased the pressure, rubbing her clit harder. "Come for me, little one."

She would have given anything to have been able to disobey him, to have been able to deny him the satisfaction of making her orgasm a mere three minutes after he'd entered the chamber, but her body had a mind of its own. And it wanted to come.

"Oh god." Nellie screamed as her nipples stabbed upward, then groaned long and loud as her orgasm jolted though her belly. Her hips instinctively rocked back and forth, giving her as much friction on her clit as was possible.

When the intensity began to wane, when she was once again aware of her surroundings, she warily looked up, her gaze clashing with his.

"They will definitely be punished," he said hoarsely. "No man but me will ever touch you again."

Nellie blinked. She'd forgotten that before her captor had brought her to peak, they had been discussing the fact that the teenage boys had been touching her without permission. She nibbled on her lower lip. They were just boys. In a world where any male higher than she was in the Hierarchy was allowed to play with her body at will, she didn't see the harm in a couple of teenagers wanting to see and feel what a naked woman looked like. "They were just curious," she said quietly. "They didn't hurt me."

A tic began to work in his jaw. "You would defend them?" he growled.

"I wouldn't defend any of you," she hissed. "Least of all you!"

He ignored her not so subtle reprimand. Releasing her labial lips, he stood up, his eyes flicking over her nude body. He studied her broodingly for a long moment, one palm running gently over her belly, then higher to graze over her nipples.

His dark head came up. His eyes found hers. "You can't escape me, Nellie," he softly vowed. "Even if you ran, even if you somehow managed to get away from me for a time, I'd always find you." His gaze flicked down to her breasts, then back up to her face. "But then, you know that already...don't you?"

She looked away, refusing to answer. She knew the truth, of course. He'd proven the validity of his claim when he'd disarmed her sector's security system just to steal her away. But that didn't mean she had to respond to his question.

Silence filled the cold stone chamber. For a long moment Kerick said nothing, though she could feel his eyes boring possessively into her.

"I grant you five hours time to come to terms with your fate, Nellie," he at last murmured, ending the quiet. "There is something I must see to, but I will return for you."

There was a pause and then she asked warily, "What exactly *is* my fate?"

The pad of his thumb lightly grazed the tip of one nipple. She shuddered. "In five hours time I will return for you. You will be waiting for me," he informed her, his voice thick with arousal. "And you will be both welcoming and compliant."

She took a deep breath. Her eyes closed briefly. "You mean to claim me as your sexual chattel then?" she whispered.

His hand stilled on her breast. "I would have thought that much was obvious."

Her head whipped around. She narrowed her eyes at him. "Do not mock me," she gritted out. "I meant that I have a career—I have a life!" she snapped. She looked away, refusing to make eye contact. "And you've taken everything away from me," she whispered. "And for what? To what end? To have a sexual plaything," she said bitterly, answering her own question.

He took her chin in his hand and gently nudged her face to look at him. "You belong to me now, Nellie." His harsh features didn't even waver, didn't show any sign of weakness or a willingness to let her go. "Now *I* am your life."

Her nostrils flared at his arrogance. What made his arrogance that much worse was the fact that she honestly didn't think he was trying to be a jerk—he simply wanted her and to his way of thinking that was just that. "You have no idea what you've just done," she bit out.

"Oh?" One dark eyebrow rose. "Were you the mistress of a leader in the Hierarchy? Do you think he will come here to find you?" His laughter was bitter, angry. She could surmise he didn't much care for any talk of her being intimate with another man, which she found odd. She'd thought all males realized that females rarely to never came to them as virgins. "I promise you, little one, that you will never be found. The weak males of the Hierarchy would never survive outside the protection of a biosphere."

Nellie gasped. Her eyes clashed with Kerick's. "We are..." She wet her lips. "We are on—on the...*Outside*?" Good god, she thought in a panic, any number of horrid things could happen to them outside the protection of the biosphere's perimeter. They could be killed by mutant animals—or worse by sub-humans. "I d-demand that you take me back," she stammered out in a wild voice. "Sweet Cyrus, but why would you sentence the lot of us to death!"

For the first time since she'd known him, she could have sworn his eyes gentled a bit. Just a bit. "I take care of my possessions," he said in low tones. "You have nothing to fear, Nellie."

She snorted at that. "How comforting," she said acidly.

"So as I said," he continued, his eyes narrowed, "your lover will never find you."

Nellie sighed. She shook her head slightly. "I don't have a lover."

Now it was Kerick who did the snorting.

Her jaw clenched. "Don't you think I'd tell you if I did? Holy Cyrus, but I'd love to make you as angry as possible," she gritted out.

Strangely, that appeased him. She could have sworn she'd seen one side of his mouth curl upward in an awkward semi-smile for a threadbare moment before he stifled the reaction and wore his stone façade once again.

Nellie blinked. Had she actually made the grim giant...smile?

She sighed. Why should she give a yen if she had?

"If you have no lover," Kerick rumbled out, his large hands palming her breasts and gently kneading them, "then why did you say I had no idea what I'd just done?"

Stubbornly, she refused to answer him. She harrumphed instead and looked away.

"You will answer me. Now."

She bit down onto her tongue as hard as she could to keep from screaming at his arrogance. Again, she didn't think he was *trying* to be an arrogant jerk because he'd gentled his voice in a way that said her reply mattered to him, but nevertheless the man had the social manners of a hybrid pig let loose at an elegant techno-opera party. She had to keep remembering that he had the upper hand here. For now.

"Nellie…" he warned.

She lay there for a protracted moment feeling petulant, refusing to answer. But she could feel his eyes boring into her as he stood beside her with an inhuman patience waiting for her to answer. She sighed. "I was developing a serum," she quietly admitted. "And I was close to perfecting it."

His large hands stilled on her breasts. "A serum?" He paused. "What kind of a serum?" he murmured.

Nellie's forehead wrinkled at the way he'd asked the question. He actually sounded interested in her answer, which was more than she could say about any other male she'd ever known. Typically the only time a male ever discussed her career with her was to give her his opinion on how selfish she was to keep one. "Sub-humans," she said quietly. She shrugged dismissively, but the gesture was far from casual. "My mother was…infected." She looked away, refusing to say more.

There was a long pause.

"We will discuss this at a later date," Kerick said softly. His palms cupped her breasts and kneaded them. "After you've come to accept your place as my possession."

Nellie's head flew to the side. Her gaze clashed with his. "Why? Why me? Why did you steal me and not another woman?" Her nostrils flared. There had to be more to this than mere sexual longing. "Were you sent by the Hierarchy to murder me?" she gritted out. "Because if you were I'd prefer to get it over with *before* you fuck me."

Another long pause.

"Why would they want you dead?" he asked softly.

It dawned on her what she'd just said to him, what she'd just told him in so many words. Her eyes widened at her own stupidity. How could she have given away so much information? Stupid! Stupid! "I—I…" She glanced away. "I was only jesting," she lied.

Silence filled the cold stone chamber.

"Your skin is chilled," Kerick at last murmured, dismissing her earlier remarks. A single finger traced the outline of an erect nipple.

She blew out a breath. Relief that he hadn't pressed for an explanation? Arousal at being touched so intimately? She no longer knew. "I am," she quietly admitted.

He released her breasts and pulled a small virtual computer device from the pocket of his black cloak. Three button sequences later, the locks on her legs unclicked, freeing them. A second after that she felt the chain that held her arms pinioned above her head give way. She cried out when her arms fell down to her sides, pain jolting through them as they came back to life.

Kerick sat down beside her and began to gently work the knots out of first her arms and then her legs. She averted her gaze the entire time, uncertain what to do or say.

"So long as you are a good girl and do not disobey me, I permit you to wander the length of both this stone chamber as well as the large underground dirt chamber most adjacent to the doors." He waved a hand toward the doors in question. "But you are to go no further. The other five chambers that comprise the catacombs we dwell in are off limits for the time being."

Nellie's eyes flicked around the stone chamber she'd been sequestered in. She sighed. Where was Cabel Modem when a woman in distress needed him? "There's not even a comfortable pillow-bed to sleep on," she grumbled. Given the fact that not having a pillow-bed to sleep on was the least of her problems, she wasn't even sure why she cared, but there it was.

Kerick finished working a large knot out of her arm, then stood up. "I've seen to it that we will have a comfortable pallet for sleeping." Her lips turned down at the word *we*. "But for now I must go. I will return to you in five hours time. Until then, feel free to wander the two chambers." His eyes narrowed. "But do not venture beyond the dirt chamber, Nellie. Be a good girl while I'm gone."

She gritted her teeth at his usage of the word *girl*. That was the second time he'd called her thusly. He truly did have the social manners of a hybrid pig. Had the man been raised in a damn cave? Oh that's right, she thought on a sigh, they were on the Outside. He probably *had* been raised in a cave. Sweet Cyrus.

She turned her head to look at him. His fingers idly sifted through her mane of dark red hair.

"I will not remove the sensory collars," he informed her, dashing her last hope of escape. "You will wear them always that you might remember who it is your body belongs to," he said thickly. His brooding eyes flicked once more over the length of her nude body, his gaze openly hungry.

As then, as if he'd just remembered a prior engagement, he abruptly stood up to take his leave of her. "Five hours," he reminded her, his voice once again steeled and in command. "I grant you but five hours. It's best if you use them wisely."

"Oh? And what do you consider a wise use of my time? Thinking of ways to pleasure you?" she asked bitterly.

He shrugged. "I admit the idea pleases me."

Her jaw dropped open as she watched him walk toward the stone doors. She couldn't believe the man's arrogance. "By what name do I call you?" she ground out. She knew his name, of course, but she wanted to hear him confirm it.

Kerick stopped when he reached the stone doors. He turned his dark head to look at her, his intense gray eyes finding hers. "Master," he murmured. "Your permanent one."

Chapter 12

"Kalast? How in the name of Cyrus did the wench ever make it to Kalast?" Kerick rumbled out the question to Elijah as he helped him transfer the unconscious woman they'd just stolen from the Altun Ha biosphere to the black land conveyance the trio had "borrowed".

Xavier raised an eyebrow. "I must have missed something vital to the conversation, amigos. How could the woman be on Kalast if we're stealing her away for Elijah to master even now?"

Kerick grunted. "Not this woman," he rumbled out. "Elijah was referring to that Kora Williams wench whose name keeps coming up on the virtual memory searches we ran."

Xavier's lips formed an O.

"Don't know how she escaped Earth," Elijah admitted as the trio took their places inside the rough terrain land conveyance. He jumped in behind them from the top of the vehicle before sealing the overhead entrance. "But she obviously had some help from within the Hierarchy, amigo."

Kerick's eyes narrowed in thought as Elijah engaged the land conveyance. The vehicle ignited and took off, hovering a few inches above the ground. "I wonder why she ran," he murmured.

"Dunno." Elijah's mouth, which was typically as glowering as Kerick's, curved upward in a slight smile. "And for tonight at least I don't give a yen."

Xavier snorted at that. "I don't want to hear about it. The two of you already have wenches to master and the best I can do is visit a droid Pussy Parlour," he muttered. "I haven't felt a real pussy in over ten years. Ten years! And when I finally break outta Kong, what do I get? Droid cunt. Very unfair, amigos."

Elijah's deep laughter echoed throughout the conveyance. Kerick's eyes twinkled good-naturedly but he didn't smile. "The Auctioneer will bring in a new crop of wives to bid on in a month's time. You'll have a better selection to choose from then, my friend."

"Shit, Riley," Xavier mumbled, "my cock will have fallen off by then." His head came up as he glanced at Kerick. "You sure you won't share? It's done all the time in poor households amongst brothers." He shrugged his shoulders. "Growing up, my own mother called five men master. My father and all four of my uncles."

Kerick's jaw tensed. He didn't like the idea of other males looking at Nellie, let alone sharing her body with them. Not even a friend who was practically a brother. "I don't share."

Xavier heard the subtle warning in his tone. He nodded once, dismissing the subject. "In a month then."

The males were silent for the next twenty minutes while the conveyance ventured toward the biosphere's perimeter. This was the tricky part, steering out of it without setting off any security devices within Altun Ha. Tricky, but not impossible. Indeed, they had already made this trip from the biosphere to the catacombs seven times since they'd escaped. This was the eighth time.

The seventh trip to the biosphere was, in Kerick's estimation, the best yielding one for it had been the same occasion that he'd unmanned the security system to reach Nellie—Nellie Kan.

And, as it turned out, *Doctor* Nellie Kan.

He had wanted her from the moment he'd broken into Vorice Henders' office chamber looking for information, but had ended up viewing Nellie through the sensory cameras instead. He had thought her a lab technician or perhaps a protégée for she had looked young to him. But no—as it turned out she was a full-fledged scientist within the Hierarchy who had seen thirty-two years.

Kerick had watched through the sensory cameras that night as Nellie had stripped off her clothing. He had lusted for her as he'd never lusted a woman in his life when she'd bent over into the laboratory closet, searching for—whatever it was she had been searching for. And when she had turned around and started playing with her tits and pussy...

He had known then and there that he would steal her away. Those large, heavy breasts, her ruby red nipples, and that rare breed of dark red hair—the sort of female he'd spent fifteen years in Kong fantasizing about owning.

Now he owned her, he thought possessively.

Kerick had decided upon stealing Nellie away that same night he'd viewed her through the sensory cameras, but she had thwarted him. Unknowingly on her part, most likely.

It had been fifteen plus years since he'd been within touching distance of a human woman, so seeing Nellie, smelling her scent, hearing her voice—it had shaken him enough to make him momentarily forget what he'd set out to do. By the time he'd mastered his wits, she'd been halfway to the atrium.

That evening he had cursed himself an idiot for allowing her to escape him so easily. It was a fact that would eventually inflame him, for getting to her after that had been no small feat. That night in the lab she had been easy pickings. But from that evening onward, she had been careful, very aware of her surroundings while coming and going, often having an armed guard escort her to and from the atrium.

Finally, not knowing what else to do, and desperate to keep her away from other males after having watched those Hierarchical scientists touch all over her body at the Fathom Systems party, Kerick had decided on taking her by force — at home. Elijah and Xavier had called him mad, but he'd ignored them and carried through with the course he'd set for himself just as he always did.

It had paid off. Nellie was in the catacombs even now. And she was all his.

"There's something I forgot to mention to you," Xavier said, ending the silence.

Kerick arched an eyebrow but said nothing.

"About that female named Kora who escaped to Kalast…"

"Yes?"

"She was a scientist within the Hierarchy when she fled."

Kerick's body stilled. "You are certain?"

"Very." Xavier frowned. "The virtual memory searches I ran were conclusive. I don't know what that means, if it means anything at all, but for some reason the correlation doesn't sit well with me."

"Nor with me," Kerick murmured. He thought back on Nellie, and how in a moment of fright and anger she had accused him of being an assassin for the Hierarchy. She had believed her own words without a doubt. Which meant that she had been expecting to die. Just like his mother had been expecting to die back when he'd been a small boy.

The question, of course, was why? What did she know?

"You better get your female to talk," Elijah warned. "She might know something without even realizing it."

Kerick inclined his head. Half of what Elijah had said was correct — Nellie probably did know something. But the other half of Elijah's sentence was most likely false — Nellie not only knew something, but she was aware of what that something was. "She'll talk," he rumbled out.

Xavier grinned. "Awfully sure of yourself, amigo."

"I am." Kerick stared straight ahead, his grim features concealed in the shadows. "It just means I shall have to master her sooner than I expected to is all."

Elijah looked doubtful. "Not sure that's possible, old friend, or even recommendable. Females are like pets—takes time and a lot of patience on your part for them to trust you enough to allow themselves to grow dependent on you."

"Under normal circumstances, perhaps." Kerick hated the harsh tactics he knew he'd have to use to bring Nellie to heel, but it was necessary. Her life might depend upon it. All of their lives might depend upon it.

Tonight he would greedily fuck her as many times as her body could handle, but tomorrow, in the morning, her mastering would begin. "But then these circumstances are not precisely normal," he murmured.

Chapter 13

AND ALWAYS, NIGHT AND DAY, HE WAS IN THE MOUNTAINS AND IN THE TOMBS, CRYING, AND CUTTING HIMSELF WITH STONES...

Stones.

Of course.

Nellie's teeth sank down into her lower lip. Her eyes widened as comprehension slowly dawned. Tara Riley was, if nothing else, too clever for her own good. She'd hidden her analogies well, had used ancient religious text to throw any potential and unwelcome journal thieves off the scent, but they were there as plain as a summer day in the Scandinavian biospheres are long if you knew what it was you were looking for.

Problem was, Nellie thought on a sigh, for the most part she still didn't know what she was looking for. Clues, yes, but clues to what?

For years she had believed that the worn diary would help her unravel how the sub-human had come into existence, which would help her create an effective serum. And although she still believed the journal held the key to the answers she sought, she now understood that Dr. Riley had been trying to tell her more. But what more?

She closed her eyes briefly, not wanting to deal with the implications of her suspicions. If what she was beginning to suspect was accurate, then it was very possible, in fact probable, that the journal not only answered the question of how sub-humans had been infected, but why...and worse yet, by whom.

AND JESUS SAID UNTO HIM, COME OUT OF THE MAN, THOU UNCLEAN SPIRIT.

AND HE ASKED HIM, WHAT IS THY NAME? AND THE DEMON ANSWERED, SAYING, MY NAME IS LEGION, FOR WE ARE MANY.

"Do you really want to know the answer, Nellie?" she whispered to herself. She brought her knees up and wrapped her arms around them, the stone pallet underneath her feeling cold against her naked buttocks.

She might be a captive today, she thought, but there was always tomorrow and with it a new chance to flee. By continuing her study of Dr. Riley's journal when she did escape, by purposely seeking out the answers she knew the diary held, she would, in effect, be changing the course of her existence forever. She would always be on the run, just as Tara Riley had been. She would be forced to remain in the frightening Outside world, a place where the only laws were the ones violent outlaws and equally dangerous sub-humans had created for themselves. She would—

Sweet Cyrus, nothing would ever be the same again. The chip, the sub-humans, the Hierarchy—somehow all connected.

Nellie took a deep breath and expelled it, her hand idly sifting through her mane of dark red hair. If she didn't do the right thing, she'd never be able to look at herself in the image map again. But if she did…well, she might not be alive long enough to do anything about the answers she dug up.

One thing was for certain, she thought as she glanced around the stone chamber she'd been thrown into: she had to get out of here. Now.

AND ALWAYS, NIGHT AND DAY, HE WAS IN THE MOUNTAINS AND IN THE TOMBS, CRYING, AND CUTTING HIMSELF WITH STONES...

"The zida stone," she whispered, her eyes round.

Nellie's heartbeat picked up rapidly and went into overdrive. A small smile tugged at the corners of her lips when the first piece of the puzzle clicked definitively into place.

The zida stone was a rare and costly gem strewn throughout the catacombs and mines of a few South American biospheres. The rock was not indigenous to Earth, for in reality it wasn't actually a gem but the scattered remains of a felled meteorite that had been blown to bits by the Hierarchy about forty years past.

Not much was known about the zida stone by the average scientist, for none would be so bold as to venture out of the perimeter of a biosphere to obtain and study one, but a few facts were known about it amongst Nellie's peers. Only a few, she realized, but they were important.

She stood up, hands on her hips while she paced, trying to remember the exact wording of the lecture Treymor Lorin had given her concerning the zida stone.

She sat on his lap naked, her back to his chest, her legs spread open, the fingertips of his right hand sifting through the triangle of dark red curls covering her mons. His fingers went lower, pressing against her clit, making her gasp. The two scientists who sat opposite Dr. Lorin chuckled, grateful to him for providing a show with a rare human female for their viewing pleasure.

"Ride me," he whispered in her ear before licking it. "My friends have traveled all the way from Biosphere 5 just to watch me fuck a real female." His free hand moved aside the silken white robe he wore, exposing his penis. He nudged Nellie's buttocks with the tip, telling her without words to impale herself on him.

Eighteen-years-old, and naively trusting of her mentor, she'd unquestioningly done what he'd wanted her to do. Raising her hips, she sank down onto his cock with a groan, impaling herself to the hilt.

She tried not to blush when, in a moment of lust, a seventy-year-old scientist began pulling at her young nipples and laughing while he told her to ride Dr. Lorin harder so her breasts would jiggle for him. She tried to feel no embarrassment when his colleague, a scientist of approximately fifty, stood up and stuffed his cock into her mouth.

"Suck on me," the fifty-year-old scientist groaned in a thick Irish lilt. He was dangerously close to coming already, his fingers threading through the hair on her head. "Oh yes, Nellie, what a good girl you are…"

Dr. Lorin's fingers painfully dug into the flesh of her hips, a reminder that she had better not forget to pleasure him as well. Still sucking on the scientist's cock while feeling her nipples get tugged on by the other one, she slammed her hips down hard and rode Dr. Lorin as fast as she could.

Her breasts jiggled up and down as she rode him, making the seventy-year-old hiss with pleasure as he watched the soft globes bounce up and down. He tweaked at her nipples harder.

Dr. Lorin made a soft purring sound, then continued his lecture while she fucked him. "The properties of a zida stone…

1. *The inside of the charcoal gray zida stone is said to contain a milky gray substance with a highly hallucinogenic solution.*
2. *The hallucinogenic solution is believed to be indigenous to the planet Xiom, a trader world on the eastern cusp of the Vega Star System,*

> *where the wilds of the mountains are so dangerous that not even native lifeforms will explore it.*
> 3. *The density of the zida stone is quite heavy, for when the rocks first hit the Earth's surface, they sunk below ground and ended up in catacombs and mines..."*

And that, Nellie thought, her breath catching in the back of her throat as she continued to pace the chamber, brought her to point number 4:

> *Nellie drained the fifty-year-old scientist's cock of sperm with her mouth, the sound of his gasps echoing throughout the terrace as she drank him dry. Dr. Lorin clutched her hips, his fingers imprinting the flesh there as he came on a loud groan, emptying himself of seed inside of her pussy.*
> *"And," he panted, taking a kerchief from his robe and mopping his brow with it, that brings me to the final property of a zida stone...*
> 4. *A strong magnetic force surrounds the outside of a zida stone, one so powerful that any electrically charged and/or radio-wave induced communications device within twenty feet of its position becomes shifty at best and non-effective at worst..."*

Her eyes flicked down to the sensory chains she wore, sensory chains that had been programmed using the most advanced electrical and radio-wave technology.

Advanced or not, she thought, her heartbeat thumping madly, a zida stone could polarize it.

Her eyes flicked toward the doors. She nibbled on her lower lip.

It was her only shot. She needed to escape. And, she thought as she slowly made her way across the stone chamber, she needed Tara Riley's journal back in her hands.

Nellie opened the doors quietly, her head poking out to ascertain if she was being watched. Sensing that the coast was clear, she was careful to make as little sound as possible as she inched her way out into the corridor.

Grabbing a lit torch from off of a nearby wall sconce, she kept her eyes alert for hybrid animal activity as she made her way deeper into the bowels of the Earth.

It was time to explore the adjacent dirt chamber.

* * * * *

"Steady," Kerick murmured, his eyes never straying from the pack of sub-humans surrounding them. "Keep it nice and steady, amigos."

Xavier swallowed a bit roughly. "I think I just shit myself," he muttered.

Elijah softly snorted at that as his grip tightened around the flash-stick he'd palmed when they'd first been ambushed. The land conveyance had short-circuited, leaving the group no choice but to trek through the jungle by foot. The woman he'd stolen began to quietly cry, so he drew her closer against his side with his free arm. "Give the word when you're ready, Riley," he said under his breath.

Kerick's gaze remained fixed on the largest of the creatures, the female he assumed to be the pack's leader. Her deadly black claws were fully visible, one spiking up from the tip of each finger. Her fangs were bared, indicating her hunger. A thick, viscous saliva frothed from the naked female's mouth, dripping down her chin and between her breasts. The crimson pupils in her slate black eyes held no warmth, no compassion or pity, no guilt.

But the rest of her looked as human as she'd once been. And that, Kerick admitted to himself, was what made killing a sub-human so difficult. This female had been infected by no fault of her own; indeed some human somewhere was probably mourning the loss of her still to this day, so much wanting their mother—or sister—or daughter—back, yet knowing in their heart that eventually she would die. Like this.

Did my mother die like this?

Kerick's eyes gentled with pity, even as he took a deep breath and opened his mouth to give the command that would sentence these creatures to death. His gaze flicked from the large female toward a smaller female child who looked to be no more than ten. Either the Hierarchy had purposely infected her or she'd wandered off from her family's domicile and gotten bitten by a sub-human, but either way the pathetic creature would never live to see another tomorrow. His nostrils flared at the injustice of it all.

Steeling himself against his emotions, and mollifying himself with the promise of retribution on behalf of those that would die today, Kerick aimed one brief nod in Elijah and Xavier's direction. "Let's do it, amigos," he murmured.

Xavier closed his eyes briefly, expelled a deep breath, then nodded back. "I got your back, old friend."

Three feet away, a low growling sound emitted from the little girl's throat as fangs exploded through her gums. Screaming the most horrific, blood-curdling sound imaginable, she squatted down upon her thighs and lunged long and high through the air, her claws spiking out as she aimed herself bodily towards Kerick.

Kerick sighed as he raised the muscled arm holding a flash-stick high into the air. He'd chosen this weapon as opposed to the others he carried to make certain that the kill was done as quickly and cleanly as possible.

He aimed the flash-stick's sites directly between the little girl's eyes as her body hovered over his head. She whimpered in mid-air, the sight of the weapon triggering a memory of a former life, and a former self.

Their eyes clashed.

Comprehension dawned in the child's gaze.

Kerick's heart constricted.

"Sleep with the angels, querida," he whispered.

* * * * *

Nellie closed her eyes and willed herself to calm down, commanded her breathing to return to normal.

This is no time to lose it, Nellie. Calm down. Start over. You can do this. You have *to do this! The serum has to be finished. You must get out of here and get that journal back.*

She opened her eyes and took a deep breath. Her gaze flicked around the underground dirt chamber. It was a large hollow within the earth, approximately twenty feet high and forty feet across. Three pools bubbled up from pits in the ground, two of them filled with precious mineral water and one with what she assumed to be boiling tar.

She held the torch up as her gaze narrowed at the pit of bubbling black sludge. Her eyes widened in comprehension. "That's not tar," she murmured. She stood up, then walked slowly across the chamber. When she'd reached the bubbling pit, she leaned over, crouching down upon her knees. "Definitely not tar."

The pit, she could surmise, had once been filled with virgin mineral water, just as the other two pits were. But something had caused it to change, to become blackened. Perhaps, she thought as she leaned in closer to the dark pool, perhaps something from the heavens had landed in it, forcing the mineral pool to change. "A meteorite," she whispered.

Nellie took a hard look at the underground chamber surrounding her, asking herself while she did if it was possible this underground hollow she was in had been carved out within the belly of the earth when a chunk of alien meteorite had struck it. "Very possible," she muttered to herself. "In fact, probable."

Her gaze flew wildly about the chamber. There had to be some sort of stick laying around. Or something—anything—she could use to dig into the black sludge with.

Nothing.

Taking a deep breath, she closed her eyes and ordered herself to find the courage to do what needed to be done. She had no idea what the chemical breakdown of the bubbling black pool was, or even the temperature of it, but she knew she had to stick a finger in it regardless, to see if it was temperate enough to place her entire arm in.

A zida stone, or perhaps many zida stones, could be wedged down inside the frothing pit. All it would take was one rock—just one—and her chances at escape would increase a thousandfold.

Her eyes flicked open. She took one more calming breath. "It's now or never, Nellie," she whispered.

Slowly, she lowered her hand toward the bubbling pool. Her heartbeat accelerated and perspiration broke out onto her brow and between her cleavage. She took a deep breath and expelled it, air coming out in a rush, as she quickly dipped her index finger into the bubbling ooze.

Her eyes widened. "It's temperate," she murmured.

Chapter 14
December 23, 2249 A.D.

Kerick couldn't remember ever being more tired. The walk through the jungle had taken hours — hours he could have spent with Nellie. It had been his intention to spend last night giving her endless pleasure and seeking his own in return, but now there was no time left for generosity. He had to get down to the business of mastering her. He had to break her to his will. His encounter with the sub-humans had only further solidified that fact in his mind, for he needed Nellie to talk.

Pulling himself out of the stream he'd been bathing in, he walked toward a hidden break in a nearby boulder that led to the catacombs below. Naked, he crept quietly into the break, stopped long enough to light a torch, then made his way down the rocky dirt path that led into the belly of the Earth.

The sound of a woman moaning made his heart stop. He came to a halt, his eyes narrowed.

It couldn't be Elijah and his newly acquired female making all that noise, for Elijah had taken his wench down into a deeper chamber, the same one he'd lived in for years whenever they'd had "business" to see to near the Altun Ha biosphere.

The moaning grew louder, causing Kerick's nostrils to flare. The voices, he surmised, were coming from the chamber he'd placed Nellie in. Enraged, he walked quickly toward where the sound was coming from, his muscles cording in preparation of a fight.

He would kill Xavier with his own two hands if he was fucking Nellie, he silently vowed. He'd gut him. Flay him. Strangle —

He stopped abruptly when he reached the stone chamber. His gray eyes widened fractionally. Where in the name of Cyrus was Nellie?

There were but two occupants within the stone chamber and neither of them was the woman Kerick had stolen for himself. His eighteen-year-old brother Kieran was one of the people in the chamber, and the young boy was greedily sucking the cunt of a gorgeous tied up blonde female who looked to be in her late thirties.

One corner of his mouth lifted in a small smile. He could gather from the fact that the wench wore no nipple chains — yet — that she was unmarried. Which meant the female had managed to make it for close to forty years before getting hunted down and claimed as a male's possession.

Now she was a possession. His brother's property.

Kerick shook his head and walked away, a grin tugging at his lips. Apparently after young Kieran has tasted Nellie—an occurrence he still got angry about when he thought on it—the boy had decided to go out and find a pussy of his own to lick and fuck. Kerick could well imagine what Xavier's reaction would be when he found out, which was why the grin. The thirty-six-year-old Xavier had made a direct path for the first droid Pussy Parlour available when they'd come out of the jungle, while eighteen-year-old Kieran was about to get the real thing.

Kerick made his way toward the dirt chamber, assuming it to be where he'd find Nellie. His cock stiffened at the thought of being inside of her, at the knowledge that after fifteen years of sexual deprivation he would finally be able to sink his manhood into a warm, welcoming cunt.

He hoped the beautiful scientist had spent the hours-long reprieve she'd been given to come to terms with her fate. She belonged to him now, she would always belong to him, and Kerick would never give her up.

After he buried himself balls-deep inside of her, he'd get her pregnant. And then, he thought, his cock stiffening all the more, he'd be permitted by the laws of the Underground to chain her nipples.

Then they would be official. And everyone would know she irrevocably belonged to him.

* * * * *

She prided herself on her cunning, on her ability to slip in and out of potentially threatening situations. When she had left the Underground safe haven of Xibalba, which was a network of ancient catacombs within the bowels of the Earth that learned females used to go into hiding within, she had done so with the intent of quickly slipping in to help Dr. Kan escape, then to quickly slip back out with none the wiser.

But Dr. Kan had apparently escaped before she'd even shown up. Either that or the scientist was being hidden away in a chamber she hadn't yet located.

And then the unthinkable had happened. She, a ten-year veteran of *locate-and-rescue* operations—and a lifelong veteran of throwing males of the species off her trail—had been captured.

She couldn't believe it. After thirty-seven years of managing to thwart the efforts of every male who had ever sought to claim her, she had finally been caught. And worse, she had been captured and claimed by a teenage boy who'd tracked her down with a cunning she hadn't thought males possible of.

Sweet Cyrus.

She groaned when yet another orgasm tore through her belly. Gasping for air, her eyes flew open and her gaze trailed down to where the boy—Kieran—was sucking on her pussy. Her clit was so sensitive she felt like it would explode if her captor didn't stop toying with it. Her nipples were so stiff that she feared even the softest of touches would be painful.

But he didn't stop—he never stopped. He sucked on her pussy again and again, wringing orgasms out of her that were so intense as to be painful. She could tell he was a virgin, knew that he'd never fucked a female before. His eyes were closed in bliss as he lapped at her, growls of pleasure erupting from his drenched mouth as he kept his face buried between her thighs for the better part of an hour.

By the time he was finished, by the time Kieran had sucked her pussy to his heart's content, she was a writhing, moaning, gasping, convulsing, half-hysterical female in dire need of being fucked. Whomever it was that had lectured to this boy on the ways of mastering had known what he was about.

He raised his dark head from between her legs. Panting, she watched as his handsome face bobbed into her line of vision. Their gazes clashed.

She watched in helplessness, in lust, as Kieran grabbed his swollen cock by the base and guided the tip toward her opening. Her nipples stiffened even more just from seeing the look of awe on his face, hearing the way he gasped when he slid the head inside of her wet cunt.

"Sweet Cyrus," he moaned.

"Go deeper," she heard herself whisper. "Slide all the way inside of me."

On a groan he complied, his heavy-lidded eyes squeezing all the way shut as he sank his young swollen cock into her pussy all the way to the hilt. His breath came out in a hiss as he began to move, his teeth gritting as he slowly stroked all the way in and all the way out of her flesh.

Her eyelids grew heavy. She shuddered when he lowered his face to her breasts and began licking her nipples as he continued to slowly thrust in and out of her body. "Faster," she gasped. She put her needs into terms she was certain even a naïve boy could understand. "If you want my pussy to make more juice for you, you have to fuck me faster."

He moaned from in between her cleavage, his heavy head coming to rest on her large breasts as his fingers played with her nipples. He continued to thrust slowly in and out of her, his eyes closed tightly. "I don't want to," he said shakily. "If I go faster my cock will spurt. I want it to last."

Sweet Cyrus, she thought, she'd never before considered how lust-provoking a virgin male could be. His face was pillowed on her breasts, so she could only see one side of it, but the view was enough to allow her to glimpse the dreamy expression on her captor's face. He looked as though he'd died and gone to the heavens.

Even the way his innocent fingers plucked at her nipples was a turn-on. He played with them intently, as if they were two new toys he'd just acquired and would never let go of. And then there was the slow, heady, mind-numbing sex he was giving to her…the expression writ across his face said it all: he wanted to savor every stroke.

She, on the other hand, was being driven insane.

"It's okay if you spurt," she whispered. She wished she wasn't tied up. Not only because it would make escaping easier, but perversely, because she also had a mad urge to run her fingers through his dark hair. "Your cock will stiffen up again and make more juice to shoot inside of me."

He raised his head from her chest and trustingly met her gaze. "Are you certain?"

Holy Kalast but she was certain. "Yes," she said thickly. She wet her lips. "I'm certain."

Kieran cupped her breasts as best he could, and then settled his large body atop hers. "I love you," he said with heart-wrenching innocence, almost making her feel guilty for planning to run from him. "I'm so glad I captured you."

She took a deep breath and expelled it. He was too young to separate affairs of the heart from affairs of the flesh, so would it kill her to give him back the words his expression said he was desperate to hear?

"I love you too," she murmured, her heart squeezing at the look of joy on his face. "And I'm glad that if I had to be claimed, it was by you." That, at least, was the truth.

Kieran grinned down at her as he rotated his hips and slid the head of his eager penis inside of her flesh. A moment later his expression turned serious when he sank into her pussy balls-deep on a groan.

He fucked her long and hard, moaning and groaning while he pounded in and out of her cunt, greedily filling her up with his swollen cock. He came quickly the first time, and again the second time, but he never stopped his fast, hard thrusting.

When she finally came for him, when her flesh began to contract around him and milk him of more seed, he somehow knew this was the last time he'd be able to come — for now. Squeezing his eyes tightly shut, he picked up the pace of his thrusting and crammed his cock harder and deeper and faster into her flesh.

He growled as he burst, frenziedly fucking her while his balls drained of cum.

A few minutes later, when they'd both come down from their mutual high and after he had removed the ropes that had bound her hands over her head, Kieran was too exhausted to do anything but sleep. Drowsy, he snuggled his face into her cleavage and popped a nipple into his mouth. He sighed contentedly, his large body pinning her smaller one to the animal hide bed.

She took a deep breath and blew it out, one hand leisurely stroking his mane of midnight-black hair while he slept.

Kieran and Kora. Kora and Kieran.

Holy Cyrus, she thought. They sounded like a singing droid duo.

Chapter 15

The sound of bellowing, of an enraged male losing control, echoed throughout the catacombs.

"What the hell?" Elijah muttered. He sat up, groggily looking around. His female, the imported English wench he'd stolen, slept quietly beside him. He sighed, then stood up and padded out of the chamber.

* * * * *

A popping sound echoed in the stone chamber as Kieran's mouth unlatched from around her nipple. His head shot up from her breasts.

"What's wrong?" Kora asked throatily, her voice thick with arousal.

"Dunno," Kieran admitted as he slid his cock out of her pussy. "But I'll be right back, querida." He grinned down at her before moving off her body.

She bit her lip. "Are you going to tie me up again?"

His eyes gentled, but he was nobody's fool. "Of course," he murmured.

Kora sighed as he went through the motions of securing her to the stone wall—sighing because her escape efforts had been thwarted or because she'd miss the feel of him stuffing his big penis into her while he was gone she was no longer certain.

He ran a large hand over her belly, then over the swell of her breasts. He plucked at a nipple before strolling from the chamber.

Her eyes flicked toward him, studying him as she watched him walk away.

He wouldn't be easy to escape from, she knew. He was young, he was in love, and he'd just claimed a pussy for his own private use.

Sweet Cyrus.

* * * * *

"This had better be good, amigo." Xavier, the first to arrive in the underground dirt chamber, swiped a hand over his stubbled jaw. "I just got back from the Pussy Parlour," he muttered. "Shit I'm tired." When

Kerick said nothing, when he simply stood there staring into space, Xavier cocked his head to study him.

Kerick's jaw was tensed, his muscles corded, his nostrils flaring. He looked like he was ready to kill someone. Xavier had never seen him this angry. "Amigo?" he murmured. "What in the name of Cyrus is wrong?"

"She's gone," he gritted out. Kerick's eyes narrowed as he slowly turned his dark head to look at Xavier. "Nellie escaped."

Chapter 16
December 26, 2249 A.D.

Slipping through the hidden console within the image map of her domicile, Nellie dragged herself into the bathing chamber as she tried to catch her breath. Sleeping by day and making her way through the rough terrain of the jungle by night had taken its toll on her both physically and mentally.

She had been on the run for the better part of four consecutive days, missing out on the festive holiday celebration within the biosphere while running for her life on the Outside. Christmas had always been her favorite holiday, so she was feeling melancholy that she'd missed it. Given everything she'd just gone through she wasn't certain why she even cared, but there it was.

She was tired, she thought weakly. She was hungry. She was dirtier than she'd ever before been in her life. And, she thought with a frown, she was also sick to death of being naked. But first things first…

Stepping under the sanitized shower, she instructed the machine to wash her hair, then called for her droid to wash her body. She closed her eyes as Cyrus 12 lathered her all up, running her silver hands up and down her body. Over her breasts, over her belly, then down lower to her mons.

Mmmm, she thought, her eyes closing, *this feels so good.*

She hurt everywhere. She ached everywhere. She'd been scratched up by branches, she'd skinned up her knees on jagged rocks, and she'd been chased down by hybrid animals. The only thing she could be thankful for was the fact that she hadn't run into even a single sub-human throughout the entire four-day trek back to the biosphere. The possibility had terrified her while on the Outside for she had been weaponless, but somehow, through the grace of Cyrus perhaps, she had escaped unscathed.

When the sanitized shower was finished washing her hair, she retired into her large bathing pool and instructed Cyrus 12 to wash it again. It felt incredible to have her hair shampooed — glorious even after having been so dirty for so long. The feel of the droid's fingers expertly massaging her scalp was almost enough to lull her to sleep.

She closed her eyes and smiled as she sank down lower into the heated, bubbling water. "I'm certain you made my excuses to Fathom Systems rather than telling my employer the truth?" she ventured.

"Affirmative, Dr. Kan. I told them you were feeling unwell."

Nellie nodded. She had expected Cyrus 12 would have the smarts to do so. Suddenly she was thankful she'd spent the extra yen on an advanced model like her droid rather than on one of the cheaper, less intelligent models. "Did anything happen in my absence I should be informed of, Cyrus 12?"

"Affirmative. On the night of your departure, the slave went back online at 2300 hours, approximately twenty hours after the estimated time..."

The droid went on to list every inconsequential detail that had transpired since Nellie had been kidnapped. She sighed, wondering if robotics engineers would ever learn how to make a droid understand the difference between crucial and trivial information. She listened with half an ear while she soaked, her muscles feeling infinitely better thanks to the bubbling mineral water of the pool.

"...and then this morning, at 0813 Zulu time, Vorice Henders and two unidentified males searched your domicile..."

Nellie's eyes flew open. Her heart rate soared.

"...they left at approximately —"

"Halt!" She wiggled out from beneath the droid's shampooing hands and turned to question her. "What are you saying?" she breathed out. She began to tremble. "They searched my domicile?"

"Affirmative."

Sweet Cyrus.

She closed her eyes and took a deep breath. Her eyes flew open and clashed with the droid's. "We have to get out of here," she said shakily. She willed herself to calm down and think rationally, but her gaze rounded as a thought struck her. "Did they find the book?" she whispered.

"To which book are you —"

"The journal," she said firmly. "Dr. Riley's diary."

The droid searched her memory cells. "Negative."

Nellie chewed on her bottom lip as she stood up. "Did they realize you were observing them, Cyrus 12?" It seemed a bit odd that Henders and his men would carry on with their illegal activities right in front of the droid, realizing as they must have that Cyrus 12 would report everything she witnessed back to her mistress. Her programming would allow for nothing less.

"Negative, Dr. Kan," the droid replied in a monotone as she attempted to help Nellie step into a full-length gold silk robe that was in the height of fashion. But Nellie was too busy running into her sleeping chamber to cooperate. The droid followed on her heels. "I was deactivated. The humans believed me to be unaware of their movement."

Well that explained Henders' laissez-faire attitude, she thought as she frantically opened up the secret panel within her pillow-bed. Her sleazy employer must have believed Cyrus 12 to be a cheap model. Less expensive droids didn't host the ability to assimilate information while deactivated, but the more expensive models did. Thank the heavens.

She keyed in her code, then expelled a breath of relief when the mechanism popped open, revealing the diary of Tara Riley within it. "Thank Cyrus," she muttered as she snatched up the worn book.

She whirled around to face her droid. She felt ready to lose it, ready to collapse from fear and exhaustion, but she knew that she couldn't. If she gave in now, if she even slowed down, the Hierarchy would find her. She couldn't allow for that — not when so much depended upon her survival.

"Listen to me, old friend," Nellie said quietly. She took the droid's hands in her own. "We have to leave and we have to leave now. If we don't, those men will come back and they'll kill us both." She knew it was the truth. They'd short-circuit Cyrus 12 to keep her from telling others what they'd done to Nellie. And Nellie, well, she knew she'd be the first one expunged from existence. "I need you to go dress yourself in a nondescript robe with a hood." She didn't want others to see the droid's face — nothing that could give away who they were. "I'm going to do the same. While I'm gathering supplies I want you to find us some manner of weaponry."

The droid nodded with a perfect human affectation. "As you command, Dr. Kan." She searched her memory cells. "But statistically you have a better chance of survival if you leave without me."

Nellie's heart wrenched. If she left Cyrus 12 behind, she would no doubt be raped and short-circuited beyond repair. She hadn't realized until that moment how much the droid had come to mean to her. "No. I'll take the chance." When Cyrus 12 opened up her mouth to cite more statistics, Nellie held up a palm. "Besides, your memory cells are citing probables that would be true if we were remaining in the biosphere." Her heartbeat picked up dramatically. "But we're going into the jungle," she whispered.

The droid hosted no pre-programmed knowledge of a jungle. "I do not understand this word…"

"The Outside," she said firmly. "Now let's go."

The droid's eyes widened as a human's would. "Statistically, the chances of survival are—"

"Please don't tell me." She turned on her heel and walked quickly to the other side of the sleeping chamber where her body décor had been draped. "I don't want to know as I've already beaten the odds once. Hurry up, Cyrus 12!" she said urgently. "We've got to get out of here. *Now*."

The droid obeyed without further argument, spinning around and making her way to the auto-kitchen to search for make-shift weaponry.

Nellie blew out a breath as she quickly donned a nondescript gray robe, then frantically threw together some supplies. Regardless to whatever statistics her droid might have spewed out, Nellie realized they only had one real shot at surviving. And that shot, she conceded, wasn't even a very good one. It was based upon the words of an infected woman—a female who might have been half delirious when she'd handed Dr. Riley's journal over to Nellie along with her small bit of esoteric advice.

"If ever you find yourself in trouble," the woman had warned, "look to the Outside and find the Xibalba."

Nellie blinked. Her brow wrinkled. "The Xibalba? What is—"

The woman's entire body began to tremble. Nellie backed up quickly, fearing a transformation would come upon the informant.

The woman bared her fangs, her body violently shaking. Nellie's hand flew up to her mouth to cover it, for she could tell the older woman was trying her damnedest to fight the insanity off and was losing. Mingled pity and fear welled in her eyes.

"Go to the Outside," the woman rasped as ten black claws jutted up from the tips of her fingers. She cried out as she gazed down at her trembling hands surrealistically, her expression horrified as blood dripped from the puncture wounds the claws had made when stabbing up from below the skin. She slowly backed away, preparing to flee before she did Nellie harm. "Look to the jungle and you will find the Xibalba."

Nellie watched as the older woman launched herself into the air and fled away into the night. She clutched the journal against her chest and took a deep breath, steadying herself.

Xibalba — the ancient Mayan word for Underworld…

The Xibalba was not real, she thought. Its existence was but a rumor, no doubt concocted by disgruntled females wishing to escape the horror of their everyday existence. An underground network run by learned women? No, it couldn't be real.

Could it?

Running back toward the bathing chamber to disappear through the image map, she stopped for a moment to take a long hard look at her sleeping chamber. Cyrus 12 said nothing, just watched Nellie mourn the loss of the life she had worked so hard to attain.

Years of hard work, years of diligent study and sacrifice...

It had taken all Nellie had to give and more to buy the domicile, the one place on Earth that had been all her own. Her eyes stung with tears that she refused to let fall.

She knew in her heart that she would never lay eyes on her home again.

* * * * *

"Well?" Kerick barked. "Did you discover any useful information?" His steel gray eyes tracked Xavier's movements as his friend alighted inside of the stolen land conveyance and sealed the overhead entrance.

"She definitely hasn't been back to Fathom Systems," Xavier said on a sigh. His features were grim. "Amigo, I think you better accept the possibility that—"

"They have not killed her," Kerick ground out. His jaw tightened. He *hoped* they had not killed her was more to the point, but he refused to allow himself to consider the possibility. If she was dead, he would never forgive himself.

Kerick had realized that Nellie was in danger from the moment she'd admitted to being a scientist within the Hierarchy. He should never have left her alone.

At the time he had thought it was the honorable thing to do— Elijah had aided him in deactivating the sector's security so he could steal away Nellie for his own, and so he had returned the favor for his old friend that Elijah might have the woman he coveted as well. He had even done as much before he'd had the opportunity to claim Nellie sexually, which was an activity his body raged from the need of. Aiding Elijah had seemed honorable at the time. Now it just seemed stupid.

"What do you want to do now?" Xavier asked as he steered the hovering land conveyance over the harsh jungle terrain.

Kerick pondered that question for a long moment. His eyes narrowed determinedly. "Return to the catacombs," he answered. It was the logical place to start. "I want to see if there has been any Underground whispers about a red-headed female scientist on the run."

The familiar mix of anger at Nellie for disobeying him mingled with worry for her safety knotted in his gut. He needed to hunt her, needed to get her back. When he claimed her this time, he'd see to it that the deed was done properly. He'd master her quickly, gain her trust and dependency, and from there he would be able to help her. He'd be able to help them all.

Kerick sighed heavily as his gaze flicked toward the wild jungle terrain outside of the conveyance.

If Nellie was out there he would find her.

He only prayed that he found her before the Hierarchy did.

* * * * *

THE HUNTER

"If women want any rights more than they's got, why don't they just take them, and not be talking about it."

— *Sojourner Truth*

Chapter 17

My Beloved Nellie,

I see the way you look at me, the fear so apparent in your eyes, and it breaks my heart as nothing else could. I know what is happening to me, lass. I know that it's just a matter of time before I am lost to you completely.

Will you ever know how much I love you, Nellie? Will you remember all of those precious years we spent together as a normal mother and daughter? Will you remember the walks in the rain, and the snowball fights every Christmas in the Winter Dome of the biosphere? Will you remember the giggles we shared every Sunday morning when we watched the virtual cyber-toons together?

Or will you remember me like this.

Like...a monster.

Oh, my beautiful Nellie, please don't remember mummy this way...

Sinead Kan,
December 24, 2230

Chapter 18

January 9, 2250 A.D.

When she was certain the coast was clear, Nellie motioned with her hand for Cyrus 12 to follow her toward the next set of large boulders. The formation of rocks, which she assumed had been scattered throughout the jungle by Underground dwellers for concealment purposes, was perhaps another four or five miles away by foot.

She had known from her studies years back that the ancient Mayans had once used the network of underground caves in their worship of the gods. She had not realized until the past two days just how many of these caves there were. It made the task of finding the Xibalba all the more difficult.

Xibalba, she thought on a sigh. She didn't even know if it existed or not. The word meant *Underworld* in the ancient Mayan tongue. The Mayans had believed that the mouths of the caves were the entrance to the spiritual underworld of the gods. Nellie just hoped that the mouths of one of these caves would prove to be the entrance to her own salvation.

She traveled through the jungle in silence with her faithful droid at her side, surrounded by the sounds of nocturnal creatures rising from their slumber to hunt. Cyrus 12 stayed on constant alert for sub-human and hybrid animal activity, while Nellie remained in the lead, going in the direction of...

She wasn't certain. She only knew that her instincts were telling her she was headed in the right direction, and instincts were all that she had to go on at this point.

If this Xibalba existed, Nellie adamantly vowed to herself, then she would find it.

* * * * *

The next several days proved to be the hardest of Nellie's life, and yet conversely, she became a more powerful woman for it. She grew stronger physically, learned how to feed and care for herself in an extreme environment, learned even how to wield deadly weapons to their best advantage.

The days were long and hot, the nights cold and lonely. She was more thankful than ever for Cyrus 12's companionship, realizing as she did that her droid was now the only manner of friend she would ever have — could ever afford to have.

Some nights, even most nights perhaps, her mind would wander back to the Underground catacombs and to the mysterious man named Kerick who had stolen her away. As she lay beside the ever-vigilant Cyrus 12, her gaze staring unblinking into the makeshift embers of the dying fire they'd built for warmth, she wondered if he ever thought about her since she'd escaped him, or if he'd simply gone out and stolen another female as a replacement.

She frowned, cursing herself as an idiot for even contemplating the question to begin with. Sweet Cyrus, did the answer really matter? Did she even care?

Nellie sighed, her eyes feeling dried out from a prolonged lack of blinking. There was just something so solid about that man, so powerful. Ironically enough, the steel resolve and physical strength that had scared her so mightily when he'd first stolen her from the Altun Ha biosphere seemed as though they'd be a blessing now, an assurance that she'd live to see tomorrow instead of dying out here in the jungle tonight. She knew death could be lurking just around the next corner, could take her unawares at any given time...

But sweet Kalast, that hardly meant she should think back on her captor! He had been interested in mastering her, in fucking her, not in helping her develop a serum, she reminded herself.

Nellie took a deep breath and expelled it, then settled in next to Cyrus 12 under the animal furs. The droid wrapped a toned silver arm around her middle, offering silent comfort while the scientist slowly drifted off to sleep.

There was no use in thinking back on the past, and especially not on the enigmatic Kerick. Chances are, Nellie knew, that she had already been replaced by another female captive anyway. But if she hadn't...

No. Even if she hadn't been replaced she could never go back. Not just because he was bound to be angry with her for escaping after the trouble he'd gone through to capture her, but also because they had different, disparate goals.

Kerick wanted sex. Nellie wanted a safe haven to work in while she developed the serum. And so she would continue down the path she had chosen, while praying to Cyrus that the path led to the Xibalba.

Nellie closed her eyes on a sigh, telling herself not to think about it. She ignored the voice in her head that reminded her of how intrigued Kerick had seemed by her talk of the serum, and slowly drifted off to sleep.

Chapter 19

January 21, 2250 A.D.

By the fourth week of Nellie's disappearance, Kerick's desire to recapture her became an all out obsession. She was all he could think about, all he ever dreamed about—all he wanted period.

For fifteen years he had controlled his bodily needs, not even allowing himself to masturbate except for on the rarest of occasions. At the time he had needed to exert that physical and mental control over himself, for it had helped him to retain his sanity in Kong. And, he conceded, it had also helped him to keep from grieving over never thrusting inside of a woman again.

But now he was free, a fact his body and mind refused to overlook. And the urge to mate, the urge to bury his cock deep inside of her tight, wet cunt, came upon him frequently and violently. His mental faculties felt no more advanced than an animal's these days, as it seemed he was finding a place to be alone every other hour just so he could violently jack himself off.

He needed Nellie, he mentally reiterated for the millionth time. He needed some information—anything—even the smallest of rumors to go on, and he would find her.

As Kerick prowled toward the commons chamber—the Underground earthen room used as a communal dining place by seven or eight different tribes of Outlaws who dwelled within these particular catacombs—he told himself he would make it through the meal long enough to ascertain if any of his men had picked up on Outside whisperings of Nellie, and then he would go. He couldn't stand to be in the commons chamber longer than was necessary anyway, for he was damned tired of watching his brother fondle all over the female he'd claimed while Kerick had been forced into celibacy, separated from his own.

Had he once thought it amusing when his nineteen-year-old brother had captured a wench for his own use? He grunted. When

Kerick himself had possessed his own woman, yes, he had found it amusing. Now that he was alone, however, the amusing had mystically devolved into the annoying. Suddenly he understood how Xavier must feel.

Upon entering the commons chamber, the first thing Kerick saw was young Kieran standing over his claimed property, pounding into Kora's pussy from behind like a battering ram. The wench was gasping from atop the stone table she'd been bent over, her breasts jiggling as she moaned during each hard thrust.

Kieran's eyes were closed as if concentrating intently on the feel of his captive's cunt, his fingers digging into the flesh of her hips as he pounded animalistically into her flesh from behind.

Kerick's eyes shuddered, lust coming upon him. He had a feeling he knew what he'd be doing after the meal, and he also had a feeling he knew who he would be doing it with — himself, he frowned.

Sweet Cyrus he needed to find Nellie.

But as lustful as he was, it was more than his need to own her, more even than his need to thrust inside of her and pound away at whim that made him obsessed with finding her. He was also terribly worried about her and was desperate to protect her.

On the Outside, and especially in the Underground, rumors abounded like wildfire. Yet Kerick had heard no whispers of a female scientist on the run. It was as if Nellie had been erased from existence.

But in his heart he knew she was alive. Knew, too, that he would find her. Only this time, when eventually he recaptured her, he would make no foolish mistakes. He would master her immediately.

And he would make certain she never escaped him again.

* * * * *

It wasn't until a bit later, a few minutes after Kieran's lust had been properly satiated, that Kerick realized he now had a sister-in-law. When the young Master and his new wife sat down to eat, he saw that the wench was wearing nipple chains. The last time he had seen her that hadn't been the case. Her nipples had been bare.

So Kieran had managed to get the wench pregnant, he mused. She had to be with babe. Otherwise his brother wouldn't have been able to marry her. In a world where males outnumbered females almost five hundred to one, the laws of neither the biospheres nor the Outside worlds would permit for a wench to be forcibly married to a male who couldn't breed her.

Kieran had proven his virility. And now his woman wore the nipple chains. No male save his brother would ever dare touch her again.

Kerick's eyes flicked down to his sister-in-law's breasts. A thin gold hoop circled the base of each nipple, the thin metal bands serving to keep her nipples plumped up. A delicate gold chain ran from the post of one hoop to the post of the other, symbolically binding her from the touch of other males.

His thoughts immediately returned to Nellie as a primordial jealousy knotted his insides. His brother now had the reassurance that no other male would ever touch his female. Kerick, on the other hand, had nothing.

His jaw tightened as he broodingly studied the new couple. He had to find Nellie. *Now.*

Kieran grinned as he flicked at one of his wife's nipples. "Notice anything new on her, brother?"

Despite his melancholy mood, a small smile tugged at the corners of his lips. The urgency Kerick felt to recapture his female before another male took her didn't lessen, yet he couldn't help but to take a moment to share in his brother's happiness. Kieran was to be a father. "Congratulations to you both," he murmured. "And welcome to the family, Kora Riley."

His sister-in-law was polite enough to quietly murmur a thank you to him, but she skittishly avoided his gaze—a fact Kerick found unsettling for reasons he couldn't quite pinpoint. It was as if she was hiding something, or perhaps plotting something, and was worried he would see right through her.

Or perhaps he was seeing conspiracies where they didn't exist, he sighed. Ever since Nellie had fled from him, his grim mood had grown all the grimmer.

Still, he would keep an eye on Kora Riley. A naïve male in the throes of an all-consuming lust and love (and who'd been nineteen-years-old for approximately five hours) could be fooled. Kerick could not.

"She didn't get her blood this moon cycle," Kieran arrogantly informed him. The muscled arm that lay across his wife's shoulder tightened, drawing her in closer to his side. "My babe is in her belly. Best birthday offering I've ever had."

Kerick's gaze flicked towards the new bride. She was pale as a sheet and slightly shaky. Almost as if she was in shock from the realization that she was pregnant. What had the wench expected to happen when Kieran had been eagerly mounting her day and night? Surely she was old enough to know how babes came to be in a female's belly. She had to be nearing forty, close to Kerick's own age.

"I'm happy for you, brother." Kerick's steel gaze trailed away from his sister-in-law's and back to his younger sibling's. "In truth, I am."

And, Kerick realized, he really was happy for him. Kieran had been deprived of everything growing up, including a home and most of his family. Their maternal grandmother had raised him, and had dutifully brought the younger Riley to visit Kerick in Kong once a year. She had been old and frail, but she had also been smart enough to never let the Hierarchy get wind of how Kerick and Kieran were related.

Now their grandmother lie dead, her remains lodged deep within the belly of the earth. She had held on for as long as she could, but in the end old age and grief over having lost her only daughter to infection overtook her. While their grandmother had been alive, she had dutifully prayed to Cyrus every day, begging for a cure, pleading with the fates to spare her daughter...

Tara Riley had done the unthinkable and gone into a remission of sorts for many years. Yet inevitably, tragically, his mother's illness had reclaimed her body and soul a final, shattering time. Kerick simply counted his blessings that Kieran had not picked up their mother's infected gene. His brother had undergone extensive testing from Underworld scientists and was without a doubt clean.

Kieran's birth had been the result of a rape, of a male who had forced himself upon their mother until her belly had swollen with child. It was true that in their world forcing a wench to have sex was as commonplace as breathing, but nevertheless there were still rules governing the act. Kieran's father had broken them all.

The sadistic bastard had shown their mother no kindness. He hadn't even married her after she'd ripened with child, insisting he'd never wed with an infected freak. He had even gone so far as to inform Tara that he had enough yen to buy a biosphere-raised female whom he could breed, so he had no intention of ever laying eyes on Kieran after his birth.

Not that his mother had given a yen, Kerick remembered. Tara Riley had always been a fighter and pregnancy hadn't changed that facet of her personality. If anything it had made her tougher and a thousand times more determined to invent a cure for her infection. But in the end she had been lost to them, Kerick had been so grief-stricken that he'd immediately taken out those he knew to be responsible for her regression, and Kieran had ended up being raised by their grandmother.

Marion Riley, Kerick thought nostalgically; were it not for their grandmother, the brothers would be virtual strangers today. But she had intervened and had made it possible for them to develop their brotherly affection. She had dutifully sent virtual messages to Kong once bimonthly, allowing the brothers to speak to one another as if they had been occupying the same chamber. The wily wench had even managed to make the virtual messages untraceable so the Hierarchy could never find Kieran. Their grandmother had done all she could do and more, and for that Kerick would always hold her memory in the highest esteem.

Kieran grinned, his next words breaking Kerick from his thoughts. "Alaisdair wants me to share her, you know. But I ain't." His smile devolved into a scowl. "I don't share."

Kerick snorted at that. Kieran had obviously inherited his possessiveness. "I don't blame you, brother," he mumbled, his mind wandering back to Nellie as it was prone towards doing. "I don't blame you at all."

Kieran sighed. "You'll find her, Kerick. Nobody doubts it, you know."

Kerick nodded but said nothing. If it was possible to find her, he would. He just needed a lead, any lead...

Xavier entered the communal stone chamber with a naked woman and her five Masters. Kerick immediately recognized the smiling and very pregnant female as Xavier's younger sister Madra. Madra had been purchased with five hundred stolen yen by the Tomi family about a year ago, so she now served in the role of wife to the fifty-year-old patriarch of the clan, as well as to all four of his grown sons.

By whom the babe in her belly had been sired of was anyone's guess, for it went without saying that all five of her husbands had mounted her. It was common for brothers to pitch in their yen and buy a communal wife, the general feeling being that so long as the males were of the same direct bloodline it didn't matter who sired the wench's children for the babes would still be of their line.

Kerick idly wondered how he'd grown to be such an oddity. Where most Underground men accepted, even expected, to share a wench, Kerick knew he'd kill any male who ever thought to touch Nellie.

Nellie, he mentally sighed. It always came back to Nellie. She might have escaped, but he still considered her to be his possession. He had no idea why he was so obsessed with her, a wench he barely knew, but there it was.

Perhaps it was because Nellie reminded him of his mother in fundamental ways—both were scientists, both were fighters. Perhaps he hoped that where he hadn't been able to save Dr. Tara Riley, he would be able to save Dr. Nellie Kan. That Nellie possessed an earthy, exotic lure didn't exactly hurt matters, he conceded.

Xavier motioned toward him, inducing one of Kerick's eyebrows to raise slightly. He murmured to his brother that he would bring his birthday offering down to him later, then stood up and walked towards his longtime friend.

Xavier O'Conner was roughly the same age as Kerick, thirty-eight to be exact. When Xavier had been captured by the Hierarchy and sent to Kong to work as a slave laborer for Federated Earth until his execution, Kerick had already been imprisoned for five years and their mutual friend Elijah for one year.

He had never expected to see either Xavier or Elijah again. When Kerick had first arrived at Correctional Sector 12 he had fully expected to be executed within a fortnight of arriving—when he learned he had been sentenced to fifteen years of slave labor before being put to death in the pit...well, that was when his plans for escape had begun to formulate.

Being reunited with his trusted friends had been both a solace and a sorrow. A solace because he was again surrounded by men he could trust, men he vowed to escape with. A sorrow because he knew there was no longer anyone on the Outside trained enough to continue the systematic assassinations of the Hierarchy leaders that the three of them had begun so many years back.

But they were free again. A fact every Hierarchy leader of Federated Earth was surely aware of by now. A fact that would cause every Hierarchy leader from Altun Ha to Dublin to exist in a constant state of paranoid wariness, inducing them to double their guard and tighten the security within their sectors.

As if that mattered. As if Kerick Riley, known as "The Grim Reaper" amongst his enemies, hadn't considered the fact that they would do that very thing. Stupid, the lot of them.

"I've got news, old friend," Xavier said on a grin.

Kerick grunted, then followed him to where they could converse in private. Growing up, Tara Riley had often teased the boys that their personalities were like yin and yang, light and dark. Where her son Kerick was brooding and intense, his friend Xavier was easily humored and laid back. Elijah Carter had been somewhere in the middle, neither dark nor light of mood and expression.

Tara, his mother, had often referred to them as her three babies, her prides and joys...her little killing machines, Kerick thought with a small, nostalgic half-grin. Ah — the wonders of boyhood.

"What the kong are you smiling about?" Xavier grumbled, now frowning. In truth, he only frowned when Kerick smiled — probably because the gesture mightily confused him.

Kerick shook his head slightly, snapping back to normal. "Nothing," he muttered. "I was just thinking back on when we were boys."

Xavier nodded. By mutual, silent understanding they never spoke of Dr. Tara Riley aloud. And especially not to Elijah. Where Kerick and Xavier missed her as sons missed a mother, Elijah missed her as a lover who'd had his soulmate cruelly snatched from him.

Elijah and Tara had never consummated their relationship, both Kerick and Xavier knew. The ebony giant had been deeply in love with Kerick's mother, a short, pale woman twice his age, but he had honored her desire not to be mastered when she could go out of remission at any time and turn on the only man she had ever known love of the heart with.

If Elijah regretted having given Tara Riley the choice to gainsay him, he'd never said as much aloud. But then Kerick and Xavier were thoughtful enough not to question him. The memory of Tara Riley was a sacred one to Elijah, one he'd allow no man to cheapen.

Indeed, when Tara Riley had been lost to them a final time, it had been Elijah, not Kerick, who had dealt the deathblow to Kieran's father, the man directly responsible for his mother's devolution. Kerick had managed to track down and exterminate all of the Hierarchy leaders responsible for Tara's demise save Maxim Malifé, Malifé having gone into hiding and thwarted him. By the time Elijah had hunted the sadistic man down and done away with him Kerick had already been captured and imprisoned within Kong for four years. Elijah had joined him not long thereafter.

"You said you had news." Kerick motioned toward an empty stone table away from the throng of Outlaws. "Get on with it."

Xavier grinned, taking the cold slab of a seat beside him. "It's amazing what one can learn at the Pussy Parlours, amigo."

Kerick grunted but said nothing. It was by now a bit of a running joke amongst Xavier, Elijah, and Kerick that Kerick was the only one of the three of them that hadn't been inside of a cunt since their escape. Elijah had the wench he'd stolen to release himself into — a wench who bore a strikingly eerie resemblance to a young Tara Riley — and Xavier had become a connoisseur of droid Pussy Parlours.

But Kerick didn't want to empty his seed into an emotionless droid. He was saving everything he had, not to mention every bit of stored up anger, pent up jealousy, and prolonged frustration, for Dr. Nellie Kan.

He knew the intensity would be hedonistic for him and frightening for her. But a certain level of fright was needed to successfully master her in a short period of time. It would cause her woman's heart to appreciate the gentleness he'd show her towards the end of the mastering, cling to it and thereby to him.

"Here's the bones of it, amigo," Xavier said in low tones, breaking Kerick from his thoughts. "Two Outlaws claim to have run into a redheaded woman and a droid out in the jungle a few days back."

Kerick stilled, his jaw clenching. "Run into her?"

Xavier sighed. "They didn't fuck her if that's what you're thinkin'." He grinned. "Seems the doctor and her droid made short work of them. She knocked them out with makeshift weaponry when they tried to claim her, but apparently she couldn't bring herself to kill 'em since they're alive to talk about their humiliation. Sweet Cyrus, how embarrassing!"

Kerick snorted at that. "I'm surprised they spoke of it with you," he rumbled out. His eyes twinkled with an odd sense of pride upon hearing of Nellie's escape.

Xavier's easy grin faded. "Not willingly they didn't, amigo."

Kerick nodded, the silent implication that Xavier had tortured the information out of them not a surprise. It was the way of the Underground, a place where only the strongest survived. In a bleak, desolate world where the majority of men grew old and died without having ever thrust inside of a real woman's flesh let alone impregnated one, shedding the catacombs of one or two more males was hardly frowned upon. In fact, just the opposite.

"Did they give you coordinates?"

Xavier frowned, scratching his chin thoughtfully. "Yes."

Kerick absently flicked a hand toward him. "So why the frown then?"

"Because the coordinates were near the Crossroads." He sighed. "If that redhead and her companion truly are Nellie Kan and her droid, they could be anywhere, old friend."

Kerick agreed, yet he felt his hope rekindle despite the news, felt the familiar adrenaline surging through his veins. The Crossroads was an area within the belly of the earth where seven Underground passages converged, allowing Outlaws to choose from seven disparate routes that all led to far reaching points of the biospheres within this part of Federated Earth.

It was true that Nellie could have taken any of those routes, but it was also true that she was still alive. She had to be, Kerick thought with mingled impatience and possessiveness. Redheads were a rare breed of female. That the two Outlaws had spotted one was a good sign of her survival.

But what was she doing on the Outside? Kerick uneasily asked himself. Surely the wench would have headed back to the Altun Ha biosphere...

The droid was with her, he remembered, his body stilling. She *had* returned to the biosphere. Which meant someone or something had forced her hand into fleeing from the perimeter of protection.

She knows something. Find her before the Hierarchy does...

Kerick rose from the slab of stone, impatiently shooting up to his feet. He waved off Xavier's assistance when his friend prepared to stand up. "I hunt alone. You need to remain behind to watch the others." He turned his head, his gaze narrowing at his sister-in-law. "Keep your eye on that one," he rumbled out.

Xavier followed his line of vision. "All right. But why?"

Kerick's answer was slow in coming, thoughtful. "I don't trust her. She's going to try to escape or...something." He didn't know what, only that his instincts always seemed to be on full alert whenever he was occupying the same chamber as her. "Just watch her," he muttered.

Xavier nodded. His gaze strayed to where his sister Madra was seated naked on the lap of her eldest husband. He absently watched his sister groan as a second husband sat on his knees before her outspread thighs, lapping at her cunt. The eldest husband rubbed her ripe belly, then massaged her stiff nipples as she shuddered and climaxed.

"Consider her watched," Xavier promised, his gaze flicking back to Kora. "I won't let the wench out of my sight."

Kerick nodded, satisfied. Xavier was always as good as his word. "Tell Elijah where I've gone," he threw out from over his shoulder as he strode away. "When I return, we will resume our planning."

As he made his way deep into the belly of the earth, Kerick half wondered if one of the reasons he was so desperate to find Nellie was out of the primitive desire to insure that his bloodline carried on when he died. The final battle with the Hierarchy would most likely be the final battle he ever fought in the mortal realm. Getting Nellie ripe with his child before the onslaught would at least allow him to rest in peace, knowing as he would that a fundamental part of him had managed to survive and would flourish.

Nellie might have been biosphere-bred, but she was capable, cunning, and strong. Any child he put in her womb would live to see old age.

Of this Kerick was certain.

Chapter 20

"Happy 14th birthday, Nellie," Nicoletta Kan murmured. She turned to Nellie's mother, then gently squeezed her hand. "She's beautiful and brilliant, Sinead, as are you."

Sinead Kan smiled proudly, tears that would never fall making her eyes glisten. She squeezed Nicoletta's hand back. "Promise me you will always care for her. Promise me…"

Nellie's smile faded as she listened to her mother's troubled voice. She had tried to forget for a moment — just for a moment — that her mother's devolution was growing worse, that Sinead would soon be lost to her, and to Nicoletta, for all time.

Nicoletta. Her father's second wife. It was illegal within Federated Earth for a male to possess more than one wife, yet the Hierarchy always overlooked the law where wealthy, powerful males were concerned. Nellie's father had proven to be no exception for he owned a grand total of five.

"Of course, bella," Nicoletta whispered in her throaty Italian accent. Her eyes softened, grew worried. "Do not think upon what has yet to transpire, my friend."

Nellie drew in a deep breath and shakily expelled it. She was thankful indeed for the friendship Nicoletta had gifted her mother with. She supposed the two women, "rivals" for Master Kan's affection, should have hated one another. But they didn't. They adored each other.

Perhaps because Nicoletta hated Master Kan with as much venom as Sinead did.

The Master's other three wives, all of them shallow and vain wenches, worshipped their husband. But then they were more interested in the elevated status marriage to him had brought them than in concerning themselves over trifles…such as the fact that they were wed to a demon wearing human skin.

"I know," Sinead answered, trying to hide her pain behind a smile. She forced a chuckle. "I need to quit sounding so morbid and so…" Sweat broke out onto her forehead. She closed her eyes tightly and expelled a raspy breath.

Nicoletta instinctively shot up to her feet, her hand reaching for the flash-stick she had made a habit of carrying.

Nellie's breathing grew labored as she slept. Her head thrashed back and forth, violently ramming against Cyrus 12's silver breasts. "Oh no, mommy. No, please don't…"

"Oh God!" Sinead cried out, pain lancing through her. "Help me, God!"

Nellie's piece of birthday cake fell from her plate, forgotten. She paid no attention as the honey-cake plopped onto the floor of the auto-kitchen, the thick sugary frosting sticking to the expensive tiles. She was too busy crying, too busy softly weeping as she watched her mother turn into…a monster.

"Sweet Cyrus!" Sinead screamed as she shot up to her feet.

Nellie's hand flew up to cover her mouth as she watched blood spurt from the puncture wounds her mother's jutting fangs caused.

"Why would your father leave you here with me?" she cried out in a tortured voice. "He knows what I am!"

He made you what you are, mommy, *Nellie thought. She said nothing, just watched as she prayed to Cyrus that her beloved mother might be spared.*

"Fight it!" Nicoletta pleaded, even as she grabbed Nellie by the arm and backed up a few steps. "For the love of the ancient saints, Sinead, fight it!"

Sinead screamed, clawing at her face with the dagger-like nails that shot up from her fingers. "I cannot!" she wailed. Her voice turned deep, demon-like. It reverberated throughout the chamber. "For the love of my daughter, Nicoletta, kill me!"

Nellie shook her head back and forth. Oh no – please no!

"Do not do this to me!" Nicoletta screeched. "Fight it, Sinead! Fight it!"

But there was no more battle to be fought, Nellie realized on a sob, as she watched her beloved mother turn on the woman who had been Sinead's best friend.

Sinead picked Nicoletta up off of the ground like a doll, her hand wrapped around the other woman's throat. Nicoletta's face swelled up and turned purple, her throat issuing hellish gurgling sounds as she was slowly strangled to death. The flash-stick dropped from her hand, clanging on the hand-painted tiles…

Nellie's gaze darted toward the weapon.

"I told you," Sinead said to Nicoletta in the darkest, deepest voice Nellie had ever heard, "to kill me." Her mouth twisted into a cruel smile, her unblinking eyes glowed a blood-stained crimson. "But now I'm hungry."

Her breathing labored, her young breasts heaving up and down, Nellie watched in horror as her mother's mouth slowly opened, revealing two rows of serrated teeth. Oh no. Sweet Cyrus, please –

Nicoletta's brown eyes widened in terror as the suffocating woman watched her best friend reel her into the awaiting mouth. She tried to scream, Nellie could tell, tried to call out for help, but she was being strangled…

Nellie scrambled to the floor. She reached for the flash-stick.

Sinead pulled Nicoletta closer. And closer…

Nellie's heart rate shot up. Perspiration dotted her brow.

"Mommy, no!" Nellie called out in anguish as she jumped up from the tile floor and pointed the flash-stick at Sinead. "Let her go! For the love of the woman you once were, I beg you not to make me do this!"

But it was like bargaining with an animal – a predator whose instincts were telling them that they needed to feed.

Or a demon being demanded by its master to kill.

The gurgling sounds Nicoletta made grew raspier, more tortured. Sinead's mouth opened wider, her claws digging into Nicoletta's neck and puncturing the skin…

"Noooo!" Nellie screamed as she raised the trembling hand holding the flash-stick. "Noooo!"

Nicoletta fell to the floor like a broken doll, forgotten. Sinead turned on Nellie, her mouth twisting into a lunatic's smile, a low hissing sound issuing from the depths of her throat. There was no Sinead left. There was only a monster.

"Forgive me, mommy," Nellie murmured, a single tear tracking down her cheek. She aimed the flash-stick directly at Sinead's heart. "I will love you forever."

Closing her eyes, unable to watch as she murdered her own mother, Nellie detonated the weapon. A beam of energy pulsed out from the flash-stick, killing Sinead Kan instantaneously, charring her flesh until it fell from the bone.

Nellie stood there, in shock, for what felt like an hour. She couldn't move, couldn't speak, couldn't even cry.

A murderer. She was a murderer.

Her beloved mother was dead.

"She loves you," a soft, raspy voice whispered as a gentle hand came to rest on her shoulder. "Sinead will always love you, bella Nellie."

The tears came all at once, making Nellie gasp for breath. "Nicoletta," she sobbed as she turned into the other woman's embrace. "Oh Nicoletta…"

Nellie cried out as she shot up into a sitting position, waking up in a cold sweat. Her breathing was labored, perspiration covered her forehead.

Her mother was dead. She'd killed her own mother…

Her nostrils flared in anger. In hatred. *You are the murderer, father. Not me. How could you do that to your own wife? To your own daughter?*

Nellie fell back onto the animal furs, breathing deeply to steady herself. She gazed up into the night sky, unblinking.

She would end it. She had always known it was her destiny to end it.

"Let's resume trekking," Nellie murmured to Cyrus 12. She swallowed against the lump of emotion in her throat. "We must chance venturing into the Underground again," she whispered. "We must find the Xibalba."

Chapter 21

January 22, 2250 A.D.

The Crossroads

Kerick followed the tracks of two sets of foot impressions — one left behind by what had to be a droid, the other left behind by what was no doubt, at least in his mind, a human wench.

The foot impressions could belong to none other than Nellie and her machine companion, he told himself, his sharp gray eyes flicking about the cavern. Underground dwellers could not afford to own a droid. And even if they could afford to, they had no legal means for purchasing one.

Kerick came to a halt when he reached the large Underground portal of the Crossroads. Outsiders carrying torches trekked on foot all around him, some of them accompanied by a communal wife, but most of them traveling alone.

His gaze flicked about, considering the seven different routes she could have taken. Tracking foot impressions would be impossible from this juncture forward, he realized, for too many travelers were even now leaving behind their own marks, unwittingly covering up the tracks Nellie Kan and her droid had left behind.

If I were a wench traveling by foot without a Master, which way would I go?

His eyes narrowed in concentration as he considered the options. Cavern 1 led to the northeast, Cavern 2 to...

His body stilled. Adrenaline coursed through his blood. There could be but one path.

The path less traveled by...

Kerick walked slowly toward Cavern 7, the route that led into the deepest part of the Earth's belly. He stopped when he reached it, his eyes flicking over a stone sign with Spanish writing carved into it.

AVISO: ZONA PELIGROSA. (*WARNING: HAZARDOUS ZONE.*)

Squatting down on his muscular thighs and using his torch to shed light on the dirt ground, Kerick's gaze methodically studied the packed mud of the cavern's floor. His eyes narrowed in concentration as he searched for clues that would tell him whether or not Nellie had traveled down this route—foot impressions, fibers from body décor—anything would give him the answer he sought.

"I'm going to find you, Nellie Kan," Kerick murmured, his eyes scanning the ground with the efficiency and detail of a hawk's. "One way or another you will be—"

His words came to an abrupt halt when the light from the torch hit upon…something. He reached toward the object, carefully picking it up between his thumb and forefinger.

Hair, he thought, his body stilling. He had found three strands of dark red hair.

Kerick's jaw clenched in resolve. He had been led a merry chase, but the hour of Nellie's mastering was within his grasp once again.

His gaze flicked down the long, wide corridor of Cavern 7. "One way or another, you will be mine," he murmured.

* * * * *

"Cyrus 12?" Nellie whispered. She swallowed roughly as her eyes attempted to adjust to the darkness. The torch had gone out at least fifteen minutes ago, the light from the wick having been snuffed out during the small avalanche she'd managed to survive. Now she understood why Cavern 7 was considered a hazardous zone. She just prayed to Cyrus that her droid had managed to survive the impact, for it had been her droid who had shielded her from the falling rocks.

Nellie bit her lip. She would never forgive herself if Cyrus 12 had been crushed beyond repair. The droid was a machine, true, but she was also the scientist's faithful companion. "Cyrus 12?" she asked again, her voice a bit shaky.

She knew that they had fallen into some manner of antechamber, but hadn't a yen as to what it was or where it could possibly lead to. If only she could find a way to ignite another torch—

Nellie's heart all but stopped when three men bearing torches entered the antechamber. The trio looked to be brothers, for all of them were possessed of the same blonde hair, lanky build, and scratchy body décor. She tried to shield herself, tried to duck behind a boulder before they saw her, but she didn't move quickly enough. They came to an abrupt halt the minute they spotted her, their faces shocked. And then their expressions changed...

Her cat-like green eyes widened in alarm, recognizing those expressions for what they were.

Lust. Gluttony. Malicious intent.

She swallowed again, her heart rate soaring. Without Cyrus 12's protection, Nellie realized she would never escape this antechamber without being raped.

Or worse yet, raped and claimed.

"Well lookie at what we got here, amigos," the tallest one said on a chuckle. His grin widened, showcasing his rotted teeth. "And here I thought we was just gonna find us some more flint today. Looks like we're gettin' us a cunt instead."

Nellie gulped. Her gaze darted nervously about the dimly lit antechamber as she tried to find a method for escape. And a weapon to defend herself with.

"Sweet Cyrus, but ain't she pretty!" the youngest one said excitedly. "We're gonna have us the hottest pussy in the Underground!"

"Not so fast," the third man said warningly. He was shorter than the other two, but the gruffest looking of the bunch. This was obviously the trio's leader. "We gotta get her pregnant before we take her back to the tribe, otherwise everybody will wanna poke her. Nester," he said conversationally, as if Nellie wasn't standing there listening to all this, "go build us a fire. We're gonna be here a while. Zeb, you help me corner the wench."

Nellie closed her eyes briefly, steeling herself. The thought of being mounted and continuously impaled by these three disgusting males was enough to induce vomiting. She had to find a way out! she thought hysterically. Sweet Cyrus, please...

"Come here, little wench," the tallest one said quietly, holding out his hand to her. He made kissing sounds with his lips, as if calling to a dog.

Her nostrils flared at the insult. Obviously he'd never been around many females. She scurried back, yelping when she accidentally hit her head on a boulder behind her.

Now she did sound like a dog, she thought grimly.

"Look at them big breasts," the tallest one — Zeb — said in awe. "Holy kong, she must be biosphere bred."

Nellie's heart rate picked up, thumping against her chest. She took off, madly dashing away as fast as her feet could carry her. "Help me! Somebody help me!" she cried out as she ran between boulders.

She was tackled a few seconds later, inducing her to scream. Two sets of meaty hands dragged her to the ground, simultaneously covering her mouth. She gasped when her stomach hit the rough earthen floor, the wind knocked out of her on impact.

By the time she could breathe again, it was too late. Nellie closed her eyes and softly cried while the two men tore at her tattered body décor.

Chapter 22

It had taken the trio of Outlaws less than a minute to discard her body décor. It had taken them less than five additional minutes to gag her and then subdue her flailing body.

Staked out spread-eagle on the ground, her arms pinioned above her head and her ankles tied to her thighs and bolted to the ground so she couldn't straighten out her legs, Nellie could only lie there and watch as the two males stared at her exposed cunt.

She flinched when one of the males grabbed his own erection and squeezed it, his meaty hand pressing against the rough wool of his trouser-like body décor. She tried to scream, but the gag made it impossible.

"Where the kong is Nester?" Zeb asked, his voice incredulous. "I'm gonna fuck her without him if he don't hurry."

The leader of the brothers looked around the antechamber and sighed. "Don't know. I'll go find him." He turned to Zeb and, in a lightning-fast motion, wrapped a hand around his neck and pulled him in close. "If you fuck her before I do, I'll kill you. Y'hear me, boy?"

Zeb nodded between gurgling sounds. The leader released him. "I'll be right back."

Nellie closed her eyes briefly, thankful for the small reprieve. She tried to calm down, for she knew her labored breathing was causing her large breasts to heave up and down, which was only serving to snag Zeb's undivided attention. Attention she most certainly didn't want.

The brothers were truly the ugliest males she'd ever laid eyes on. But it was more than the ugliness, more even than the rotted teeth and oniony breath, that had all of her senses on full alert. It was that bizarre gleam that haunted their eyes…

They had been infected, she knew. The disease was only in the beginning stages, so there was no guessing how long it would take before they turned. She could only hope that she managed to escape them before it happened.

Otherwise, today's rape victim would be tomorrow's dinner. And then there would be no serum. She chilled at both thoughts.

Ten minutes later, Zeb was pacing the antechamber floor, clearly torn between following orders by waiting on his eldest brother to return, and using Nellie before the brother did make his reappearance. He was growing more and more anxious and agitated as each second ticked by, a state of chaos that was making Nellie more nervous as well.

It was getting chilly inside of the antechamber, inducing Nellie's nipples to harden. She could feel cold air hitting her pussy, which was quickly making her all the colder. She wanted to ask for an animal fur, but the gag prevented her from doing so. She couldn't even motion with her hands or legs that she needed to ask a question because she had been well secured to the dirt ground.

Finally, Zeb stopped his pacing. He turned his head toward Nellie, his hands on his hips. "I'm gonna go find my brothers. Don't even think about gettin' away, wench. Horan would kill you. He ain't right in the head sometimes."

Which meant the eldest brother's devolution was growing more acute than the others'.

"I'll be right back." Zeb reached down and pinched her nipples, making her flinch. "Then I'm gonna suck on these babies all night." With that he stood up and stalked from the antechamber.

Nellie laid there, cold and shivering, for what felt like hours. Perversely, her mind often wandered back to her first captor, a grim reminder that if she had to be held against her will by a male, at least she would have been detained by an attractive one not showing signs of devolution had she not fled from him.

But that didn't matter. And, she reminded herself, she wanted to be captured by no man. What she wanted was to escape.

Think, Nellie! Think!

Nellie began to systematically check the binds for weaknesses. She struggled against the hemp ropes, hoping to tatter them against the nails the brothers had used to stake the bindings into the ground.

But by Kalast, it was no use. The harder she struggled, the tighter the binds became.

She cried quietly from behind the gag, praying for help.

Just then she saw the shadow of a large male appear against the far wall of the antechamber. He was carrying a torch—

Nellie blinked. He was carrying a torch, a satchel, and he was…hooded.

Sweet Cyrus. Could that be—

No. No, it wasn't possible.

Nellie's cat-like green eyes widened as she watched the male slowly walk towards her. It felt like it took forever before he finally came to a standstill before her splayed out body, but when he did, he at last lowered the black hood…

Kerick.

Nellie gulped from behind the gag as she watched those intense, familiar eyes trail up and down her naked body. He looked at her with lust, with need—with anger.

"I told you once that you could never escape me for long, Nellie Kan." His words were rumbled out in that dark, forbidding voice of his. The voice that said she had reached the end of the line and that she would belong to him until the day she died.

That explained what had become of the brothers. He had picked them off one by one, systematically hunting them down like prey. That way there had been no screams.

She swallowed nervously.

Kerick's steel gray eyes flicked from her cunt up to her face. His jaw was clenched, his muscles visibly corded. He removed the satchel he carried from off of his shoulder and flung it down to the ground beside her. "One thing I am not, wench, is a liar."

Chapter 23

Nellie screamed from behind the gag, her body thrashing madly against the binds to no avail. Kerick made no move to stop her, just stood over her like a grim guardian and stoically watched as she wore herself out. He had removed his cloak several minutes ago, and now wore nothing save the black woolen pants that were molded to his muscled lower body like a second skin.

By the time she calmed down and quit fighting, she was exhausted. The fact that she was having difficulty breathing was visible by the dramatic heaving of her breasts.

Kerick came down on one thigh beside her, a callused palm running over her belly. "I'm removing the gag that you might catch your breath," he murmured. "I'd advise you not to scream." One eyebrow rose slightly. "Unless you desire to watch me kill any male who might enter this antechamber."

Her body stilled. She hesitated, then shook her head no.

"Good girl."

His muscled arms reached up, the roped veins there bulging as he worked at the knot behind her neck. The familiar scent of him reached her nostrils—a clean but masculine aroma that was both oddly comforting and understandably frightening.

Comforting because it was familiar. Frightening because she had no idea how roughly he would handle her.

Given the circumstances, given the fact that to him she was but an escaped piece of sexual chattel he'd managed to recapture, she expected that his anger was bound to manifest itself and that a great deal of pain would be forthcoming. Masters in general were not known for their kindness. The reputation of Underworld Masters didn't even bear dwelling upon.

Would he beat her? Nellie nervously wondered as the gag came off and she was able to suck in a deep breath of air. Would he use her roughly, then pass her around to others to do the same with?

She closed her eyes briefly to steady herself, her thoughts tracking back to her sire and some of the severe punishments he had handed out to each of his five wives over the years. At some point or another he had beaten them all within an inch of their lives—some were whipped, some caned. He'd even infected one...her mother.

Kerick placed one large palm on her belly, breaking her from her thoughts. She sucked in her breath when his fingers began to lazily trail downward, knowing as she did what he meant to touch.

Nellie took a deep breath and blew it out. Her gaze was fixated on her captor's throat, for she wasn't feeling quite bold enough to look him in the eye just yet. "I suppose you mean to punish me," she whispered a bit shakily. It wasn't like her to show a weakness, but there it was. She was tired and cold and—

"Of course," he rumbled out. "Whether or not you earn further punishments is entirely up to you, little one."

Little one. Nellie blinked and looked away, hating how secure she felt by his patronizing words. She was hardly a little girl anymore, yet the words conjured up an imagery of a naïve young lass being guarded by her strong, invincible protector.

Kerick's callused fingers ran through the thatch of dark red curls at the juncture of her thighs. Softly. Soothingly. Over and over. Again and again. It felt so relaxing that she almost—almost—drifted off into slumber.

His fingers trailed down further, inducing Nellie's muscles to clench, her mind again worried that he would handle her roughly. His callused thumb settled against her clit a moment later, making her gasp. He worked his thumb in slow, methodic circles, arousing her within mere moments.

Nellie's breasts began to heave up and down in a slow, sensuous gyration. Her rouge nipples stabbed upward, achingly swollen.

"That's a good girl," he murmured, his intense eyes raking over her exposed cunt and nipples. "Let go for Master, Nellie." He applied more pressure to her clit with his thumb, simultaneously speeding up the circles he was making on it.

Nellie gasped, her eyes closing on a soft moan. She was irrevocably lost in a whirlwind of arousal a moment later—too turned on to be frightened about what punishments might await her, too turned on to care about the precarious position she was in, spread-eagle and splayed out before him.

"Let go for Me, Nellie," Kerick rumbled out again, his voice dark and coaxing. He rubbed her clit faster, his saturated thumb running easily over the slippery piece of flesh. "Let go for Master."

With her hands tied together and staked to the ground above her, and with her thighs and ankles tied together and staked out at either side of her body, fighting her captor wasn't an option. But then judging by the way she felt now, she doubted she would have fought him even if she hadn't been.

Nellie gasped, her back arching and her breasts thrusting up on a groan. "Please," she whispered. "Faster."

He complied, his thumb working faster and faster still. She moaned low in her throat, her eyes squeezing tightly shut as her body prepared to orgasm. She could feel the climax coming on quickly and knew it would be violent. Faster and faster his thumb rubbed. Faster and firmer and—

Kerick removed his thumb, allowing her no release.

Nellie's eyes flew open. She whimpered. "What the kong are you doing?"

His steel gray eyes clashed with her wide green ones. "You will not come," he murmured, "until Master is pleased with His wench."

She gulped as she watched him stand up and shed the remainder of his body décor, wondering how long he meant to torture her this way. She was to find out all too soon.

Over the course of the next half hour, Nellie was turned into a writhing, gasping, moaning, groaning, begging, pleading, wanton woman. Kerick kissed her everywhere, sucked on everything, teased her with the promise of being impaled, but allowed her to feel no more than the head of his manhood before pulling back.

She didn't know how he could stand it, for she could see the clenching movement his jaw made every time he withdrew, could see too how corded and tense all of his muscles were.

He was like a machine. A gigantic machine with the mental and physical resolve of a droid.

She was going to go mad.

"Please," Nellie groaned for what felt like the thousandth time. She moaned as she watched him palm her breasts as best as he could, then swirl his tongue around her aching, jutting nipples. His hard, naked body was settled atop hers and she could feel his thick erection poking against her belly. *"Please,"* she begged louder.

But he paid her no attention. He popped a rouge nipple into his mouth and suckled hard from it, making her moan. He sucked on it until it was so ruby-red and swollen that it was painful. Then he switched to the other one, his mouth latching onto it and suckling while his hips gyrated back and forth in slow, methodic circles, teasing her with what could be but wasn't quite hers.

"I'm going mad," she dramatically declared, her voice a pathetic sob. Her head began to thrash from side to side, her moans tortured. "Please!" she groaned, unable to take it anymore. She took her pleading a step further, begging him for what it was she wanted in more precise terms. "Please fuck me!"

The torture grew worse. He unlatched his mouth from her nipple, releasing it with a popping sound. Kerick then ran kisses all the way down her body, his tongue darting around her labial folds to lazily lap at them while his hands gently kneaded her breasts and plucked at her nipples.

"Sweet Cyrus, please!" Nellie sobbed, pathetically close to crying. Her head resumed its thrashing, the jarring action growing more and more violent, more and more desperate. "Please fuck me! I beg you to fuck me!"

Nothing.

"Please!" she screamed, her voice frantic as her head thrashed harder and harder. *"Master please fuck me!"*

Kerick impaled her pussy, driving his cock in to the hilt.

Nellie cried out, coming violently and instantaneously. *"Yes! Yes! Oh yes!"* She knew she sounded pathetic, but no longer cared. She groaned long and loud, gluttonously loving every moment of her release.

Only when it was over and the tremors of climax began to wane a bit, did she realize that although Kerick's cock was buried deep in her flesh, he was purposely keeping his body still, granting her no friction in order to come again. And she did want to come again — sweet Kalast but she felt like she had ten gallons of juice stored up for him.

Her breathing was labored, inducing her breasts to heave up and down beneath his palms. She softly moaned at the feeling of having them kneaded so expertly by his large, callused hands. She glanced up at him, noting the steel resolve of his clenched jaw, the tenseness of his well-honed muscles, the seriousness of his intense, forbidding expression...

He wasn't going to give her more, she knew. Not unless she gave him what he wanted in return. But what could he possibly want from —

Nellie's breathing stilled. Her eyes widened as she remembered the magic word that had gotten her impaled.

Kerick had finally buried his cock in her pussy when she'd called him...

Master.

She swallowed roughly, realizing as she did that she would get no more release without showing him more obedience. She groaned, any resistance she might have put up quickly thwarted by the callused hands kneading her breasts, the palms running over her aching nipples, the motionless but pulsating cock she could feel buried deep inside of her, teasing her with what could be...

"Master, please." Nellie took a deep breath and expelled it. "I — I'm sorry I ran from You. I'll be a good girl. I — I promise."

Kerick rewarded her words, his hips gyrating slowly back and forth. He moved in and out of her flesh in long, leisurely strokes — enough to make her moan, yet not fast enough to produce the friction necessary for orgasm.

"Please, Master," she begged, frustrated by her lack of ability to throw her hips back at him. "Please fuck me hard."

His hips moved a bit faster, yet still not fast enough. She didn't know whether to grit her teeth or sob like a martyr. Or both.

"My body is Your vessel." She gasped when he gave her one hard stroke, rewarding her continued compliance. "My cunt and nipples belong to You and only You—*oh yes.*" She groaned when he gave her one more hard bang, simultaneously realizing that she knew she'd never have to worry about him passing her around to others to share of. He was far too possessive.

"I will obey You always and never run from You again—*oh yes! Oh yes!*" Nellie moaned when he gave her three hard, deep strokes in rapid succession. She reveled in the grunting sound he made, understanding the sound meant that he too was near the end of his limits. Assuming, of course, that he had any.

Sweet Cyrus, but she was taking no chances, she thought hysterically.

"I accept the nipple chains without proof of Your ability to breed me—*Please! Oh yes! Oh—more!*—I accept the brand of your line without You having paid yen unto my sire…" She gasped when he gave her five hard, fast stokes, her head falling helplessly back onto the dirt ground. "I will never touch, submit to, desire, or think of another male…"

Kerick fucked her hard, plunging his cock into her flesh in fast, deep strokes. She cried out at the hedonistic friction, coming violently and instantaneously—again.

"My good and obedient wench." He ground out the praise, his muscles flexed and jaw clenched as he rode her body ruthlessly. He pounded into her long and hard, fucking her in the way they both wanted it, needed it. "Come for Master again, Nellie."

She did—over and over, again and again. Unable to move, unable to do anything besides lie there and take the gluttonous fucking he was giving her, she moaned loudly, her head thrashing from side to side as he impaled her cunt time and time again. "*Yes!*" she cried out. "*Yes! Yes! Yes!*"

He mounted her impossibly harder, groaning as he repeatedly buried his thick cock in her flesh. She could hear the suctioning sound her pussy made on each of his upstrokes, could feel how hard her nipples were jutting up to stab against his chest.

Nellie gasped when she came again, having never known a woman could orgasm so fiercely and so many times in one session. She threw her head back and moaned, greedily loving it when he fucker her harder and harder and—

Kerick's muscles tensed from above her, the roped veins of his musculature prominent. "I'm coming," he growled as he mercilessly fucked her. *"I'm coming."*

He closed his eyes and groaned long and loud as his body convulsed atop hers. His teeth were clenched and his muscles corded as he spurted hot cum deep into her cunt. "My pussy," he growled, plunging in and out of her flesh until he'd drained every last drop from his sac. *"All Mine."*

It was long minutes later before Kerick finally pulled out of Nellie's body. Even more time went by before he cut away her binds, allowing her body to move about for the first time in hours. It gave Nellie time to think about all of the vows she had made while in the throes of uncontrollable lust — vows she knew she would be expected to keep.

She swallowed nervously as she watched him reach into the satchel he'd brought with him and pull out a piece of ornamental jewelry. He placed first one gold hoop, and then another, around her stiff nipples. A delicate but strong gold chain threaded with rubies was next laced from one nipple ring to the other, the chain dangling down a bit so as not to be in the way of his mouth when he desired to suckle of them.

Nellie glanced up at him curiously, surprised that an Outlaw could come up with the yen to buy such an expensive piece of matrimonial body décor. Kerick didn't satiate her curiosity with an answer, of course. He leaned his grim face into her breasts instead and placed a soft kiss on either nipple. "Mine," he murmured. "All mine."

The branding came next, an electro-tattoo that was impossible to remove with any manner of technology. But then brandings had been created with the purpose of never being able to get rid of them, for males weren't likely to steal away a female whose body was permanently marked by another Master's brand.

On her hands and knees before him, her buttocks raised high into the air, Nellie offered Kerick no resistance as the electro-tattoo was carved into her right buttock. It didn't hurt, not really. She could feel a slight pinching sensation, a bit of pressure perhaps, but nothing more than that.

She found herself wondering what the carving looked like, but knew she wouldn't have the answer until she happened upon an image-map. All that she could be certain of was that his first and last name were permanently engraved on her right buttock...

Her curiosity grew. She didn't even know his last name, she thought, that realization occurring to her for the first time.

Kerick ran a possessive palm over the electro-tattoo, his hand coming to a rest on the side of it. "Mine," he murmured as his lips came down and kissed the branding. "All mine."

Chapter 24

The two female scientists emerged from the shadows, crawling out from behind the scattered boulders after the new Master steered his wife from the antechamber. A pair of intense gray eyes watched Kerick's retreat, mourning from the loss of not being able to call out to him.

They had been so close — Dr. Kan had almost been within their grasp. But then Kerick had come in before they had been able to reach her and now Nellie Kan belonged to him, to Kerick, irrevocably.

Kerick.

The scientists located the crushed body of the droid and, after ascertaining that she was salvageable, hitched her up to an electro-cart to be taken back to the Underground lab.

"Should we follow them so we know where she's been taken to?" Dr. Patricia Reddy asked in her native Spanish tongue. "Dr. Kan still has the journal, I'm certain. My readings gage that it's contained within a vacuum-sealed container in the satchel she still carries." She sighed. "If Dr. Kan won't be joining the Xibalba, then we need that journal back."

The intense gray eyes flicked towards her. "We need Nellie's help, my friend. The journal is not enough. If it were then we would have developed a serum long ago."

Dr. Reddy arched a shapely black eyebrow. "I saw the way he looked at her. That male will never let her escape him."

"No. He won't."

"Then —"

"But he'll still bring her to us. When she tells him what she knows, his curiosity, if nothing else, will bring him back to Cavern 7."

Dr. Reddy blinked. "This is a *male* we are speaking of, my friend. They are not a species well known for their cunning intellect. Or their compassion."

"That male is different," she murmured.

Dr. Reddy snorted at that. "How so?" she asked dryly, her arms crossing under her breasts.

The intense gray eyes flicked toward the other female scientist. "Did I tell you his name?" she whispered.

Dr. Reddy hesitated, her curiosity piqued. She shook her head.

"Kerick." The gray eyes briefly closed, as if savoring the name on her lips. "Kerick Riley."

"Sweet Cyrus." Patricia Reddy clapped a hand over her mouth, her shock evident.

"He'll come back," the other scientist murmured, her usually stoic eyes showing a bit of vulnerability. "I know he'll come back."

Chapter 25

January 23, 2250 A.D.

The trek back to the catacombs felt as though it was taking forever. Kerick hadn't wanted to gamble with Nellie's life by stopping to fuck her en route. It was taking every last bit of resolve he had not to give in to his more primal urges and mount her every way imaginable.

But good Cyrus, it had been fifteen years since he'd plunged into a wench — fifteen years. And the wench he could now plunge into at whim was Nellie Kan...Nellie Kan *Riley*.

He owned her, he thought possessively. She would never spread her thighs for any male but him.

Sinking into Nellie's pussy back in Cavern 7 had felt as exquisite as Kerick had known it would. She had been tight and wet and greedy —

And he wanted more.

And more. And more. And more.

He wanted to suck on her stiff nipples — nipples that were now adorned with his rings. He wanted to lap at her puffy cunt, then turn her over and fuck her hard from behind, the proof of his permanent ownership visible on her buttocks as he repeatedly sank into her.

He wanted to do a lot of things, he thought, his manhood growing swollen. Yet at the same time he knew it was necessary to never let himself forget that he needed to maintain a rigid control where she was concerned — at least until she'd been totally mastered by him.

First things first, he needed to get her into the security of the catacombs. Once there he would isolate her from all other humans but himself, allowing her no contact with anyone until he was certain he had her unequivocal trust and devotion.

Both ingredients were necessary. Both ingredients would insure her survival. He could then get her to talk about what she knew in regards to the Hierarchy.

"Are we almost there?" Nellie asked quietly. She cleared her throat. "I'm very tired," she whispered.

He believed her. She sounded more than a wee bit drained.

His steel-gray eyes flicked down, scanning her naked body. She wore no body décor but the nipple chains, a fact that he and his cock couldn't help but to notice and appreciate. "Soon, Nellie. Perhaps another half-hour at best."

She nodded, but said nothing.

Kerick ran a possessive palm over her backside, his hand settling on the branding. "How does it feel?" he asked with genuine concern, though Nellie probably didn't yet know him well enough to recognize the barely perceptible difference in his tones. "Does it hurt?"

She shook her head, but again she said nothing.

His eyebrow rose. Ah. The silent treatment. So that was how it was to be.

She was a stubborn wench, Kerick realized, but then that was one of the many reasons he had been so attracted to her from the beginning.

His callused hand squeezed her buttock, the subtle reminder of who owned her clear. "I will let it go this time," he said softly, "but in the future when I ask a question with words I expect an answer that also contains words."

He saw her jaw clench and wanted to sigh at the telling reaction. But he didn't, of course, for he had known from the beginning that Nellie would not be mastered so easily.

Under normal circumstances he wouldn't have given a yen, for he would have let the mastering progress at its natural pace. But there was no time for that now. Her life, whether or not she yet realized it, depended upon his strength.

And on his ability to get her to talk.

* * * * *

AND I STOOD UPON THE SAND OF THE SEA, AND SAW A BEAST RISE UP OUT OF THE SEA...AND THEY WORSHIPPED THE BEAST, SAYING, WHO IS LIKE UNTO THE BEAST? WHO IS ABLE TO MAKE WAR WITH HIM?

AND HE CAUSETH ALL, BOTH SMALL AND GREAT, RICH AND POOR, FREE AND BOND, TO RECEIVE A MARK IN THEIR RIGHT HAND, OR IN THEIR FOREHEADS: AND THAT NO MAN MIGHT BUY OR SELL, SAVE HE THAT HAD THE MARK...

HERE IS WISDOM. LET HIM THAT HATH UNDERSTANDING COUNT THE NUMBER OF THE BEAST FOR IT IS THE NUMBER OF A MAN; AND HIS NUMBER IS SIX HUNDRED, THREESCORE, AND SIX.

Nellie's eyes flicked up from Tara Riley's journal to the stone and thatched door she was hoping Kerick wouldn't be walking through for a while. He had said he would return in a couple of hours with food, which should give her enough time to study the diary — an activity she hadn't been fortunate enough to do while trekking through the jungle with Cyrus 12.

AND JESUS SAID UNTO HIM, COME OUT OF THE MAN, THOU UNCLEAN SPIRIT.

AND HE ASKED HIM, WHAT IS THY NAME? AND THE DEMON ANSWERED, SAYING, MY NAME IS LEGION, FOR WE ARE MANY...

"My name is Legion," she murmured. "For we are many." Her eyes darted from the passage Tara Riley had scrawled out from the Book of Mark back to the original passage copied from the Book of Revelation.

AND I STOOD UPON THE SAND OF THE SEA, AND SAW A BEAST RISE UP OUT OF THE SEA...AND THEY WORSHIPPED THE BEAST, SAYING, WHO IS LIKE UNTO THE BEAST? WHO IS ABLE TO MAKE WAR WITH HIM?

"Who is able to make war with him...?" Nellie bit her lip as she considered which of the many Hierarchy leaders that description fit. The problem, insofar as she could see it, was that the description fit at least five men of Federated Earth.

1.   Kalif Henders—the owner of Fathom Systems and her former boss, Vorice Henders, brother. His estimated personal holdings, she recalled from a virtual program she'd seen on him, were in excess of 2.7 trillion yen. Although he had never been appointed the High Chancellor of any particular biosphere, it was implicitly understood by all and sundry that he owned the United Americas of Earth.

2.   Creagh O'Malley—a Dublin biosphere born multi-billionaire who was the High Chancellor of the United Republic of Europe. O'Malley and Henders were thought to have strong ties to the other, but rarely were the two ever seen together in public.

3.   Maxim Malifé—No. Scratch him off. He's dead, Nellie thought.

4.   Tozeki LeJuene—born in the African Congo biosphere, he was High Chancellor of the United African States, and was reportedly the man Henders was most dependent upon for the import of Erodium from planet Kalast—Erodium being necessary to manufacture the yen chips

hosted in humanoid brains for buying and selling purposes.

5.   Abdul Kan — *my sire*, she thought with a heavy heart. Master Kan, a citizen of the United Americas of Earth, had been born and bred in the Arabian biospheres. His personal assets were near the range of 1.3 trillion yen and he held a close connection to Creagh O'Malley, the two having roomed together at virtual university years back. Master Kan was the owner of Kan Technology, a conglomerate organization that provided Fathom Systems with, among other things, the necessary human guinea pigs to test yen chips and other technology on. The guinea pigs were often taken from correctional sectors, or bought from poor families with too many sons.

Nellie ran a punishing hand through her hair, feeling, for the millionth time, indirectly responsible for the torture and death of so many males. She knew she couldn't have said anything that would have stopped her father from selling slaves to Fathom Systems, of course, but she could have gone public with what she knew about the illegal activity and stopped it that way.

She took a deep breath and blew it out. So many valuable years and so many valuable lives had been wasted. And all because she had once believed, naïve as it sounded, that her father would change and see the error of his ways with a wee bit of coaxing.

Stupid. She had been more foolish than she felt comfortable admitting.

Nellie closed Tara Riley's journal and vacuum-sealed it up. That accomplished, she secreted it away within the hidden chamber of her satchel and placed the satchel where it had been before Kerick had taken his leave.

She glanced around the chamber that was her new home — at least for the time being, making certain that all was as it should be. Yes, she thought, everything looked right.

The underground earthen and stone room, though smallish, was comfortable enough. Lit torches sat in sconces, providing light. Animal furs were strewn all over the chamber, providing warmth. A crude nonautomated kitchen sat to one side of the chamber, a rudimentary entertainment area to the other, and the bedchamber at the far corner. Her gaze next fell to the large, and rather decadent, pillow-bed.

She had been surprised upon seeing it, for she was fairly certain that there hadn't been such a lush looking bed here when she'd escaped. Which meant that Kerick had acquired it just for her—which also meant that he had spent time thinking about how to make her more comfortable here while they had been separated.

She didn't know what to make of that fact. She didn't know how to *feel* about that fact.

Kerick was an enigma to her. She was wed to him—wed for Cyrus sake!—yet she didn't even know what his last name was. (Or what her last name now was for that matter.) He was grim and brooding, yet also gentle and protective—she knew he would protect her with his life.

And he was now her husband—her Master. Which meant he would expect her to carry on as his wife. He would expect her to be docile and submissive, to regard his word as law and truth, and to cater to his every desire and whim.

Or at least that's what she'd been taught at the elite deportment school she had attended all those years ago. For two solid years she had been trained in the art of being a proper wench and wife—trained against her will, of course—so she knew all there was to know about pleasing a Master.

Theoretically speaking, anyway. She had no practical knowledge for she'd never actually been mastered by a male. She'd had obligatory sex with Dr. Lorin, of course, but that was far different from being mastered.

Nellie sighed, rubbing her temples. Did she want to please Kerick? Could she trust him enough to open up to him and ask for his assistance that she might create the serum, or should she carry through with the first plan she had concocted, which consisted of trying to find yet another way to escape him?

She chilled at the thought of how displeased he would be if she tried to run from him again. So far he had dealt with her in an unexpectedly gentle fashion, given that he was a male at any rate, and she had no desire to mess that up.

Nellie knew that one thing was for certain: even if she did manage to escape Kerick again, he'd find a way to hunt her down and bring her back to the catacombs. Only the next time...

She frowned. She knew he wouldn't be so gentle with her if there was a next time.

Nellie plopped down onto the pillow-bed with a sigh, the sensory chains she once again wore making a jingling sound. She had two choices, she knew. She could run and break his trust or she could stay and try to gain it.

If she ran from him, she would be facing not only his wrath but also the possibility of dying out in the jungle. But if she stayed then she could theoretically be wasting a lot of time because, if after trying to gain his confidence he decided not to help her so she could finish the serum, she'd have to make a run for it anyway.

Nellie bit her lip, weighing the options. Running would be very difficult, especially since the cavern she had found the zida stones in had been sealed off. That meant that the only other true choice was to stay — and hopefully win him over.

Her gaze flicked down to the pillow-bed she was sitting on, her thoughts backtracking to the years she'd spent in deportment school. She knew Kerick would want some pussy when he returned...

Nellie took a deep breath and expelled it, her mind made up. She would stay. She would prove herself to be loyal and obedient in order to gain his trust. And somehow, some way, she would get his help.

Chapter 26

Kerick entered the chamber, his expression remote and grim. He threw his satchel into the corner, then turned to look at her. His steel-gray eyes were as harsh and intense as ever, perhaps more so. Nellie bit her lip as she regarded him, wondering what he was thinking.

"Nellie, stand up."

The command was barked out, his voice broaching no argument. She immediately complied, determined to gain his confidence. She shot up to her feet from the pillow-bed, and then stood there before it as he'd ordered her to do.

Kerick blinked. He looked...confused by her quick compliance. She supposed she couldn't blame him for that. Cyrus knows she was hardly the docile, biddable type.

His eyes raked over her nude body, hovering at her nipple chains then on downward to the thatch of dark red curls at the apex of her thighs. She cleared her throat and glanced away, uncomfortable with the knowledge that her body had reacted to his stare.

"When the Master enters the chamber," he began, his eyes flicking up to her face, "it is the duty of—"

"Oh yes, I forgot," Nellie interrupted. Deportment school had been a long time ago after all. "I apologize."

He blinked again.

Nellie turned on her heel and climbed into the pillow-bed. Her back to him, she got on her hands and knees, pressed her face in close to the bedding, and raised her buttocks high into the air. She even wiggled her butt invitingly, having remembered that small bit of advice doled out by the drill instructor.

Apparently it worked. His next words were spoken thickly.

"Yes—well...that's good." She could hear his footfalls growing closer, so she wasn't surprised when she heard him come to a halt behind her. His callused palms began kneading her lightly tanned buttocks, making her wet.

One of his hands left her buttocks and began stroking her pussy from behind. She moaned, throwing him another inviting butt wiggle.

She heard him sigh as if exasperated, which both confused and embarrassed her. Perhaps she hadn't done this correctly after all, she thought. Sweet Cyrus, she hadn't been in deportment school for years! What did the arrogant man expect?

"Nellie," he barked. "Turn around and face Me."

She hesitated for a moment, but then complied. Exasperated herself, she threw her hands up in the air, the jarring action causing her nipple chains to make a twinkling sound. "Is this not what You want? What have I done wrong now?"

His jaw clenched. "Perhaps you are doing this just a bit too right," he hissed.

Now she was the one doing the blinking. "I—um...I do not follow."

"Where did you learn this!" Kerick bellowed. His nostrils flared. "Who has mastered you before Me? And how is it that you do not bear a brand from any but Me?"

Ah—he was jealous. The outrageous emotion shouldn't have aroused her, but it did.

Nellie frowned disapprovingly—whether at him for growling at her or at herself for being aroused by an emotion she had no business desiring, she couldn't say. "So if I was mastered by another, then does that mean You wish to let me take my leave of You and the catacombs?"

His gray eyes narrowed menacingly. "Not a chance," he said distinctly, each word spaced out. "Not a chance."

She sighed, running a hand through her hair. "You are the only Master I have ever known," she admitted.

"Then how—"

"Deportment school." She shrugged. "My sire sent me to deportment school for two years so I'd know what a Master would expect of me."

Kerick grunted. He sounded both irritated and appeased. "The males of the biosphere are too weak to break their own wenches?" he asked incredulously. "They rely upon droid schoolmarms to see to the task?"

She nodded. "I suppose that about sums it up, yes."

He grunted again. "Tell me, are they able to actually fuck their wives, or does it upset their delicate constitutions too much to do that as well?"

Nellie hid a smile. This was the first time Kerick had ever shown a sense of humor in her presence. That he had decided to develop one when she was doing her damnedest to keep her emotional distance was a bit off-putting. "I assume they are able to breed their wives, yes."

He sighed, surprising her. Kerick wasn't given to showing weaknesses, and that sigh clearly stated that he was exasperated.

"Nellie…"

"Yes?"

He pinched the bridge of his nose. "I will be right back."

She blinked. She was having a kong of a time trying to figure him out. She wanted to ask him where he was going, but decided he probably wouldn't answer her anyway so why bother to ask. She'd only get irritated when he didn't. "Are we not going to eat dinner?" she inquired instead.

Kerick threw a dismissive hand toward the corner of the chamber closest to the door. "In My satchel you will find provisions. Ready them for us to eat and I shall return in a few minutes."

Nellie had to wonder at the calculating expression on his face, but she said nothing. She nodded instead, leaving it at that. "It will be ready when You return."

* * * * *

Kerick wanted to hit someone or something — namely the weak male who had sent Nellie to deportment school. Didn't her sire understand how strong the bonds between the Master and the mastered became when all was said and done? It was a mental process as much as a sexual one — a process he had effectively been robbed of before he'd even known Nellie had existed.

He supposed he could go through the motions of mastering her, yet he doubted the result would be as powerful since she had been desensitized to it at a young age and knew what to expect.

That meant that he needed a new game plan—another way to engage Nellie's emotions. Docile compliance spawned nothing but stoic acceptance. Emotions—especially extreme, severe emotions—would give him the result he needed to make her cling to him in a short period of time.

He needed her to cling to him. And if he were honest with himself, the reasons weren't totally for Nellie's benefit. He had his own selfish reasons for wanting to be cherished by her, though he hated admitting needs so romantic in nature were a part of him.

He realized, of course, that Nellie would prefer to keep her emotions under lock and key...

Kerick's jaw clenched. He also realized that he'd never allow that to happen.

Chapter 27

January 24, 2250 A.D.

It was a little after midnight when Kerick returned to the chamber. Nellie immediately went to the pillow-bed and got in the *head-down-ass-up* position. She heard Kerick mutter something about droid schoolmarms, which she found decidedly irritating. There was simply no pleasing the man, she thought with down-turned lips.

"Nellie, come to the table and share dinner with Me," he rumbled out.

Her belly clamored at the reminder of food. It had been hours since she'd eaten. "Okay."

When she turned around, the first thing she noticed was that the calculating look Kerick had sported upon leaving the chamber had grown even more acute. She stopped cold in her tracks for a brief moment, a bit alarmed. But not wanting to give away her fright, she quickly recovered and walked the rest of the space that lay between them.

His callused hands found her breasts and began to gently knead them. She blinked a few times in rapid succession, trying her damnedest to ward off the arousal she was experiencing. And then his fingers began to pluck at and tweak her nipples and she knew she was a goner. It was all she could do not to moan like a wanton.

"My rings look beautiful on them," he murmured, his expression intense and brooding. "I've never seen nipples of this rare rouge color before."

"Oh." It was all she could think to say. She was having a hard enough of a time trying to keep her eyelids from hooding in desire and her legs from going weak.

He gave her a deeper nipple massage, forcing her to moan for him. "Do you like that?" he murmured, his voice thick. "Would you like to sit on My lap while you eat, that I might massage your nipples and cunt?"

She wanted to scream out a yes, but refused to. It was her objective, she reminded herself, to gain his trust without breaking to his will. "If it pleases You," Nellie hedged. She closed her eyes briefly, arousal making them difficult to keep open. "Then it would please me as well."

The next thing she knew she was in his lap with her legs spread wide apart, her back to his chest, while she dined on cheeses, a tasty meat she wasn't familiar with, and a flat bread. He leisurely toyed with her nipples — plucking at them, plumping them up with his fingers — and occasionally ran a callused hand down her belly, then onward to her cunt to play with it.

Within minutes she'd had her fill of food and was moaning instead of eating. She dropped a piece of meat onto her trencher and turned around in his lap. Straddling him, she could feel his erect cock poking through the black body-molded braies he wore.

"Please," she whispered, her eyelashes lowered. "Will Master please fuck me?" She ground her hips against him, letting him know how much she wanted it.

"Look Me in the eye," Kerick murmured. "Always look Me in the eye when asking for a boon."

A boon? Nellie thought incredulously. A *boon*? She sighed. Considering how worked up he'd purposely gotten her, it probably was a boon, she thought grimly.

But look him in the eye while asking to be mounted? It was the very thing she didn't want to do. It was easier to guard herself, after all, if she could pretend that the man whose confidence she wanted to gain was a nameless, faceless entity.

A fact he was no doubt aware of. *Damn him.*

No — she couldn't look him in the eye, she realized. It made her too vulnerable. If he rejected her, which she highly suspected he was going to do in order to prove his power over her, then she would feel humiliated.

Which was no doubt the point of all this, she thought acidly.

His thumb found her clit. He applied pressure to it, rubbing her intimately in lazy, but firm circles.

She gasped, her head falling back and her eyes closing.

His mouth latched around a plump nipple and suckled it vigorously, heady *mmm* sounds coming from low in his throat while his thumb continued to stroke her clit.

She moaned, her fingers threading through his dark hair. "Please," she breathed out. She opened her eyes slowly, hesitantly making eye contact. She swallowed when their gazes clashed, having never felt more naked than she felt at this moment. "Will Master please fuck me?" she asked quietly, her voice vulnerable.

He looked pleased—arrogantly pleased. Her nostrils flared as she looked away, preparing for rejection.

"Of course," he murmured.

Her breathing stilled. Her head shot back, and she looked at him dumbly. "Err...you will?"

"Yes." Kerick reached into his braies, freeing his cock. The thick piece of male flesh jutted out from his groin looking ready and eager. "So long as you are honest with Me, and always give honest reactions, I will deny you nothing. Save the right to leave Me, of course."

She wet her lips. She hadn't been expecting that. "Naked honesty?" she muttered.

He nodded slowly, his steel gray eyes clashing with hers. "Naked honesty," he murmured.

She cleared her throat and glanced away, unable to hold his gaze. "All right," she whispered.

Kerick cupped her chin, forcing her head up until she met his gaze again. "Always look Me in the eye," he reminded her.

It took a long moment, but eventually she nodded. She had no idea why he wanted her to look at him and couldn't decide what to make of it. "All right," she repeated, this time meeting his gaze. "Naked honesty."

His hands found her hips. He nudged her body up, telling Nellie without words to mount him. She did, guiding the opening of her pussy to the head of his cock. She closed her eyes at the same time she threw her hips down, doing her best to impale herself on him. But he stopped her with his hands, his muscled biceps flexing.

"Look at Me while you fuck Me," he said in low tones. "Do not close your eyes, Nellie. I am your Husband, not a body part."

She flinched as though she had been struck. This was more difficult than even she had thought it would be, but at the same time she didn't want him feeling badly because of her. She supposed she shouldn't care of his feelings, but found that she did.

Nellie opened her eyes, her gaze slowly clashing with his. He allowed her to sink down on him then, which she did, enveloping his cock on a groan.

"Your pussy feels so good," Kerick murmured, his intense eyes narrowed in desire. One callused hand came up, threading through her dark red mane of hair. "Cyrus smiled on Me the day he delivered this intelligent, wonderful woman into My safe-keeping."

She maintained his gaze, but suddenly felt like crying. No male had ever spoken to her so sweetly. No male had ever spoken to her as though she mattered. "Thank you," she said a bit shakily. She cleared her throat and blinked a few times in rapid succession, trying her best to rein her emotions in.

They began to fuck—slow and leisurely. And always they maintained eye contact. Nellie rode up and down him, moaning as she enveloped his cock into her suctioning flesh, over and over, again and again.

And always they maintained eye contact.

Kerick played with her nipples, murmured words of praise and thanks to her, told her how beautiful she was, how much he admired and cherished her...

And always they maintained eye contact.

The naked honesty, Nellie admitted to herself as she threw her hips down and grinded her cunt onto his cock, was getting to her. She'd never felt more vulnerable, more exposed. Everything was right there for him to see—the years of loneliness she'd spent since her father had forced her from Nicoletta, the deep-seated fear of abandonment she'd carried around inside ever since her mother had died, the bleakness she'd felt at knowing she'd never be able to have both her treasured career and the security of family every woman wants...

When you look another person in the eye for an extended period of time, there is no way to lie. All of your emotions, all of your vulnerabilities, no matter how greatly you might wish to mask them, are there for the other person to either cherish or tatter.

Kerick was choosing to cherish them. She felt her eyes well up with tears.

"You are so perfect," he murmured. "Inside and out."

And then there were his eyes to consider, she thought shakily. They were dead — unless she was around. Bleak — unless she was around. Guarded — unless he was making love to her.

Loneliness — he had known so much loneliness...

A single tear tracked down Kerick's cheek, causing Nellie to lose it completely. She began to softly cry as she rode him, tears streaming down her face unchecked. "Kerick..."

She reached for him then, threading her fingers through his hair and bringing his face down to meet hers. She kissed him with everything she had in her, the very first time she had allowed, let alone wanted, a male's lips to touch her own.

If he had meant to break her with naked honesty, it had worked, but in the process he had broken himself.

She slipped her tongue past his lips, needing to be as connected to him as possible. The kiss was unguarded in a way Nellie had never been before, a freeing, intimate experience she hadn't allowed herself prior to this moment in time. Kerick was just as caught up in it, his tongue aggressively thrusting into her mouth to take over the lead.

When they finally let each other go from the kiss, they fucked hard — animalistically.

And always they maintained eye contact.

Nellie arched her back as she rode up and down him, her large tits jiggling from the fast movement. Kerick's jaw clenched, the vein on his neck prominent as he cupped and kneaded them.

"Come for your Master, Nellie," he ground out, his callused palms kneading her breasts as though he meant to brand them. "I need to feel your sweet cunt coming for Me."

Nellie rode him harder, her pussy making suctioning sounds as she repeatedly enveloped him. "Kerick," she breathed out, her eyes widening, "*Master.*"

She came hard, screaming as they stared into each other's eyes, the orgasm more intense than she'd ever known. He followed quickly, his nostrils flaring and his breathing heavy as his fingers dug into the flesh of her hips and he poured his hot cum into her cunt on a groan.

When it was over, when both of them had been drained, she collapsed against his chest and cried softly, the feel of his arms wrapped securely around her making the tears fall freely. Nellie couldn't remember having ever cried in front of another human since her mother had died, let alone in front of a man. But she couldn't seem to help herself.

He didn't take advantage of her vulnerability, didn't make light of it or try to push her away for showing a soft side. Kerick held her instead, kissing her forehead and telling her of how wondrous she was, telling her of how he'd never let anyone hurt her, telling her of all the babies he wanted to put in her belly...

Nellie clung to him, letting the tears fall until they were done, feeling more vulnerable yet more protected than she'd ever before felt. She fell asleep in his arms that eve, in the throes of a deep slumber by the time he carried her to the pillow-bed and fell asleep on it beside her.

Nellie would never forget this night—a powerfully beautiful, and powerfully frightening, moment in time.

Chapter 28

January 28, 2250 A.D.

The next four days proved to be the most intimate, and freeing, that Nellie had ever known. She and Kerick got to know each other in non-sexual, as well as sexual, ways. Nellie told him about being a scientist, about the serum she had been working on, and about her employer breaking into her domicile when Kerick had captured her the first time. She admitted that was the reason she and Cyrus 12 had fled the Altun Ha biosphere and told him that she hoped he would support her endeavor to continue her work and finish the serum here in the catacombs.

He had adamantly said of course, which elated her. Her trust in him soared higher after that.

But for reasons she couldn't quite pinpoint, perhaps because she was so used to keeping it a secret, Nellie never once told Kerick about Tara Riley or about the doctor's secret journal. Tara, her posthumous heroine, was her one final secret—for now. She knew that eventually she would have to tell him, most likely after he had stolen all the necessary equipment she would need to continue her grueling work.

Nellie wasn't the only one who talked. Kerick, contrary to her expectations, was very open about his life and experiences with her. He never spoke of his mother other than to say he'd lost her to infection, so Nellie rightly assumed that the subject was too painful for him and never broached it. She could understand his feelings, for she hadn't spoken of Sinead with him either, other than to tell him that she too had lost her mother to infection.

Where Kerick didn't speak of his childhood at length, he did, however, tell her about his detention in the Kong Penal Colony, a subject that sparked some sort of a distant déjà vu kind of feeling for reasons she couldn't place. He spoke of the loneliness, of the systematic abuse doled out to the slave laborers, of how some of the laborers were taken away to be used as guinea pigs for Fathom Systems...

She'd swallowed nervously when he'd told her that, not quite able to bring herself to admit that the man responsible for all that was her sire. Kan, after all, was a common last name in Federated Earth, as ordinary as Jones or Jackson had been hundreds of years ago. She wasn't surprised by the fact that he'd not yet made the connection between his wife and Abdul Kan.

As close as the two of them grew in those four days in non-sexual ways, so too did they further their intimate bond with constant sex. Nellie's favorite activity was to kneel at Kerick's feet while he talked to her about his life, sucking on his cock as he opened up his heart to her...

Kerick groaned as Nellie sat on her knees before him, deep-throating his cock. The smacking sounds her lips were making as she sucked on him were as exciting as the suckling itself. She was moaning low in her throat, as if his cock was the best treat she'd ever tasted, and her hands were expertly massaging his balls, tightening them up as his arousal grew.

"As I was saying..."

Her cat-like green eyes closed as if in bliss, and her lips devoured his cock. She took him all the way in, until the head of his manhood damn near touched her tonsils.

Sweet Cyrus — who gave a yen what he had been saying.

"Nellie," Kerick groaned, his fingers threading through her hair. She looked so beautiful and wondrous, sitting naked and submissive on her knees before him, wearing nothing but nipple chains and the brand he knew was on her ass. Her full lips sucked on him faster, the smacking sounds growing louder and louder.

Kerick's muscles corded and tensed as he prepared to orgasm. He had never felt so connected to another human being as he felt at this moment. He wanted to tell her he loved her, tell her that he would always love her, and yet the words stopped at his lips, perhaps afraid that they wouldn't be returned.

"*Nellie.*" He groaned loudly as he came, hot liquid spurting into her mouth on a roar. She drank every bit of it, lapping it up as though she couldn't get enough of it.

When it was over, when he had come down from his high, he picked Nellie up and carried her to the pillow-bed. He didn't bother telling her what he was going to do, he just did it. Without a word, his face dove between her legs and he greedily lapped at her cunt, licking her labial folds and sucking on her clit until she came hard and violently for him.

Even then he found that he couldn't stop. His face remained buried between her legs, sucking on her flesh until she'd come again and insisted that she could take no more. By then he was hard again.

Turning her over, Kerick murmured for her to get in the *head-down-ass-up* position. She immediately complied, further arousing him.

He sank into Nellie's flesh on a groan, the sight of the branding on her ass a powerful aphrodisiac. He possessively ran a rough palm over it, watching her ass jiggle as he fucked her hard from behind.

Her body still at the height of sensitivity from all the orgasms she'd just had, Nellie couldn't seem to stop coming. The harder he banged her, the louder she screamed — and the more she came.

Kerick grabbed her by the hips and fucked her possessively, plunging in and out of her cunt with domineering strokes. "More!" he heard her beg. *"Master, please fuck Your pussy harder."*

He went wild on her then, his hips pistoning back and forth as he greedily stuffed her flesh full of cock and cum. He broke on a roar, his teeth gritting and jaw clenching as he spurted his seed deep inside of her.

Long moments later, when his breathing returned to semi-normal, Kerick gently nudged Nellie's body, getting her to lie down on her side. He followed her down to the pillow-bed with his own body, his cock never leaving her pussy.

Side by side, their bodies still joined together, they fell into an exhausted sleep in the animal furs.

Chapter 29

January 29, 2250 A.D.

"What the kong are you doing?" Kieran bellowed.

Kora yelped, not having heard him enter the Underground corridor. Her sensory chains jingled as she turned on her heel to face him. "You scared me," she breathed out.

His eyes narrowed suspiciously. "I'll just bet I did."

"It's—it's not what You think."

"Uh huh. So you weren't trying to get into the sealed off cavern again then?" Kieran crossed his arms over his chest. "You were looking for a gift for Me, is that it?" he asked sarcastically.

Kora blushed, looking away.

"Why do you want to leave Me?" he gritted out. His anger quickly dissipated, turning into vulnerability. "I'd do anything for you," he said softly. "I love you."

Kora closed her eyes and took a deep breath. The boy was getting under her skin.

Who was she fooling? Sweet Kalast, Kieran was already under her skin and into her bones.

"If I ever left," she quietly admitted, "it would only be for a while. And I'd always come back to You, Master."

Kieran's nostrils flared. His eyes searched hers. He uncrossed his arms and pushed away from the corridor wall. "You ain't leaving Me—not ever."

She put up a palm, then softly rested it on his chest when he stood before her. Her head came up and she met his eyes. She told him the truth, or as much of it as she could tell without betraying the Xibalba. "I have to go, Kieran. I *must*. For You, for our unborn child…I have to go," she murmured.

His jaw clenched. "Why?"

She sighed, knowing she could never divulge her reasons to him. For if he did know why…

She couldn't even imagine what would become of her.

Kora shook her head, looking away. "I can't tell You." She sighed again. "I wish I could, but I can't. You must trust me in this and let me go."

"No," he ground out. "I will never—"

"I vow I will come back," Kora promised, her eyes meeting his once again. "I vow it," she adamantly repeated.

Kieran closed his eyes briefly, sighing. "Tell Me why you must go."

"I've told You that I cannot—"

"Then the answer is no." His jaw clenched. "If you cannot trust Me, Kora Riley, then I cannot trust you."

His expression grew remote, which she found oddly depressing. She had grown to cherish the unguarded manner in which he dealt with her. "Kieran…"

"No!" he barked.

She offered him no resistance as he forcibly steered her from the corridor.

* * * * *

Naked save the nipple chains and the ever-present sensory chains she wore, Nellie felt a bit anxious as Kerick led her down the long earthen corridor that led to the commons chamber. This was the first time since her arrival in the catacombs that she was obliged to be near other Underground dwellers. She wasn't certain of what to expect.

Dozens of male eyes were on her as she and Kerick made their way into the commons chamber. Their eyes seemed glued first to her dark red pubic hair and then to her large breasts. It occurred to her that most of these males had probably never seen a female who had been biosphere engineered and bred. Either that or it was the rare coloring of her nipples and pussy hair that they enjoyed. She felt a bit embarrassed when they began applauding, cheering Kerick on for having recaptured her.

"Way to go!" one shouted out. The others followed suit, praising Kerick for the capture of his rare prize.

They were celebrating the fact that Kerick had proven to be more cunning a hunter than she was an escapee. Her nostrils flared at the perceived insult.

"Stop it," Kerick murmured, steering her toward a table where a young but heavily muscled male was seated on an animal fur covered stone chair. A female wearing nipple chains, a woman in her late thirties that she could safely assume was his wife, sat at the young Master's feet, suckling his cock as he ate his meal from a trencher. "They are not making jest of you. They are but congratulating Me."

She sighed, realizing as she did that this wasn't worth fighting about. "Fair enough."

"Did your droid schoolmarm tell you of what is expected from a wife when partaking of a meal with unmated males not of her or her Master's line?"

"Of course," Nellie sniffed, suddenly feeling defensive of her schooling. "I had a high-class education."

He grunted, obviously unconvinced where the merits of her educational background were concerned. "I will introduce you to My comrades after the meal, as is the way of it," Kerick said in low tones so nobody could hear them. "Until then, I ask as a favor to Me that—"

Nellie stopped in her tracks. She turned to face him. "I won't embarrass You," she said, a bit hurt that he'd thought she might even consider it. "I know what is expected of me in public, Kerick. Having the manners of a hybrid pig is Your field," she said sweetly, "not mine."

He frowned, but leaned down to kiss her. "Let us eat."

"Kerick," she said weakly, feeling a bit overwhelmed by all of the eyes on her.

"Yes?"

"Can we leave as soon as we're done eating?" She cleared her throat, glancing away. "This is a bit much a bit too soon," she whispered.

He took her hand and squeezed it. "Of course." He waited for her to look back up at him. "I have a stolen virtual movie chip in My satchel. If you'd like, we can watch Cabel Modem's latest show after the meal."

Her eyes widened. "I didn't know You owned a virtual movie lab. I didn't know one could in the catacombs."

"Well now you do."

She grinned, the first time she'd ever done that in front of him. His eyes widened a bit, then softened as if studying it. "Which show is it?"

He blinked, returning to normal. "*Savage Alien Love*, or some such drivel. It's a wench-flick. You will like it."

She nodded, then followed him to the table. She deeply suspected he had stolen the virtual movie chip expressly for her, but said nothing.

Kerick took his seat at the communal table. He sat in an animal fur covered stone chair that was actually quite comfortable to lounge on due to all of the padding. Once there he motioned for Nellie to follow suit.

Nellie took her societal place at his feet, kneeling down onto the lush animal furs that had been splayed out on the dirt ground for her to sit upon. She waited for Kerick to remove his stiff cock from his black braies, then immediately began to suckle it while he ate his meal and talked with his friends.

She wasn't precisely certain why females were expected to do this when dining in public. The only thing she could figure was that it stemmed from a primal need Masters had to remind unmated males who it was that owned the wench sitting submissively at His feet, sucking Him off. In a world were females were rarer than uncorrupt Hierarchy leaders, she was hardly surprised.

Nellie's gaze flicked to the woman seated beside her, the one kneeling at the young Master's feet. Apparently her Master had already came for she was being fed from his hand. The woman smiled. "I'm Kora Riley," she whispered. "Your sister-in-law."

Without removing Kerick's erect cock from her mouth, Nellie smiled back at her. She obediently sucked on it even as she listened to the other woman speak. Wait a minute, she thought hesitantly. Had Kora said that her last name was…

"And you are Nellie Riley," the woman said meaningfully, startling Nellie to the point where she all but gagged on her husband's cock. "It's my humble pleasure to meet you, Doctor."

Nellie Riley. Nellie...Riley?

The woman's eyes sharpened. "Yes," she murmured. "*That* Nellie Riley." She accepted another food bit from her Master's hand and swallowed it quickly, watching as Nellie feverishly suckled Kerick's cock. "We must help each other," Kora said in a barely audible whisper. "And soon."

No, Nellie thought, her heart thumping like mad in her chest while she sucked her husband off. Surely Kerick couldn't be...*that* Kerick? Tara's *son*?

"Elijah," Kerick said, turning Nellie's attention to what was transpiring above-table. "With Maxim Malifé dead at your hands, that leaves only four more that we must take out."

Nellie's eyes widened. She suckled Kerick fast and furiously, wanting him to come so she could whisper with Kora.

"True," Elijah's deep voice concurred. "Tozeki LeJeune, Kalif Henders, Creagh O'Malley, and..."

Nellie's heart began pounding in her ears.

"...Abdul Kan," Elijah finished. He snorted, his tone arrogant. "I'm enjoying this, amigo. Those bitches all know by now that you have escaped from Kong. They are aware that the Grim Reaper has returned from the land of death."

Sweet Cyrus. Nellie closed her eyes and sucked faster. Her head bobbed up and down in lightning-fast motions that made her dizzy. She was rewarded for her hard work a few moments later when Kerick's cock spurted, hot cum shooting down her throat.

She drained him dry, making certain no juice was left, and then turned wide eyes on Kora. "What is going on?" she whispered. She accepted the piece of meat Kerick handed down to her as he continued the conversation with his comrades, eating it out of his palm. She chewed quickly. "Who are you?"

Kora listened to the talk above-table for a protracted moment, making certain her Master was embroiled in the conversation. "A scientist like you," she whispered back. "I came here to bring you to the Xibalba but was captured by your Master's brother in the process."

Nellie closed her eyes briefly, overwhelmed by all that she had learned in what amounted to less than five minutes time.

"The serum, Doctor," Kora whispered. "It must be finished. *Now.*"

"I agree," Nellie whispered back, accepting another piece of meat from Kerick's palm. "Kerick will be acquiring the necessary equipment that I might—"

"We've no time for that. We must flee. Together. Tonight." Kora's nostrils were flared, her expression one that would broach no argument to the contrary. "More rides on this than you can possibly know," she said, her voice breaking into a quiver.

Nellie wanted more information, but realized that time was of the essence. When the males were finished with their conversation, the women would be brought above-table. Who knew when they could speak freely again after that. "I cannot," Nellie whispered. "But I can promise to get that equipment just as soon as—"

Kora held up a palm, silencing her. *"Please,"* she begged. "Please come with me." She spoke the rest quickly, accurately guessing that the conversation above-table was almost finished. "Meet me at the corridor that leads into the cavern with the zida stones this eve at midnight. I've figured out a way to break its seal."

Nellie was given no time to reply for Kerick was bringing her up to sit in his lap, as was Kora's Master doing to her. She sat in his lap, her back to his chest, his hands kneading her large breasts and massaging her nipples for all to see while he introduced her to his friends.

"It's nice to meet you," Nellie politely murmured first to Elijah, then to Xavier, and finally to her brother-in-law Kieran. Her eyes shuddered as arousal gnawed at her. "The pleasure is all mine."

Chapter 30

Nellie climbed out of the pillow-bed at ten minutes of midnight, careful not to wake Kerick in the doing. She had never been more frightened, more on edge, than she was at this moment. For if he caught her...

She swallowed against the lump in her throat as she collected her satchel. If he caught her he would never forgive her.

Stopping only long enough to make certain he was softly snoring, she quietly exited their chamber, then ran down the corridor to where she knew Kora would be waiting. Just as she'd known she would be, the scientist was there, looking as nervous and uncertain as Nellie felt.

Kora's eyes lit up when she saw her. She motioned with her hands for Nellie to hurry.

By the time Nellie reached her side, she was panting for breath. "I cannot go with you—not without telling Kerick," she told a defeated looking Kora. "But," she said quickly, "I've brought copies both of Tara Riley's journal and my own notes. There's enough information here to get started on the serum. I vow to you that I will follow soon on your heels to finish it." She sighed. "With or without Him."

Kora looked hopeful again. "Thank you," she murmured. "But you do not know how to find the Xibalba—"

"Cavern 7?"

Kora's eyes widened. "Yes," she whispered. "The third boulder on the right in the inner most antechamber."

"Go quickly." Nellie handed over her spare copy of notes to Kora then shooed her toward the sealed off entrance of the cavern containing the zida stones. "I've already figured out why you need that serum— now go!" she whispered fiercely.

Kora nodded. She stopped long enough to kiss her cheek, then opened the trapdoor she'd figured out how to break the seal on. "Tell

Kieran I'll be back, Cyrus willing," she murmured. "I..." She glanced away and sighed. "This will hurt Him and I don't want Him hurting." Their eyes clashed. "Make Him understand," she whispered.

Nellie smiled. "I will," she said reassuringly, though she didn't know if that would be possible or practical. She glanced over her shoulder, freezing when she saw the shadows of men coming upon them. She turned back to Kora. "Go!" she adamantly whispered. "Go!"

Kora disappeared through the trapdoor and Nellie sealed it behind her. She was so worked up by the time the trapdoor had been resealed that she felt as though her heart was going to beat out of her chest.

She turned on her heel, preparing to go back to her chamber, when four grim looking faces stopped her dead in her tracks. Nellie's eyes widened. Her gaze flew up to meet the only one here that mattered to her, the one who was looking at her as though she'd ripped out his heart. "Kerick..."

"Do not," he hissed, "speak to Me, wench." His nostrils flared. "Go back to our chamber and await Me there."

Nellie swallowed roughly. "I didn't try to run from You—"

"So you say." His jaw clenched. "Remove yourself from the trapdoor that My brother and My men might collect Kora."

"No don't!" Her chin came up determinedly. "It's vital that You let her go—"

"Go to the chamber!" he bellowed. "Go now!"

Her nostrils flared. But, deciding that she wasn't likely to sway either him or the three other males determined to recapture Kora, she walked away from Kerick, then ran down the corridor.

Apparently he decided not to take any further chances where she was concerned, for by the time she had reached their chamber he was stalking in behind her, slamming the thatch and stone door in his wake.

Minutes ticked by. Neither of them spoke.

Unable to endure the bleak quiet any longer, Nellie turned around to face Kerick. Her jaw was clenched as tightly as his, her nostrils were flared as outrageously as his, her breathing every bit as labored as his. "I said I didn't try to run!" she shrieked. "I expect to be believed given this past week we've spent together!"

His intense eyes bore into hers, looking more desperate and more vulnerable than she'd ever thought possible. "I want to believe you," he said hoarsely. I want to—"

Her eyes gentled, but she remained firm. "Then believe me, Kerick. *Please.*"

She broke eye contact and began to pace the chamber. She threw her hands up in the air, aggravated that she had no real way to prove her words. "I admit I helped Kora to escape, but her reasons for needing to go are valid—I will explain them to You later," she said quickly before he threw out some arrogant, irritating line about wenches belonging with their Masters. "But—*but!*—I did not run from *You.* If I had, I'd have been gone long before *You* entered that Cyrus-forsaken corridor!"

Kerick's nostrils were still flared, his breathing still harsh, but he looked as though he was calming down a bit. And better yet, he looked as though he was finally starting to believe her.

"I've never felt so broken in My life," he murmured, his gaze clashing with hers, "as I felt when I woke up and thought you had run from Me."

Nellie hung her head. "Kerick...I won't leave You." Her face came up. She sighed as they resumed eye contact. "I vow it."

He nodded, letting the silence stretch out between them for a protracted moment. But finally he said, "You have much to explain to Me."

"Yes."

"You can explain in the morn."

She blinked. "You don't want to know right now?"

"No." He slowly began to shed his body décor as he backed her up toward the pillow-bed. "I need to be inside of you, Nellie," he said hoarsely. "I need *you* period."

Nothing else needed to be said. She felt the same way. She'd never felt so alone inside as she'd felt during those tense minutes when she'd thought Kerick wouldn't believe her innocence.

Within moments Nellie was lying flat on her back, her thighs spread wide for his thrusts. Neither of them was ready to speak of romantic love to the other, yet the emotions were in their every kiss, their every touch.

Kerick wrapped a palm-full of her dark red hair around his hand, and then sank into her cunt on a groan. Nellie groaned with him, frantically meeting him thrust for thrust.

She wrapped her legs around his waist, holding on while he gave her a hard ride. His buttocks clenched and contracted as he repeatedly plunged into her pussy, drilling into her mercilessly.

They fucked hard that eve, sexually bonding with each other in an almost desperate fashion. Nellie never wanted the sweetness to end, never wanted the night to turn into the dawn, for she knew that once she told Kerick everything, their lives would forever be changed.

She and Kerick would stay together forever, she realized. That wasn't the problem.

The problem as Nellie saw it was figuring out, given all the obstacles that lay ahead, how to make forever last until they were both old and gray.

She fell asleep in his arms pondering that question, clinging to her beloved Kerick as he had hoped she one day would.

Chapter 31

January 30, 2250 A.D.

Kora ran into the middle antechamber, knowing that the men were fast on her heels. Her breathing was labored, her breasts bobbing up and down, as she dashed toward the Xibalba.

Just one more antechamber, she told herself firmly. *Keep running!*

The sounds of three sets of footfalls grew closer, frightening her. She rounded a corner and almost screamed when she bodily clashed with her leader. "Oh thank Cyrus," she breathed out, her hand flying up to cover her heart. "You frightened me."

Intense gray eyes clashed with hers. "Let's go," the woman said. "In here."

The two women filed behind a boulder, hiding themselves away in a large crevice. They remained totally still as they listened to the males run into the antechamber.

"Fuck!" Kieran swore. "I've lost her."

Kora closed her eyes at the sound of his voice, hating that she had to do this to him.

"Let's break up, amigos," she heard Elijah call out, a voice that induced Kora's leader to flinch. "Xavier, you take the outer antechamber, Kieran hunt the middle one. I'll search the inner one. Let's meet in the middle antechamber in twenty minutes."

The males split up and went about their work. Kora and her leader stood quietly, unmoving, scarcely even breathing for the next twenty minutes. When the specified rendezvous time at last came upon them, the women quietly scurried from the boulder's crevice and made their way into the inner antechamber.

"Let's go," the leader murmured, opening the third boulder on the right for Kora to sneak through. "You first."

Kora nodded, doing as she had been instructed, the notes still firmly in her grasp. She turned around once she was in, preparing to help her leader climb through the trapdoor, when it suddenly swung shut and was sealed off with a dull thud.

What the...?

* * * * *

Elijah's hand clamped down on the wench's shoulder. He had known that if he waited long enough his patience would be rewarded. He hadn't recaptured Kora yet, true, but if this wench knew what was good for her then she'd tell him how to get to her.

"Where is she?" he gritted out as he turned the female around to face him. "Where is — "

Elijah's words faltered as his jaw dropped open. Wide brown eyes clashed with intense gray ones.

In shock, his hand fell from the woman's shoulder and he stumbled back a few paces. "Sweet Cyrus," Elijah murmured. He ran a hand over his jaw, his eyes unblinking. "Is it — is it..."

He swallowed hard against the lump in his throat. "Is it you?"

* * * * *

THE AVENGER

"That little man in black says woman can't have as much rights as man because Jesus wasn't a woman. Where did your Christ come from? *Where did He come from?* From God and a woman. Man had nothing to do with Him."

– Sojourner Truth

Chapter 32

I FEEL THE DARKNESS COME UPON ME NOW MORE THAN THE LIGHT. THE MONSTER MORE SO THAN THE WOMAN...

EVIL MORE SO THAN GOODNESS.

I WANT TO SCREAM. I JUST WANT TO FUCKING SCREAM. BUT I CANNOT LOSE MY CONTROL. I CANNOT AFFORD TO EVER LOSE MY CONTROL. FOR IF I DO I WILL BE LOST TO MY SONS FOREVER...

AND THEN THEY WILL HAVE WON.

TARA RILEY
DECEMBER 24, 2238

Chapter 33
January 30, 2250 A.D.

Elijah was so stunned he couldn't speak, could barely breathe. "I don't believe it," he rasped out. Feeling lightheaded, he backed himself up against the nearest boulder for support. "It isn't possible..."

Clear gray eyes found his and softened just a bit. A hand he hadn't thought to see again in this life reached out to him.

"It's me," she choked out, her voice catching in the back of her throat. "I'm alive."

"Sweet Cyrus," he murmured, his expression surreal. "Sweet Cyrus..."

* * * * *

"What happened?" Dr. Patricia Reddy asked. Her brown eyes widened. Anxiety radiated off of her in waves. "Where is she?"

Kora took a deep breath and expelled it. "I don't know," she muttered, wringing her hands. She began to pace, an ominous feeling settling in her stomach. They needed Tara Riley back *now*. Without her, the child in Kora's belly stood no hope at all. Neither did Kora herself for that matter. "She had me go through the portal first. When I turned around to help her through it, the door slammed shut."

"Outsiders?"

She felt like she was going to be sick. "I think so," Kora murmured. This couldn't be happening. Not now. Not when so much was riding on the development of the serum.

"Shit."

Her thoughts exactly. "What in the name of Kalast do we do?" She stopped pacing, her expression searching.

Dr. Reddy sighed as she slid a charged flash-stick into the worn leather holster she wore at her hips. "We go get her back."

Kora slowly nodded. "And Dr. Kan?"

Her eyebrows rose. "We get her too."

She released a pent-up breath. This would work. It had to work. She didn't know how much time she had left, but she conceded it couldn't be long. She could feel the metabolic changes coming upon her regularly now—especially in the eves. Slowly but surely, the beast was engulfing her. "It's about damn time."

Chapter 34

Kerick's warm lips pressed against Nellie's temple. She feigned sleep, not wanting him aware of the fact she had awakened long ago. With wakefulness would come questions—questions she wasn't ready to answer.

Last eve had been bliss—they had loved each other the whole night long, clinging to one another as though they would never let go. She didn't want it to end, but suspected when the truth came out it would. There was the issue of his mother's diary, the need she had to go to the Xibalba and continue her work...

And the irrefutable fact she was the daughter of Abdul Kan. *The* Abdul Kan.

Her husband's mortal enemy.

Sweet Cyrus, she thought, her stomach muscles clenching, *how can I possibly tell my husband his beloved mother's death most likely came at my sire's hands?*

Nellie kept her eyes closed, letting herself enjoy the feel of Kerick's lips pressed against her skin. She realized full well the sensation might be a foreign one after she told him everything.

* * * * *

Stretched out on the harem bed, a beautiful, naked wife pressed against his left, a beautiful, naked wife pressed against his right, and a beautiful, naked wife sucking his cock, he looked like the emperor he thought himself to be, the master of all he surveyed. A trembling girl of eighteen stood next to the bed, scared out of her mind by what was to come. She had been purchased on the marriage auction block by Master Kan just this eve and was to become his fifth wife—sixth if you counted the dearly departed Sinead.

Sinead. The eighteen-year-old girl shared a striking—and haunting—resemblance to her beloved, deceased friend. The same wine-red hair, same creamy porcelain skin, same blue eyes. Same everything. Almost.

Naked and hungry, her dark hair in disarray, Nicoletta Kan stared at the husband she hated from the cage she had been locked up in. Over the years she had grown rather accustomed to being caged for every little offense she committed, so in truth the punishment no longer bothered her. Or at least it didn't bother her to the extent that it bothered Master Kan's other wives.

Pathetic milksops, the lot of them, she thought, frowning. Every time one of those three was caged you'd have thought life as they knew it was coming to an end. They would weep and beg and promise to be good girls—everything the Master wanted to see and hear.

Everything Nicoletta would never do or say.

The cage. This time Master Kan had sentenced her to a full week in the wretched thing. Well, a week or until she begged his forgiveness. In other words, a week...

"Abdul!" a male voice boomed out, snagging everyone's attention.

Nicoletta glanced down from where her gold-gilt cage hung suspended from the ceiling. Because she was across the bedchamber from the harem bed, she was closest to the intruder and able to recognize him immediately. Her dark eyes narrowed at him, disgust churning in her stomach. He was as vile as her husband, perhaps more so.

"Kalif," Abdul murmured. He shooed his fourth wife away from him, plucking his cock from her mouth with a popping sound. He snapped his fingers and the three on the harem bed scurried away from it, taking the trembling and untried fifth wife with them into an adjoining chamber. "It's been a long time, old friend."

Kalif Henders, the owner of Fathom Systems, inclined his head. "I try to stay away from the New York biosphere as much as possible." His eyebrows rose. "By Cyrus, I swear I do not understand why you remain here when you could afford a palace in any biosphere of your choosing."

Abdul shrugged as he stepped into his flowing white silk pants. "I like it here. So long as you don't venture below level eighty, it has much to recommend it."

"If you say so."

"I do."

Abdul slowly made his way across the bedchamber, his prowl reminding Nicoletta of a panther's. It was a shame he was so wretchedly disgusting, she thought, for her husband had always been extremely handsome in face and form. Unlike most soft men of the Hierarchy, Abdul Kan was strong and well-muscled. His dark hair and olive complexion only added to his sinister, but sexy, appearance. She blinked, chastising herself for finding anything appealing about him whatsoever.

He was evil. Pure, unadulterated, evil.

"So what brings you to New York?" Abdul murmured, his intense green eyes raking over the slight form of Kalif Henders.

A seemingly benign action if you didn't know Master Kan as Nicoletta knew him. But because she did know him — very well — her eyes narrowed thoughtfully as she wondered what he was up to. It was almost as though he was assessing Henders, sizing him up...for something.

Kalif cleared his throat. His chin notched up. "You haven't delivered the chattel to the Belizean biosphere. My scientists were expecting a shipment of prisoners to perform experiments on a fortnight past." He inclined his head, an arrogant gesture. "As per our contract, you will recall."

Abdul came to a standstill before him. At six-foot-three, he stood a head taller than the other man, and then some. "I never break my word," he murmured. His eyebrows rose. "Unless the other party breaks theirs."

Kalif stilled. His eyes widened almost imperceptibly. "I don't understand..."

It happened so fast, Nicoletta barely had time to register the fact that her husband had plucked Kalif Henders from the ground by the neck with one hand and thrown him up against the nearest wall. The slight man was gurgling, his face quickly turning a hideous purple. Her eyes widened as she watched, her heart thumping against her chest.

"Where," Abdul bit out, his words distinct and precise, "is my daughter?" His nostrils flared. His fingers tightened around the man's neck. *"Where?"* he bellowed.

Apparently Master Kan was too angry to notice that the other man could not possibly answer. His lungs were slowly being drained of air, blood vessels popping in his face.

"You have to release him, Abdul," Nicoletta said in an urgent whisper. Her voice was scratchy from five days of not using it. She sat up, grabbing the gold bars of the cage. "He can't answer otherwise."

Abdul glanced up, his green eyes that were a dead ringer for Nellie's widening a bit, perhaps recalling for the first time that one of his wives was still in the bedchamber. He blinked, and then released Henders. The slight man plummeted to the ground. He was wheezing and sputtering, his lungs fighting for air to suck in.

"I swear to Cyrus," Kalif gasped, his body shuddering, his face contorted, "I do not know."

"You lie," Abdul hissed.

"I swear it!" Kalif dragged himself up into a sitting position. His breathing was drastically labored.

Master Kan seemed to wait with inhuman patience for Henders to catch his breath when all Nicoletta wanted to do was beat the answer out of him. *Nellie*, she thought, her hands tightening on the bars. Sweet Kalast, she would give anything to hold the daughter of her heart again. She could only pray to the ancient saints that she wasn't already dead.

"I give you the truth," Kalif panted, too weak to stand. "She disappeared from Altun Ha with a droid companion. That's all my holo-cams picked up."

Silence.

"I give you one sennight to find her," Abdul said, his composure seemingly restored. He pulled Henders up by the hair, ignoring the other man's cry for mercy as he pushed him against the wall.

"But what if she can't be found? I—"

"One week," Master Kan murmured. "I will come to Altun Ha in seven days." His intense green eyes bore into the other man. The muscles in his arms were tight, corded. "No Nellie, no chattel. Do you hear me?"

"Yes," Kalif quickly agreed. His eyes rounded. "I'll send out scouts immediately."

Silence.

Abdul inclined his head before releasing him. "Go. Now." He turned on his heel, giving the relieved Henders his back. "If you don't find her," he said without inflection, "you will rue the day you ever met me, old friend."

Kalif's expression told Nicoletta that he believed him.

"I'll find her," Kalif whispered. "I vow it."

Master Kan said nothing. Henders took the silence as his cue to leave. He quickly scurried from the bedchamber, the doors sealing shut behind him.

Nicoletta stared at her husband's back. She knew her jaw had dropped open a bit, but she couldn't help it. "Why?" she whispered. "Why do You want Nellie back?"

He cocked his head and stared at her from over his shoulder. "I do not speak to a caged wife. This you know."

Her dark eyes narrowed. She ignored him. "Why?" she barked. Her nostrils flared. "Do You care about Your daughter at all or do You fear losing the yen she could bring to You on the auction block?"

The muscles in his back stiffened. He looked away. "The yen, of course," he murmured. "What other reason could I possibly have?"

Nicoletta knew he was lying. A realization that stunned her so mightily it took her a moment to find her voice. Her eyes round, she watched him walk away. She swallowed hard against the lump of emotion in her throat.

"If You had shown," she rasped out, "any caring for Nellie at all whilst she was growing up, I might have loved You. If even just a little bit."

He stilled, his back to her.

"Go to Your mindless whores, Abdul," Nicoletta whispered. "Unlike Sinead and myself, they will tell You all the lies You crave to hear."

He turned his head and stared at her from over his shoulder. His nostrils flared as his light gaze clashed with her dark one. "I'll come back to feed you later," he growled.

Chapter 35
January 31, 2250 A.D.

Kerick clasped the manacles around Nellie's wrists before securing them to a sensory chain. He paused for a moment to bury his face between her large breasts, to run his tongue over her stiff nipples and listen to her breathy sighs.

She shivered, her nipples tightening up even further. "That feels so incredible," she whispered, her nipple chain making a jingling sound.

"Mmmm...they taste so incredible," Kerick murmured from around a plump nipple.

Nellie raised her manacled hands high enough to run them through his dark hair. She spread her thighs wide open from where she sat on the bed, beckoning to him. "Let us love each other one last time before You go?"

He stilled. His head slowly rose from between her breasts. "One...*last* time?"

She swallowed.

"Do you think to run from Me again, Nellie?" His jaw steeled as he stood up and pushed away from her. "Because I'll hunt you down again if you do," he growled. "Only the next time—"

"No!" Nellie quickly assured him. She wasn't quite ready to tell him about her sire yet. She needed the time he'd be gone with his brother to look for Elijah and hunt for Kora to work up her nerve. "You took the meaning of my words and twisted them," she said quietly. She sighed as she slowly stood up. "I have no intention of running from You, Kerick."

Silence.

"Where has she gone?" he murmured. His commanding gray eyes flicked down to meet hers.

Nellie didn't pretend not to understand his meaning. She rubbed her temples and glanced away. "If You find Kora, then You find her. But do not expect me to betray mine own race."

Within Federated Earth there were but three races: male, female, and sub-human. Amongst uninfected humans, it was the male race that turned on each other. Females didn't do that. At least not any females

Nellie had ever known. Even her sire's wives—none of whom she'd had a care for besides Nicoletta and her mother—hadn't betrayed one another to their Master when push came to shove.

The problem as Nellie saw it was there was no way to go to the Xibalba without giving away the secret hiding place of so many runaway females...or breaking her vow and running from her husband. Soon—very soon—she would have to decide which of those scenarios was the lesser of two evils. She was needed in the Xibalba to work on the serum. This Nellie knew. Kora had told her as much in no uncertain terms.

But her husband. He'd never forgive her...

Kerick frowned. He took a slow, measured breath and blew it out. "I shall return before nightfall," he muttered. His eyebrows rose. "Make certain I find you here within our bedchamber upon My return."

She nodded in a distracted fashion, her thoughts in too much chaos to concentrate.

Silence.

Nellie glanced up. Her green eyes widened questioningly at the intent expression on his face.

"The *zida* stones have been removed from the caverns, little one," Kerick said softly. Too softly.

Her teeth sank into her lower lip as she nervously studied his face. The man seemed capable of anticipating her every possible thought. Not that she had decided to run from him. She still didn't know what was the right thing to do. The lesser of two evils...what an impossible decision. Break one's word or betray one's race—both were considered vile in the biospheres as well as the Outside.

"Do not force My hand, Nellie. I've no desire to punish you."

She cleared her throat. "Well," she breathed out, forcing a smile to her full lips, "I suppose that makes two of us for I've no desire to be punished." She had seen some of the punishments her sire's wives had received over the years. Every last one of them had left much to be desired, to say the least. "Go to Your brother," she whispered. "All will be well."

"Will it, Nellie?" he murmured. "Be well?"

She was given no time to answer that question for a moment later he had seized her by the shoulders and pulled her tightly against him. He claimed her mouth, kissing her roughly on the lips, branding it in the way he'd branded her body last eve. His kiss, she thought sadly, was as desperate as she felt.

By the time he pulled away, his breathing was heavy and his nostrils flaring. "I love you, Nellie Riley. Do not betray Me."

Her eyes widened at the love words. She opened her mouth to give them back, but to no avail. The chamber door slammed shut, barring her inside alone.

* * * * *

Kerick's eyes narrowed at Xavier as his friend made his way into the Commons. He had that look about him. A look that told him without words that something was not as it should be. "What is it?" Kerick barked, one eyebrow slowly arching. "What have you learned?" His gut clenched as he considered the very real possibility that Kieran had met a bad end while searching for his runaway wife. "Is it my brother?"

Xavier's demeanor, typically lighthearted, was serious. His expression, typically teasing, was intense. "No," he murmured, coming to a standstill before Kerick. He placed the torch he'd been carrying in a nearby wall sconce and gave him his full attention. "It is your wife," he sighed. "Holy Cyrus. You are never going to believe this, amigo."

Kerick stilled. His jaw clenched as he regarded his friend. Kerick had been gone from Nellie less than an hour. If she had already attempted to run from him after giving her word that she wouldn't, there would be hell to pay. "Go on."

"I was at a Pussy Parlour last night. Particularly, I was at the one Old Gingus owns near to the Crossroads."

Kerick shrugged. Xavier was always at one Pussy Parlour or another. Such was not precisely breaking news. "And?"

Xavier took a deep breath and blew it out. "And I spotted some biosphere scouts, so of course I had to find out why they were there. They pretended to be businessmen looking for one of the men's runaway wife." He snorted. "We both know better."

Yes. They did. No biosphere-bred businessmen would dare venture to the Outside, let alone to a sector within the Underground so far removed from aid. Not even for a wife. He would consider her lost yen and purchase another one when money and availability allowed. Unless the men in question had been well-trained and arrogantly believed themselves invincible. Which meant that any way you sliced it, they could not be businessmen.

Kerick said nothing, just nodded, indicating Xavier should continue.

"The name of the runaway wife," Xavier said softly, his eyes flicking up to meet his friend's, "was Nellie Kan."

Kerick's eyes slowly narrowed, a feeling of unadulterated possessiveness swamping him. "I see," he muttered. As jealous as Xavier's words had made him feel, it was the sense of urgency creeping up his spine that was alarming. He had known all along that Nellie was valuable to the Hierarchy. He just didn't know why—still didn't know why. He had been a fool not to press her for that information right from the start.

"There is more."

He had been afraid of that. "Go on."

Xavier reached into the pocket of his woolen black cloak and pulled out a holographic image roughly the size of his hand. "The scouts were dispensing these holo-cards at Gingus's last night." He placed it into Kerick's callused palm. "I think you better take a deep breath before you read it, amigo."

He didn't like the sound of that. Kerick's eyes bore into Xavier's as he closed his hand around the card. He slowly tore his gaze away, then glanced down to read it.

A photo of Nellie—three photos actually. The images flicked back and forth to show his wife's face and body at all angles. In Spanish beneath the photos were the words: *one million yen reward for the safe return of Dr. Nellie Kan.*

Kerick's breathing stilled when he saw the name of the man posting such an outrageously huge sum of money for Nellie's capture. His gaze flicked up to meet his friend's. His heart felt as though it might pound out of his chest.

"Abdul Kan," Xavier murmured. His eyes narrowed. "*The* Abdul Kan."

* * * * *

Nellie bit her lip as she searched for Tara Riley's diary. She knew it was here. She just didn't know where. Her nostrils flared as she continued to search the earthen bedchamber. It was bad enough she had to choose between the lesser of two evils. It was unthinkable that, should she choose to run, she do so without the journal.

She searched under the pillow-bed…nothing. She looked again under the animal hide chair nearest the small kitchen—nothing. Damn! Damn! Damn! She frowned. Apparently all those orgasms last eve had left her utterly witless.

She stilled as the answer came to her. The diary was behind one of the wall sconces. She blew out a breath before investigating them, wishing she could recall which wall sconce. Not that it mattered, she conceded. It would be nightfall at best before Kerick returned.

Ten minutes later, Nellie pulled the vacuum-sealed pouch containing the diary out from behind the last wall sconce in the chamber that she checked. She snatched it out, a reverent hand running over the faded leather journal. She sighed as she did so, her thoughts turning to the man who meant as much to the diary's author as he did to Nellie.

Kerick.

Twice he had saved her life. The first time she hadn't known it until after the fact—the night when he'd stolen her away from the biosphere. That eve she hadn't yet known the Hierarchy was hunting her. She hadn't known until she'd escaped the man who had inadvertently thwarted their deadly intentions that they wanted her erased from existence.

The second time her husband had saved her had been in the catacombs. That night she could have been raped or worse. Those brothers had been devolving. Had Kerick not killed them, it would have been only a matter of time before one of them had turned and killed them all.

And this was how she was to repay him? By running? She sighed as she rubbed her temples, feeling as though no matter what choice she made it would be a bad one. Run from Kerick and work on the serum, or stay and let Kora devolve.

Yes, Kora was infected. It didn't take a scientist to figure out as much. Her eyes…there was something about her eyes every now and again that was not…right. And now Kora Riley née Williams carried Tara Riley's unborn grandchild in her belly.

Decisions—impossible decisions.

Nellie needed to work on that serum. She also needed to not run from her husband—again. That left but one alternative: give him the full truth about everything and talk him into taking her to the Xibalba. She grimaced, hating that choice as much as the other two. When he knew who she was, and who her sire was in particular, everything would change. Not to mention the fact he would be angry that she'd not informed him of her background from the beginning.

Kerick's hatred of Abdul Kan would be extreme, she realized. How could it not be? Her father might not be a Hierarchy leader in title, but he was in truth. Not only was he powerful, he was a decision-maker. Not even Kalif Henders would dare piss without Abdul's permission. Which meant her father was at least indirectly responsible for Tara Riley's death, if not directly responsible.

But why? Nellie asked herself for the hundredth time. What secrets did her sire and Henders share? She knew they were in some way to blame for the creation of the sub-human race, but she couldn't begin to fathom how. If Nellie were to inform Kerick of her parentage, such questions would be the first he put to her. Would he believe her when she said she didn't know the answers? She sighed, doubting it.

Nellie vacuum-sealed the diary back up in its container, preparing to hide it again behind the wall sconce. (A kong of a good hiding place, she decided, since even she'd had trouble finding it.) She would show her husband his mother's journal later —

She frowned. Preferably after a few chalices of spirits when she was feeling less the coward.

The stone and earthen door came crashing open, taking Nellie by surprise and causing her to yelp. She whirled around on her heel, careful to conceal the diary behind her back as she did so. When her wide green eyes met very intense gray ones, she realized she hadn't been fast enough. Kerick's gaze flicked from the arms she held pinioned behind her back up to her face.

His jaw tightened. She wet her lips.

"What are You doing here?" Nellie breathed out. "I — uh — I thought You were not scheduled to return until nightfall." She forced a weak smile to her lips.

Silence. He said nothing, only stared at her.

Nellie held his intense gaze for as long as she could. Her eyelashes shuttered when the need to look away came upon her. "Please speak to me," she whispered.

He knew. Sweet Cyrus, he knew. She had no idea how, but there was no mistaking the look of anger and betrayal permeating his typically stoic if a bit grim features. She felt as though she was going to be sick. Why hadn't she told him before he found out? Why? Her heart began thumping like crazy in her chest.

"You lied to Me, Nellie Kan Riley," Kerick murmured.

Her head shot up. Her eyes widened. "I…" Her first reaction had been to deny it, but what was the point? She *had* lied. Some might try to argue that withholding information is not a lie, and technically speaking they might be correct. It still boiled down to the same thing — a lie. "Kerick…"

His nostrils flared as he thrust a holo-card into her line of vision. She blinked a few times in rapid succession as she stared at it, her brain slowly assimilating what it was she was looking at.

She sighed. He really did know. "Fuck," she whispered.

An unladylike response no doubt, but a kong of an apropos one.

His eyes narrowed. "Talk," he bit out. "Now."

Chapter 36

He wanted to kill her with his bare hands. He wanted to beat her within an inch of her life. But sweet Kalast, he wanted to cry with happiness more than anything else.

Elijah's jaw clenched unforgivingly as he guided Tara Riley through the catacombs by the back of her neck. She was alive—alive! He had been grieving her death for years and all the while she had been living and breathing mere miles from Kong. He had never been so angry, so relieved, so elated, or so hurt.

"Will you not speak to me?" she whispered as they meandered down a rocky path in the Underground.

His nostrils flared. "No!" he barked.

He steered her into a secluded cavern that they might rest long enough to eat. Once there he let go of her neck and removed his satchel to find the provisions within it. He busied himself with that chore, refusing to look upon her.

Tara sighed. "Surely you must understand why I permitted you and my sons to believe me dead? It was safer for all of you!"

She sighed again when it became obvious he was too angered to speak with her. She absently watched him pull flatbread, meat, and cheese from his satchel. "The Hierarchy would have put both you and Kerick to death upon capture had they thought me alive. *This you know*." Her teeth gritted. "And if by some off chance they did not, I could have left remission and turned on you at any hour. I couldn't have borne it had you died at my hands—claws."

Silence. Cold, harsh, angry silence. Yet there was a gentling in his eyes too. She seized him by his two strong arms, waiting patiently until he gave up and gazed down upon her.

"I love you more than life itself, Eli," she whispered. Her breathing was heavy, her heart thumping against her chest. Being this close to him again after so many years..."The intensity of it has never left nor weakened."

She felt a tear form in one eye and had to frown at it. She glanced away as she released his biceps, taking a deep breath. By Cyrus, she was not the sort of wench who ever cried! Yet the thought that Elijah might hate her made her want to do just that. When he had thought her dead, she had lived on in his memories in a reverent fashion. But now?

"I'm an old woman who has seen five decades," she said softly, staring at the ground. "My beauty has perhaps faded, but my love for you has not."

His nostrils flared impossibly further. "You betrayed me," he hissed. "I would have rather gone to my death knowing you lived than to have lived thinking you dead."

Her head shot up. Her gray eyes widened. "I'm sorry," she said softly. "When a group of scouts came in and obliterated everything within sight, they assumed I, too, had died. I had but a moment to make a choice." She nodded definitively. "And I stand by the conviction that I made the right one." She sighed as she turned on her heel and walked a pace away from him. "Today you are angry. Tomorrow you will realize the truth to my words."

"I doubt it."

"You and my sons are alive," she said tiredly, suddenly feeling exhausted and bone weary. "To me, this is all that ever mattered."

Silence.

"Tara?" he murmured.

She cleared her throat. "Yes?" she asked without glancing back to him.

"You are wrong about one thing."

She said nothing, just waited for him to blister her ears with a thousand retributions about how she never should have—

"Your beauty has grown, not faded," Elijah said softly.

She swallowed against the lump of emotion in her throat. "You lie," she said, her voice catching. Her body was still strong and toned, but there were more laugh lines around her eyes. A misnomer, she decided, given that she rarely smiled, let alone laughed. She'd also grown a streak of silver in her black mane of hair. Young she was not.

Tara turned around slowly. Her legs were shaking so mightily she felt as though her knees might give out and send her toppling to the earthen ground. "But that's a lie I can live with," she breathed out.

His dark brown eyes searched her face. He shook his head slowly. "It's not a lie," he whispered.

She looked up, taking in the sight of his heavily muscled, six and a half foot frame, until her gaze at last settled on his handsome ebony face. She took a deep breath. "I would ask you to prove it, yet you know that we cannot chance loving each other."

His eyelashes shuttered. "Do you honestly think I'll let you get out of this cavern unclaimed?" he murmured.

Her heart began pounding as her nipples hardened. Apparently she wasn't as old as she'd thought. Her very womb contracted at the mental image his words conjured. Unconsciously, she licked her lips. "Eli…"

"Take off your clothes." His voice went down in timbre. "Now."

She blew out a breath. Sweet Cyrus, how she wanted to. She could see his penis thickening against the brown leather pants he wore. For years she had wondered what it would feel like to be joined with him, to feel his long black cock impaled all the way inside of her. What he offered was no small temptation. "I…I cannot."

He sighed just a bit. "Tara—"

"Eli, please," she said in a defeated voice. She briefly closed her eyes before meeting his gaze. "Old I may be, but you know as well as I that women are breedable until death. We don't have bodies like the ancient females." She shook her head. "Scientists made sure of that."

Elijah frowned. "And your point?"

She frowned back, huffing a bit. "I got lucky with Kieran. Lucky he was not born deformed from infection! I don't think I should chance the fates twice!"

He was quiet for a long moment as he considered her words. He turned around slowly, his hands settling at his hips as he gave her his back. "Any babe I put in your belly would only be infected if you leave remission before its birth."

"That could happen," she said quietly, sadly. "You know I speak the truth."

He sighed, sounding as weary as she felt. "Many things could happen, Tara. We could walk out of here in five minutes and get blown to bits by biosphere scouts. Should we remain in this cavern for all eternity for the fear of it?" He turned on his heel and stared down at her. His nostrils flared. "When did you become so weak and afraid?"

Her eyes flared at the challenge. "How dare you," she hissed.

"You're afraid," he murmured, taunted.

"I fear nothing," she said distinctly, her words clipped and precise.

His eyebrows rose. Removing his weapons belt and satchel, he tossed both to the ground. "Prove it," he said as his fingers found the waistband to his leather trousers and began working them off his hips.

Tara's heart rate went over the top as she watched the only man she'd ever loved, the man whom she'd spent countless hours—days—

years — fantasizing about, slowly disrobe before her. He removed the animal-skin shirt he wore after stepping out of his leather trousers. His long, thick cock sprang free, jutting up against his navel.

Her nostrils flared. "I know about that wench you stole after escaping Kong. Did you claim her?"

He met her gaze, his eyes studying hers. "No."

She wet her lips. "Oh," she squeaked. She cleared her throat. "Oh," she said again, trying to sound as though the answer didn't matter so greatly.

"So," Elijah said, standing before her totally naked and erect. "Has Tara grown weak and afraid or is she still strong and fearless?"

Her chin notched up. He was using her pride to crumble her defenses and it was working like a Cyrus-forsaken charm. Her eyes narrowed. "You were always a bastard," she seethed.

He moved against her so closely she could feel the head of his cock poking against her belly. "That's why you love me," he said thickly.

Her nostrils flared even as her hand reached between them and wrapped around his thick, swollen penis. Elijah sucked in his breath. "Damn you," she whispered.

It was all the concession he needed. Grabbing her coarse dress by the hem, he tore it apart in a lightning-fast movement and sent it sailing over her head before lowering them both to the earthen ground.

Tara came down on top of him, straddling his middle while she kissed him roughly. Lips and tongues clashed and battled in a kiss as desperate as it was overdue. "Damn you," she muttered between heated kisses.

She raised her face and met his gaze as she lowered herself onto him. She grabbed his thick cock again and poised it at the entrance to her pussy. "Damn you," she breathed out as she sank down onto him, enveloping him inside of her.

He hissed. "Damn me all you want," Elijah gritted out. His fingers sank into the flesh of her hips as he flipped her onto her back, reversing their positions. "But I'm mounting you while you do it."

He sank into her to the hilt, groaning as he finally felt the pussy he'd been denied for more years than he cared to dwell upon. He took her hard, mercilessly, pounding in and out of her with possessive strokes meant to brand. He growled as he took her, fucking her harder and harder and —

Tara groaned, the first orgasm immediate and violent. She spread her legs wider as she moaned, giving him better access to her wet, aroused flesh. "Oh yes," she whimpered, moaning louder when he palmed her breasts and began tweaking the nipples as he rode her. *"Oh yes."*

She had feared the first time wouldn't last long and it didn't look as though it would. Not that she could blame Elijah for coming so quickly when she herself had come within seconds. Her nails sank into his muscular back as she felt him stiffen on top of her. His orgasm was imminent, she realized.

But Elijah was determined to savor her cunt. He moaned and groaned — in pleasure and pain of denied climax — as he sank in and out of her, over and over, again and again. "Mine," he ground out against her ear. "All mine."

She had thought her first orgasm was harsh, but the second one made her scream. *"Harder,"* she begged. *"More."*

Elijah gave her what she wanted and then so much more. She could hear her cunt sucking him back in on every upstroke, could smell the scent of their combined arousal as he impaled her with his long, thick, black cock. He pounded into her pussy again and again and again and...

He roared as he spurted, no longer able to hold himself back. His jaw clenched and his muscles tensed as his cock spewed like a geyser inside of her cunt. Tara threw her hips back at him, squeezing him with her pussy to extract every pearly droplet of semen from his cock.

They laid there joined for stolen minutes, their breathing harsh and choppy, their bodies not wanting to part. He made no move to climb off of her and she never once considered moving away from him. Forever they had waited for this moment — she feared it would take just as long before an eve like this between them would ever happen again.

"I love you, Tara," Elijah at last murmured as he bent his neck to kiss her. "Do not ever leave me again. Vow it."

She ran her hand over his face, the stubble there somehow comforting. "I wish I could," she whispered. Sweet Cyrus she felt close to crying. She had to pause for a moment in her words to keep from disgracing herself. Even then, her voice still shook a little. "I would give anything that we could live out our lives as a normal couple."

Elijah closed his eyes and took a deep breath. When he opened them, they simply stared at each other for a long moment.

"I will not claim you until you come to me willingly," he said softly. He smiled. "I give you one hour to come to me willingly."

Tara smiled back — the first real smile she'd entertained in years. "A whole hour?" she laughed. "I — "

The delight on her face faded as Elijah's eyes slowly dimmed and his massive body slumped atop hers. Her eyes widened in horror as she watched his crimson blood trickle down to stain her pale skin. She barely had time to register that the man she loved had been attacked when Patricia Reddy and Kora Williams hovered over her, a rock in Kora's hands.

"It's just a flesh wound," Dr. Reddy frowned. "He'll live."

Tara blinked.

"Your daughter-in-law, however, is another story." Dr. Reddy glanced between the two women then bent to help hoist the fallen Elijah from Tara's body. "Let's go," she said distinctly, reeling Tara's senses back in to the mission at hand. "Time is something we don't have a lot of."

Chapter 37

Nellie glanced away, uncertain where to begin. The worst part, she conceded, was over. Kerick already knew that Abdul Kan was her sire. She wondered if he hated her for it and figured that he probably did. His eyes fairly screamed of disgust. Disgust and betrayal.

"I'm sorry," she whispered. She sighed, moving the journal in front of her as she walked a pace away from him and gave him her back. "I should have told You. I wanted to—I swear to Cyrus I wanted to. But when I found out who You were…"

"You lied instead," Kerick finished for her.

She nodded, her back still to him. "Yes," she said softly. "I suppose I did." She clutched his mother's journal against her breasts. "You have every right to despise my father. He is guilty of crimes against humanity I cannot even begin to contemplate." She closed her eyes. "I suppose I feared You would think me guilty by association if You knew I'd been sired of him."

He was silent for a moment. "Nellie, look at Me."

She shook her head. "I cannot," she said quietly, her eyes opening.

Kerick walked the space that separated them, gently but firmly grabbed his wife by the shoulders, and turned her around that she faced him. Her gaze remained cast on the earthen ground, her head bowed. "Look at Me," he murmured.

"I cannot," she softly reiterated.

He frowned. "I do not hold you responsible for the actions of Abdul Kan, Nellie. No more than I hold My brother Kieran to blame for Maxim Malifé's vile life. I hold you responsible solely for your own choices." His eyes narrowed. "Twice I have asked you to look at Me and twice you have denied Me. Why?"

She took a deep breath and slowly blew it out. Here was where an already tense situation would become impossibly tenser, she thought. "Because there is more," Nellie muttered, her heart racing when she saw him frown from out of her peripheral vision. "A lot more," she quietly admitted.

It seemed like forever before Kerick at last spoke. By the time he did, her heart was slamming against her chest. With fear of what would happen next? With apprehension of how he would react to her confession? She no longer knew.

"I know," Kerick murmured, "that you are valuable to the Hierarchy. I have known that for quite some time now. I just didn't know why. It's because you are Abdul Kan's daughter, is it not?"

She slowly shook her head. "No. Hardly anyone at Fathom Systems was aware of our association."

His eyebrow quirked. His gaze momentarily flicked down to the leather-bound book she was holding, but he made no move to take it from her. "Then...?"

Her sigh was long and weary. "I told You the very day You stole me I was working on a serum."

Kerick's muscles tensed. Yes she had. Yet somehow amidst all the chaos he had briefly forgotten as much.

"I was close to perfecting it before You took me from Altun Ha. Very close, in fact."

He frowned a bit as he absently ran a hand over his stubbled jaw. "This is why you are wanted back? To finish the serum?"

Her smile was sad. She glanced up, her gaze meeting his. "They don't want me to finish it, Kerick. They never did. Only I didn't realize that until later, after You took me."

His eyes narrowed.

"They want me dead," Nellie murmured. "My own sire included, no doubt."

Kerick took a deep breath and blew it out. "They let you work on it until you got too close to the truth."

She nodded. "I didn't know it until after I ran from You the first time and returned to Altun Ha, but had You not stolen me away that eve I..." She sighed, uncharacteristic tears welling up in her eyes. She supposed the tears were due to fatigue for she had long ago come to accept that her father was evil. He had murdered her mother, his own wife. There was little point in harboring hurt feelings over the fact that he had also intended to kill his ownchild—herself. She blinked the tears away, clutched the journal tighter against her breasts, and continued. "Let us just say I would be dead," she admitted a bit shakily.

Had she not glanced away she might have seen a gentling in his stark gray eyes. "I'm sorry," he murmured. "For whatever that's worth."

Her gaze clashed again with his. "I won't pretend that growing up I didn't crave his love. I thought I could change him. That never happened." She smiled. "Idealistic youth," she whispered.

They studied each other for a prolonged silence. Kerick ran a battle-worn hand through her dark red hair, his fingers sifting through it with quiet appreciation. Her eyes shuttered. An unspoken bond was forged between them in those moments. He didn't know it yet, but the fact he was not holding Nellie responsible for her sire's actions had served to further endear him to her. Everyone else had her entire life. Why wouldn't he?

Perhaps he truly did love her.

His hand dropped, falling to rest at his side. Nellie broke his gaze. "I suppose now is the time to tell You all."

Kerick said nothing, just stood there and waited.

Nellie lowered her eyes to look down upon the journal she was holding. She ran a hand over the worn leather casing before slowly handing the book to her husband. His steel-gray eyes were filled with incomprehension. "This is the journal all of my ideas for the serum came from," she admitted. "Few know of its existence. Or at least, few did. I think the Hierarchy is now aware." She sighed. "And I think they came that eve to retrieve it at all costs. Even if they had to murder me to obtain it."

Kerick frowned as he glanced down at the diary his wife had handed him. There was something oddly familiar about it. The look of it, the scent of it, the —

His eyes widened in dawning comprehension as he opened the book to its first page. "I don't believe this," he muttered, his heart slamming against his chest. He realized it belonged to his mother before he saw her name within it. He would recognize her hurried, precise penmanship anywhere. "Where did you get this?" he asked, stunned.

"An infected woman brought it to me," she whispered.

He searched her eyes. "But how..."

"I do not know," she interrupted. "I had never seen the woman before, nor have I seen her since." She shook her head. "She said...*things* to me, Kerick. Things that made no sense. Things I didn't really believe until the truth found me in the form of Kora Williams Riley."

His head shot up. His body stilled. "What do you mean?" he softly inquired.

She sighed. "Kora was captured by Your brother while she was hunting for me. She came into the catacombs that day to retrieve me that I might finish the serum."

Here's where her decision would be made, she worriedly thought as she prepared to tell him the total truth. If he refused to aid her, whether out of denial or from a sense of misguided protection, she knew what her choice would have to be. Her heart was beating so rapidly she feared she might faint. "Kora works for the female Underground," she informed him. "She is a scientist within the Xibalba."

Kerick blinked. "The Xibalba?" He frowned. "I have heard of it, of course, though it is unlikely such a place exists."

"Kerick—"

"Kora is a liar," he said abruptly. "Nellie, think on it. If there were free, unclaimed wenches roaming about the Underground, do you not think they would have been found and ferreted out long ago by men desperate for wives?"

Her lips pinched together in a disapproving fashion. "Perhaps these females are too well trained to be caught by just anybody." Her teeth gritted. "Least of all by men," she spat.

She could have sworn she saw him smile, but if he had he quickly steeled himself to normal. "Laugh if You will," she hissed, "but I know where this place is. Furthermore, I am going there to finish the serum. With You or without You."

His eyes narrowed. "Do not threaten Me, little one."

"Then do not mock me."

He nodded, conceding the point. "Fair enough."

She sighed, suddenly feeling tired. "I'm serious in that I must go. Kora is infected," Nellie whispered. "I'm certain of it."

He closed his eyes briefly and took a breath in such a way that Nellie became chillingly aware he too had suspected as much. "I admit I knew there was something not right about her. I just hadn't realized until this moment what that something was."

"She is pregnant," she reminded him, her stare unblinking. "Time is of the essence." She blinked, then swallowed hard. "Will You aid me or will You force my hand into finding yet another way to flee from You?"

Kerick frowned as he regarded her. "I will take you to where you believe this Xibalba exists," he murmured. "Though I fear you will be gravely disappointed."

Nellie smiled, confident of anything but. "Thank You," she said quietly.

His eyebrows slowly rose. "For now I will let the issue of your lies to me go unpunished. But know, Nellie, that this subject is neither forgotten nor over."

In other words, he intended to punish her. He would leave her to wonder over when and how. Her chin thrust up defensively. "Let us be gone," she said a bit tersely. "The Crossroads is a long journey from these catacombs."

Chapter 38

AND I LOOKED, AND BEHOLD A PALE HORSE: AND HIS NAME THAT SAT ON HIM WAS DEATH, AND HELL FOLLOWED WITH HIM. AND POWER WAS GIVEN UNTO THEM OVER THE FOURTH PART OF THE EARTH, TO KILL WITH SWORD, AND WITH HUNGER, AND WITH DEATH...

AND WITH THE BEASTS OF THE EARTH.

* * * * *

He must have imagined her. Either that or a gorgeous unclaimed wench had just disappeared right out from under his nose.

Xavier's expression was grim as he entered his usual Pussy Parlour—again—to get a droid to fuck—again. His nostrils flared as he wondered where that wench had scurried off to. He knew she hadn't been a figment of an overly active, lusty imagination. In his wildest, kinkiest dreams he never could have thought up such a caramel-skinned, dark-haired beauty as that one. She didn't have the fake, manufactured look of the common human female. And if his thoughts hadn't been so focused on that holo-card he'd retrieved with Kerick's wife on it...

Damn! His teeth gritted. That gorgeous wench had been unclaimed. She wore body décor—hideous, foreign body décor but there it was. If she had a nipple chain to speak of, he certainly hadn't seen it.

Not that it mattered. That wench? He'd take her and keep her in a minute, mastered or no.

"Yer back already?" Old Gingus smiled his toothless grin as he polished the faded, chipped woodwork of the bar with a worn rag. "I ain't open yet, boy."

Xavier frowned, his gaze absently flicking up to the half broken relic of a lit-up sign that said *closed* in Spanish beneath the flicking words *G's Spot*. "I haven't been a boy in years," he muttered.

"No? Well you sure as shit got the libido of one."

Xavier plopped down in front of the bar on a stone stool. Stretched out worn leather covered it as makeshift padding. "Been locked up." His eyebrows rose as he accepted a rare, vintage cigarette from the barkeep and inhaled. "A long time."

Old Gingus laughed. "That explains it I guess."

"Not really." Xavier exhaled slowly, a ring of smoke encircling his face. He grinned. "I've always been greedy." The old man snorted at that. "Hey, G," Xavier drawled, changing the subject. His eyes squinted. "Either I'm losin' my fucking mind—always possible—or I saw an unclaimed wench roaming around down here. She stands about a foot shorter than me, maybe five foot four. She has dark brown curly hair that's almost black. Her eyes are dark too. Know anything about her?"

"No," he said quickly—too quickly. "No I don't know nothin 'bout no unclaimed wench. Hell, you think I wouldn't have poked her me self?" He laughed.

Xavier stilled. The old man was lying. But why lie if he hadn't claimed the wench? He forced a smile to his lips. "Can't say I blame you," he murmured.

Gingus handed him a skeleton key. "Stall two," he mumbled, effectively changing the subject. "The droids ain't powered up yet but go get you a virtual fuck in stall two."

"A virtual fuck?" Xavier shook his head. "Never had one of those."

"They ain't bad. They ain't bad at all. I've had me a few."

"Yeah?" *Why are you lying about the girl, old man?*

"Yeah." He cleared his throat. "It's on the house. Enjoy."

Xavier's eyebrows shot up. "Since when do you give away anything for free?"

"Since right now," he grumbled, frowning. "Don't ask so many damned questions. Besides, I owe you for gettin' rid of them troublemakers last night."

Xavier's eyes flared, recalling the biosphere scouts. Old Gingus probably wouldn't want to know just how he'd gotten rid of them. "My pleasure," he murmured.

The old man swallowed a bit heavily. Xavier could tell he wanted to be rid of him. But then most people felt that way—especially those who knew anything at all about him. For now he would oblige the old man. Standing up, he looked down at the key in his hand. "A virtual fuck?"

Gingus nodded. "It ain't half bad, boy. Go give it a try."

"I will." Xavier stilled. "Just so you know…"

"Eh?"

"I'll pay a lot of yen to own her."

He swallowed uncomfortably again, reaffirming Xavier's suspicion the barkeep knew more about the mysterious wench than he let on. "H-How much?"

Xavier's eyes flicked over the old man's face, reading him, assessing him. "A lot," he said softly. "Not that you would know anything about her, of course." His eyebrows rose. "Just put the word out."

At Old Gingus's nod, Xavier made his way toward stall two. The barkeep was hiding something and just as soon as he finished hunting down Elijah and Kieran with Kerick he'd make a point of finding out what.

He wanted that wench. He wanted her with a fierceness he couldn't explain.

The skeleton key sank in the hole. Xavier walked into stall two, which contained a small, coarse pillow-bed made from lizard hides, a virtual console with a red ON button, and little else. Discarding his trousers, tunic, and cloak, he turned on the power button, snuffed out the cold chamber's single torch, plopped down onto the bed naked, and waited.

And waited. And waited. And waited.

Xavier's teeth gritted. It was a sad day indeed when a man couldn't even get some imaginary pussy.

"Come on," he bit out. "I don't got all day." Soon Kerick would come looking for him. His jugular bulged. "Cyrus forsaken piece of shit," he mumbled. "I—"

He grunted, appeased, when the virtual program flicked on.

"Hello," a disembodied female voice breathed out.

Xavier frowned. What a cheap piece of junk. He couldn't see anybody and the breathy voice sounded more the stalking lunatic than an aroused female. "Hello," he grumbled. Sweet Cyrus this would be the worst fuck ever! "Just get to the good bits. I'm in a hurry."

The virtual wench either ignored him or wasn't advanced enough in her programming to respond. What a surprise!

"My name is…"

He winced. Ah gods. She couldn't even recall her damned name. Old Gingus had rewarded him with a virtual moron.

"My name is…"

His teeth gnashed together. "I don't care!" he bellowed. "Just get to the good bits!"

"You might try being nice, sir," the virtual wench softly chastised. "I haven't been with a man in ages and I'm a little nervous."

His eyebrows shot up, his expression surreal. He blinked. Kerick had a real wench he could mount day and night. Kieran, when he found his wife again, would have a real wench he too could mount at whim. What did Xavier have? A virtual almost-virgin who couldn't recall her programmed name and was of a mind to scold him. He sighed. This was just too much. "I'm sorry," he snapped, exasperated. He rolled his eyes. "I don't know what I was thinkin' talking to an imaginary wench like that."

"That's better."

He grunted.

"Now, where were we?"

"We were getting to the good bits," he seethed.

"Oh right. My name is…"

Ah gods, they'd never get passed this part!

"Ummm…"

He seized his hair by the roots and pulled tightly.

"My name is…"

"Arrrg!"

"Clara."

Xavier blinked. His anger slowly dissipated. "Fine," he barked. "Can we get to the good bits now?"

"Almost."

He swore under his breath.

"First we must get your mind in synchronicity with mine."

He sighed, resigned. It had taken imaginary Clara fifteen minutes to recall her name. At the rate she moved, he might get some of her imaginary pussy before his hair went silver and all the teeth rotted out of his mouth. "Fine." He waved a dismissive hand. "Just get on with it."

"Okay." She delicately cleared her throat. "What is your favorite season?"

That was easy. "Winter."

"Your sexual preference?"

"Woman."

"Do you have any sexually transmitted diseases?"

He frowned. "Any what?"

She cleared her throat again. Odd, but he found it rather sexy when imaginary Clara cleared her imaginary throat.

"Never mind," she demurred. "What is your favorite sexual fantasy?"

"I thought you were supposed to know that."

"I'm not working properly today."

"There's a shock."

She huffed. He smiled.

"You're being mean again, sir."

"I'm always mean."

"I'm about to not have sex with you."

He went back to seizing his hair by the roots. "My favorite sexual fantasy," he gritted out, obliging her, "is a woman lying down on the bed with her legs spread wide open."

"That's not very inventive."

"Then even a wench who can't recall her name should have no trouble fulfilling it."

She huffed again. He smiled again.

Silence.

Xavier released his hair and settled back onto the bed with a sigh. "Do you really want to know what my favorite sexual fantasy is?"

"Yes," Clara whispered.

"Having a woman of mine own," he murmured.

Silence.

"Oh," she at last breathed out. This time she sounded more the aroused female and less the maniacal lunatic.

"Clara?" Xavier said thickly.

"Yes?"

"Let's get to the good bits now. If you want to fulfill my sexual fantasy then be an obedient little virtual girl and come offer your imaginary body to your very hard and very real Master."

Her breathing grew heavy. Xavier's cock hardened. This virtual program was turning out better than he'd thought it would.

The dark chamber lit up, the three dimensional scene transforming the ordinary stall into a breathtaking winterscape. Naked and erect, he was lying on a polar bear fur outside in the snow. He could even feel the glistening snowflakes kissing his tanned, battle-scarred body as they fell like slippery diamonds from the sky, yet the temperature was the same as it had been in stall two.

He was in stall two, he reminded himself.

But it didn't look like he was or feel like he was. Sweet Kalast, this place was beautiful. It reminded him of everything he'd ever wanted. It reminded him of what he could never have.

And then beautiful, naked Clara was there, walking towards where he laid on the fur, her gorgeous breasts jiggling with every move she made. The sound of snow crunching under her feet reached his ears. His eyes widened when he realized Clara had transformed herself into the wench of his dreams, the honey-skinned, dark-haired beauty he'd offered Old Gingus yen for.

He swallowed roughly. Yes, this virtual program was turning out much better than he'd thought it would.

She came to a stop and stood next to where he lay on the polar bear fur. His blue eyes hungrily flicked over her body.

"Come ride your Master, Clara," Xavier said thickly. He got impossibly harder when she demurely glanced away. "I want to know what *my* sweet, tight pussy feels like."

Her breasts rose and fell as her breathing grew labored. "It's been a long time. Maybe I won't please you."

His eyes shuttered. "You'll please me," he murmured.

She moved her legs so that she stood directly over him. She hesitated for a brief moment, giving him an achingly arousing view of her cunt, before coming down on top of his heavily muscled body and straddling his lap.

Xavier ran his callused hands all over her breasts, making her gasp. His thumbs ran over her elongated rosy-brown nipples as she closed her eyes and leaned into his touch. She grabbed his cock by the root while he played with her breasts, making his breath suck in.

"Put him inside you," Xavier rasped. "I want to feel my juicy pussy."

Their gazes locked and held. Xavier found himself wishing Clara was real.

She placed his long, thick cock at the entrance of her hole. "You're so big," she said breathlessly. "I don't think I can get you all the way in."

Sweet Cyrus he'd never been so hard. "My beautiful little girl can take her Master's cock all the way in." His fingers dug into the flesh of her hips. "Come on, Clara," he murmured. "Ride your Master."

Her teeth sank into her bottom lip as her cunt sank down onto his cock. Xavier groaned, his nostrils flaring, as Clara's pussy enveloped him all the way inside. She fit him like an unyielding silk glove.

"You're so tight," he said on a half moan, half growl. His teeth gritted when she began to ride him. "There you go," he said thickly, his hands guiding her hips as she worked up and down the length of his shaft. "Mmmm my pussy feels good. So tight and sticky."

Clara closed her eyes and rode him faster, her tits jiggling as she fucked him. Her head lolled back and she moaned as she picked up the pace, the sound of her cunt fucking him reaching his ears.

"Faster, Clara," Xavier rasped. "Fuck your Master harder and faster."

She bore down onto him, sucking his long, thick cock into her juicy cunt over and over, again and again. "You feel so good," she gasped, riding him faster and harder. She bounced away like crazy on top of him, impaling herself to the hilt.

His nostrils flaring, Xavier's fingers dug into her hips as he reversed their positions. Moving her to her back, he groaned as he sank back into Clara's pussy, pounding away inside her like an animal.

"Harder," she begged, her fingernails digging into his back. "*Harder.*"

Xavier fucked her mercilessly, his teeth gritting as he sank into her cunt again and again and again and again. She screamed as she came, her pussy clenching around his cock and squeezing it tightly in a series of intense contractions that made him bellow from the pleasure of it.

"I'm coming," Xavier ground out, his muscles tensing over her. He pounded away like mad, thrusting in and out of her tight pussy once, twice, three times more. "I'm—*ah Clara.*"

He came on a roar, his entire body convulsing atop hers as he spurted hot cum deep inside her. He groaned as he kept fucking her, never wanting the orgasm to end. She felt so good, better even than the real wenches he'd had in his youth.

Xavier had expected Clara to blink away the moment he came, but she didn't. Much to his surprise and happiness, she didn't. She stayed there with him in the snowy wonderland, cleaving to him in a way that felt so good, comfortable to remain in his embrace while his eyes drifted close and he fell into a deep, contented sleep holding her close to his heart.

An hour later when Xavier jarred awake, his heart damn near broke when he realized his body was back in the drab, dreary stall two, no Clara to be found. He sighed as he stood up and relit the torch he'd extinguished when first he had entered the small chamber.

He had known she wasn't real all along. Wishing her real and having her real weren't the same thing.

As Xavier lifted his tunic to put it back on, his gaze absently landed on the broken image map in front of him, an image map he hadn't noticed before. He'd never know what made him do it, but out of curiosity he turned his gaze to the left console that he might be able to look upon his back in the reflection. He stilled as he saw them:

Fingernail scratch marks.

His eyes widened. "Sweet Cyrus," he murmured, his mind racing, his heart pounding. No—no that wasn't possible...

He forced a chuckle. Clara, real? She was real all right, but the scratches on his back had come from a virtual wench whose programmer was good at unlocking the mind's fantasies. They hadn't come from the real Clara, whatever her name was. That wench had run the very second she'd laid eyes on him.

"You're losing it," Xavier muttered, running a punishing hand through his dark hair. He sighed. "You've already lost it."

Chapter 39
February 2, 2250 A.D.

"It's wonderful to see you again, Abdul."

"I'm sure."

Kalif Henders cleared his throat as he stood up. He circled the desk in his lavish, overly decorated office and made his way toward a nearby slave. "You gave me a week, old friend," he said, coming straight to the point as he keyed in a code that would command the slave to retrieve a drink. "It has been but three days. You are early."

Abdul Kan studied him through lowered eyelashes. "I am well aware of the date, amigo. You have four days left to return my daughter to me."

Kalif mopped at his brow with the back of his silk tunic sleeve. He smiled a bit weakly, then handed Abdul the chalice of spirits the automated slave had delivered. "This drink is called Tamarish. It comes from the African Congo," he stuttered, making Abdul's eyes shutter. "A gift from Tozeki LeJeune. Drink up, amigo. It's quite good."

Abdul accepted the chalice of spirits from his longtime associate with a small incline of his head. He held the ornate gold cup between his hands, then raised it to his mouth. Kalif's gaze warily darted back and forth from the chalice to Abdul's lips. He blew out a breath when Abdul sipped from it.

A minute ticked by. "How is the search for Nellie coming along?" Abdul murmured, lowering the chalice.

Kalif smiled, his gaze continually flicking back and forth from the chalice to Abdul's mouth. "It isn't. She won't ever be found." His rat-like, beady eyes found his. "And if she is found by some miracle of Cyrus, my orders are to kill her on sight."

Abdul nodded. He had figured as much. He raised the chalice and stared at it. "You dare tell me this because you have poisoned me?" he softly inquired.

Kalif Henders chuckled. "You'll be dead outside of ten minutes. Feel free to put any questions to me you might have. *Amigo*," he mocked.

Abdul's eyes danced. "Why do you want my daughter dead?" His expression was thoughtful. "I daresay no scientist will ever find a cure for infection. Your brother made sure of that long ago. So why Nellie? Why kill her?"

Kalif's nostrils flared. "It seems my brother was dumber than I thought," he bit out. "There is a cure—only one but it does exist."

"And my daughter is the key?"

"Yes. She is the key. A key that will soon be erased from existence," he said softly.

Abdul inclined his head. He stared at the chalice before glancing up to smile at Kalif. The weak, effeminate Henders with his flowing white silk robes and idiotic taste in office decorations. "Do you know anything about erodium, old friend?"

Kalif frowned. "Erodium?"

"Yes, erodium. That is what you poisoned me with, is it not?"

The slight Henders shrugged. "Yes. What's to know? When digested in pure form it is lethal. You'll be dead at any moment," he sniffed.

"You were always a fool," Abdul sighed. "It's a Cyrus-forsaken miracle you've managed to live this long," he drawled in a pronounced Arabic accent.

Kalif was about to respond when a large tanned hand wrapped itself around his throat. His eyes bulged from around Abdul's grip.

"If I had truly sipped from the chalice, fool, I would have expired upon contact." Abdul smiled, showcasing neat white teeth. "Like this…"

Henders unthinkingly gasped as the chalice of poisoned spirits was raised to his mouth. Abdul Kan took advantage of the slight man's momentary surprise, pouring the contents of the gold cup in between his parted lips. Kalif began to shake uncontrollably, hellish gurgling sounds issuing from the depths of his throat.

Abdul released him, watching dispassionately as his former associate fell to his knees and began frothing at the mouth. Blood mixed with green vomit erupted from between his lips like a spewing volcano.

"*Veni, vidi, vici*," Abdul softly murmured. He brushed off his blue silk tunic before turning on his heel to walk away. Henders fell to the ground, his face purple as blood and vomit continued to spew. "I came. I saw. I conquered."

The vacuum-sealed door whizzed shut behind him.

* * * * *

"We are close," Nellie whispered. Her feet ached. She was tired and she was cold. Her nipples were hard as rocks from being naked—

except for a dangling nipple chain—and walking around the drafty Underground catacombs. The Crossroads were especially chilly.

Xavier's gaze flicked from Nellie's jiggling breasts to Kerick's face. "I doubt we will find anything," he muttered. "A waste of time if you ask me, amigo."

Kerick frowned as if to agree. His gray eyes narrowed at Xavier. "I daresay I am hoping my wife is right. Then maybe we can find you a wench so you can quit ogling mine," he said with a grunt.

Xavier grinned, bemused. "Maybe." His expression turned serious. "I am worried for Kieran and Elijah, amigo. Let us hope if anything comes of this excursion we are able to find them."

Kerick nodded. "On that we can agree," he murmured.

It was another hour before they were ensconced within the innermost sanctuary of Cavern 7. Xavier wielded a poisoned-tipped knife in one hand and a flash-stick in the other. Kerick was equally armed, a flash-stick in either hand.

Nellie's eyes widened as they neared the entrance to the Xibalba. Her heart was beating dramatically, her breathing slightly labored. This was it. The moment of reckoning. A voice inside nagged that the events to follow would change all of their lives forever. She didn't know what was going to happen, only that none of them would ever be the same again.

She slowly lifted a hand and pointed. "The third boulder on the right," Nellie whispered.

* * * * *

Nicoletta listened with half an ear to the boring talk above table. Politics, politics, politics—dull, dull, dull.

The Fathom Systems soiree being held tonight in Abdul's honor was proving to be even less interesting than she'd thought it would be. The only thing she cared to hear about was that Nellie had been found, yet not even once had her Kalast-forsaken husband mentioned his daughter's name.

The Master's other four wives were already above-table as they had seen to their duty and sucked him off for the assembled throng of males not of Abdul's bloodline. He had fed all of them from his hand, and now they sat with him unspeaking, no doubt making a fuss over him to appease his ego.

Nicoletta's teeth gritted. She knew why he had made her go last. Because after coming four times the fifth time would not be so easy. This was his way of keeping her below table throughout the remainder of the evening so she wouldn't embarrass him by saying something untoward in front of his business associates.

She scoffed at that. All these years later and Abdul never seemed to learn. She could suck a blind man into seeing and a sighted man into blindness. In mere minutes she would be above table.

Abdul's body tensed as she took his balls into her mouth and sucked them hard. She heard him hiss, knew from years' worth of experience he found it as painful as he did pleasurable, so she sucked even harder. He jerked up a little bit in his seat, letting her know he would punish her or at least scold her severely if she didn't handle him more gently. But by then he was hard as a rock, so it didn't much matter. She'd known that would happen, of course.

Nicoletta ran her pink tongue across the head of his uncut cock. She smiled to herself when she saw his stomach muscles clench. Taking the head into her mouth, she took his long, thick cock all the way in, deep-throating her husband in one smooth motion. His strong hand found her silky night-black hair and threaded his fingers through it.

In this at least, she had always wielded a power over him. Always.

Sucking him fast and firmly, she could feel his muscles cording already as his body prepared to come whether he wanted it to or not. His strong, callused fingers tightened in her hair, his hand guiding her bobbing head back and forth as she sucked him off.

She sucked on him harder, the sound of saliva meeting cock reaching her ears.

Harder. Harder. Harder.

He groaned, jerking up in his seat, unable to stop himself. Nicoletta's body responded to his desire the way it always did, the way she hated. Her nipples hardened and her breathing became labored as she sucked harder and faster and deeper and…

Harder. Harder. Harder.

His entire body shuddered and convulsed as he came. Warm cum shot out from his cock like a drizzling fountain and Nicoletta found herself lapping it up.

He loved it when she did that. Usually she refused him that pleasure.

Her husband lusted her in a way he never wanted the others — *had* never wanted the others. Years ago she had sometimes asked herself if maybe, just maybe in his own unforgiving way, he loved her. She had discarded the notion entirely, of course. When first she had been bought on the marriage auction block as his chattel and brought to the palace,

Nicoletta had thought him in love with Sinead too. And yet Abdul had murdered her...

Hadn't he?

Yes, yes of course he had killed her. Sinead had died at their husband's hands. That much Nicoletta was certain of. Nellie would never have lied over something of such great import as that. And because Nellie had seen the deed done with her own child's eyes, forgiveness for Sinead's death was not a possibility. Laying the blame at another's feet was not a possibility. The only possibility that existed was hating Abdul Kan for the black deed he had committed.

Nellie...ah my sweet bella, where are you?

Abdul's hand reached under the table, food bits in his palm. Nicoletta absently fed from his hand, feeling like the naked, exotic pet she no doubt looked like. But then that was probably why Abdul had purchased her to begin with...because she was a flawlessly beautiful Italian doll with large doe-like eyes and creamy porcelain skin. The perfect naked female pet.

But Abdul's second wife was no man's willing chattel. A fact her husband had a kong of a time trying to change — but never did. Nicoletta smiled to herself as she thought of how many times over the years she had been caged for her feistiness. More than all of the other wives combined and then some.

He would never break her. Never.

"Go to our rooms and await Me there."

Nicoletta's head shot up. She had been so lost in her thoughts she hadn't even realized she'd finished eating. Her chin notched up as she locked eyes with her husband. "I should like to take my place above table as is my right."

His eyebrows rose. "A right I am denying. Go, Nica," Abdul murmured. "For once let Me handle matters without your interruption."

She frowned. He sighed. A gesture of weakness he rarely made so one that left her feeling confused.

"I will find My daughter. Go to our rooms. Now." His eyelids grew heavy-lidded. "Be lying on the bed, naked and spread wide for Me, when I join you."

His words aroused her and she hated him for it. "Cage me, Abdul," she hissed, her nostrils flaring as she stood up from her kneeling position at his feet. "I will never come to You willing."

A vow she had made long ago and well he knew it.

A vow she would keep to her dying day.

Nicoletta could feel his intense stare on her naked, branded backside as she walked away, but she refused to look back.

* * * * *

Kerick's eyes slightly widened when indeed the boulder moved just as his wife had predicted it would. The vacuum-sealed airlock made a hissing sound as it opened and revealed the portal to an Underground society no man — biosphere-bred or Outsider — had known existed. His gaze momentarily flicked toward Xavier. "This airlock was not fashioned by an Outsider uneducated in engineering," he muttered.

Xavier distractedly nodded as his hand ran over the faux boulder. "Shall we continue onward?"

Kerick nodded toward the portal. "You take the lead. Nellie, you follow behind him. I'll take up the rear."

Nellie frowned at him from over her shoulder when she sensed he was staring at *her* rear. She threw him a look as if to say, *Now is not the time for that*. Kerick possessively stared at the branding on her ass cheek before glancing away.

The trio walked down a long corridor for what amounted to approximately ten minutes. Nellie realized that the female scientists of the Xibalba had to be aware of their presence. They would have met with resistance at the portal were they not meant to pass through it. Her heart rate picked up as she wondered to herself what that meant. Whatever was about to happen she understood that Kerick and Xavier felt it too. Both men seemed to tense up as they held tightly to their weapons.

The long earthen corridor grew darker and colder. Nellie shivered as she retrieved a torch from a nearby wall sconce. The frigid temperature made her nipples so hard they ached.

"There's a door," Kerick murmured to Xavier. "Do you see it?"

Xavier nodded as he prepared to open it. His jaw tensed as he studied the stone and wood mechanism. "Watch my back," he muttered.

Nellie's teeth sank into her lower lip as she waited with wide eyes to see what would happen next. She blew out a breath of relief when, a moment later, the door was forced open and nothing untoward occurred.

"Go through it," Kerick ordered.

Xavier nodded. Within seconds he indicated that the coast was clear and again the trio found themselves walking down yet another drafty, dark, earthen corridor. Nellie held the torch up high, her eyes rounding a bit when she was able to make out a small amount of light just up ahead.

This is it, she told herself. *We are almost within the heart of the Xibalba...*

Chapter 40

AND THE GREAT DRAGON WAS CAST OUT, THAT OLD
SERPENT, CALLED THE DEVIL, AND SATAN, WHICH
DECEIVETH THE WHOLE WORLD: HE WAS CAST OUT INTO
THE EARTH, AND HIS ANGELS WERE CAST OUT WITH HIM.

* * * * *

She could take the suspense no longer. Since the moment she had
first heard of Nellie's disappearance, Nicoletta had spent more time
worrying than she cared to contemplate—all tortured thoughts, no
action, and she was sicker than she didn't know what of it.

For years, ever since beloved Sinead's death, Nicoletta had
assumed the role of Nellie's mother. *She* was the one who had held
Nellie tight during the countless eves of nightmares. *She* had pushed
Abdul into letting Nellie pursue a career in lieu of marriage when he
had wanted to do anything but. *She* had been responsible for Nellie
then, and *she* was still responsible for her now.

Quickly throwing on some of Abdul's clothes—a black silk tunic
and black silk pants—she tied the bottom of her husband's body décor
off at the waist so they wouldn't fall down around her ankles while
making good on her escape attempt. That accomplished, she wound her
long raven tresses into a bun and secured it at the nape of her neck. Her
heart was beating so rapidly she felt as though she might faint.

She just had to get to the Outside. *Had to.* She had overheard some
of the murmured above table talk before being sent to her room. She
understood the Hierarchy believed Nellie to still be within the Belizean
sector, though somewhere within the Underground catacombs.

Nicoletta would find her. Were it possible, if Nellie was indeed
still alive, she vowed to herself that she would find her. Nellie would
hide from her father, but she would willingly go to her stepmother.

She could not stomach the thought that the daughter of her heart,
Sinead's own flesh and blood, might be out there somewhere needing
her. Outlaws dwelled within the catacombs. Sub-humans and
predatorial insects swarmed around the encampments, unwittingly

sealing in the bandits from biosphere interference and sealing out the Hierarchy from the catacombs.

But Nicoletta had a plan. She blew out a breath as she stared at her reflection in the image map. For once her sharp mind might come in handy rather than getting her caged for leading her into trouble.

She closed her dark eyes briefly, the giddy thought of leaving her husband and his world behind tainted by the smallest amount of guilt and sorrow. Guilt because she realized in his own twisted way Abdul needed her. Sorrow because she would have wished things could have been different between them.

But that wasn't meant to be. There had always been a longing, a hunger, between Master Kan and her, but so too was there too much proverbial water under the bridge. He was responsible for Sinead's death—for her best friend's cold-blooded murder. How could she ever forgive him for that?

Nicoletta's nostrils flared. She couldn't. And because she couldn't, she realized their destinies would never merge as one.

Stop this! she told herself, her jaw clenching. *You have been caged more times than you can count, your best friend who was like a sister to you was murdered at his hands...there is no reason to feel guilt over running! Go to Nellie – find your daughter!*

Nicoletta's gaze slowly lifted to the trapdoor above the image map, the same trapdoor she had known about since visiting this sector seven years past. She had swore to herself that if ever Abdul should bring her back to Altun Ha, and they were to stay in the same suite they had taken up temporary residence in seven years ago, this time she would get up her courage and run.

And that, she reminded herself, forcing thoughts of Abdul at bay, was precisely what she was about to do. Only instead of running blindly, she now knew where it was she would be running to...

She swallowed roughly. The Outside.

* * * * *

"Drop your weapons and place your hands above your heads. Do it now or die!"

Nellie chewed on her bottom lip as she, Kerick, and Xavier were swarmed by armed Xibalbian women. One minute there had been nothing but dimly lit passageways hidden deep within the earth's belly. A moment later, the ground had opened up, swallowed them whole, and they had been spat out into this...incredibly unbelievable place.

This world, a world of female warrior scientists, was far more advanced in terms of technology than anything Nellie had ever bore witness to in the biospheres. The biospheres were composed of black diamonds imported from planet Kalast. She couldn't begin to imagine what the transparent, silvery walls surrounding her were composed of. They were entirely see-through, allowing one to observe what was housed within each of the chambers lining the walls.

From their current position Nellie could only see two chambers, both laboratories. One, a droid laboratory where very human-looking females were being grown as if from embryos. (That was enough to make her jaw drop a little. Droids were manufactured, not grown like humans.) Two, an experimental laboratory where sub-humans quite advanced with infection were caged.

An ice-cold chill coursed down Nellie's spine as she watched a female sub-human moan and groan while...giving birth. Her hand flew up to cover her mouth. Sweet Cyrus, she'd had no idea the species was capable of breeding! What could that mean to the two races of earth? As it was, sub-humans were biologically superior to normal humans in terms of physical strength. If they became overpopulated and somehow managed to break into the biospheres...

Extinction. The two races of Federated Earth, male and female, would be erased from existence as though they'd never been.

Nellie took a deep breath and blew it out. She wouldn't pretend that she understood why sub-humans had been brought into existence by the Hierarchy to begin with, but clearly their little scientific "experiment" had taken on a life of its own. One would have hoped the Hierarchy had learned what the dire consequences of interfering with the order of nature would be when the drought of female offspring had occurred. Apparently, sadly, they had not. Her gaze flicked toward the armed scientists.

Weapons Nellie couldn't name decorated their bodies. Most of the women possessed well-honed bodies that were tight with muscle and impeccably cut. They looked almost superior to biosphere females in terms of strength and agility...

Her eyes widened. She glanced first toward the droid laboratory, then back to the armed women.

Holy Cyrus. No—no that wasn't possible...was it? Nobody could manufacture human skin...could they?

"Drop your weapons," one of the warriors repeated. "Now."

Nellie watched Kerick's jaw clench. She could tell he was unhappy about the command, but he begrudgingly complied and slowly lowered his flash-sticks to the silver floor beneath them. Xavier followed suit, warily giving up his weapons and placing his hands above his head. Nellie had no weapons to speak of, so she placed her hands above her head and awaited further instruction.

The next events happened so quickly, it took her brain a long moment to register what had happened. Kerick and Xavier, fugitives on the run from Federated Earth, were chained and shackled again, this time by fugitive females. Nellie was left unchained, then forcibly separated from her party. She turned desperate eyes toward her husband, afraid to be gone from him. Would they kill him? she wondered, her heartbeat dramatically thumping in her chest. Sweet Kalast, she just didn't know!

Kerick's nostrils flared. "Give her back to me," he murmured. "She is my wife. She stays with me."

"That is not possible," a warrior spat back, her smile humorless. "We are under direct orders to—"

"I said give her back," Kerick growled. Every muscle in his body corded like an animal preparing to pounce. *"Now."*

"She'll be fine," a lilting female voice murmured. "As will you. Do as you're told and no harm will come to anyone."

Nellie watched her husband still. Slowly, ever so slowly, his steel-gray gaze lifted, turning to the short, dark-haired woman who had spoken. His eyes widened, which alarmed Nellie, for he wasn't the type to betray his emotions, not even a seemingly harmless emotion like surprise. Or shock.

"I don't believe it," Xavier muttered, snagging Nellie's attention. "I don't fucking believe it."

Nellie's stomach muscles clenched. Jealousy permeated her soul as she wondered to herself if this woman was a former lover of Kerick's. Would he want her back? she asked herself, the knot of worry in her belly growing. Would he—?

"Mother?" Kerick rasped out, replacing Nellie's jealousy with a shock to rival her husband's with one simple word. Nellie gasped, unable to believe it.

Kerick swallowed roughly, his Adam's apple bobbing once as he did so. His eyes were wide, his expression surreal. "Is that you?"

* * * * *

Abdul Kan impatiently strode toward the hovering land conveyance, every muscle in his body tense. A missing daughter had been enough of a mission to undertake. Now he also had to find his runaway wife. Preferably before a sub-human or outlaw did.

"Nica," he murmured, the heart he'd thought long dead painfully twisting.

Always he had loved her. Never had she loved him back.

It didn't matter, he told himself, his jaw tightening as he took his place within the black tank-like conveyance, a craft that could hover at fast speeds above the Outside terrain. Whether or not she loved him didn't matter. She still belonged to him, had always belonged to him.

He'd be damned if he didn't get her back.

Chapter 41
February 3, 2250 A.D.

Kerick's eyes narrowed at the guard as the sensory door whizzed shut behind him, concealing him within some manner of a cell. Unlike the rest of the Xibalba which was lit up and admittedly quite stunning to look upon, this prison he and Xavier had been thrown into was as primitive, rough, and dimly lit as the rest of the catacombs were.

"I was hopin'," a very familiar voice sighed, "that when you found us we'd be freed, not locked up in here with you."

Kerick frowned, his eyes finally adjusting to the dark. He turned on his heel and came face to face with his younger brother Kieran. He growled when he saw Elijah chained up against the far wall, all hopes of being rescued quickly vanquished. "Why are you chained up?" he barked out at Elijah.

Apparently his old friend was of no mind to talk. Kieran, however, was. A dimple dented his cheek. "He attacked a guard when they brought us food. Now our food is dropped in through that hole in the high ceiling."

Elijah muttered something imperceptible under his breath, an agitated hand swiping over his jaw as he did so. Kerick sighed as he walked towards him.

"Don't touch his chains," Kieran warned. "I already tried that. They will sizzle you on contact, slowly but surely." He held up a palm that had sustained a burn. "Apparently these ladies don't play."

Kerick's teeth ground together. "Apparently they do not," he seethed.

Kieran grinned. "They said they'd unchain him tomorrow..." His eyebrows shot up. "If he behaves himself like a good little boy." His smile widened. "They used them exact words, too."

A tick started to work in Elijah's jaw. Kerick couldn't blame him for being angry. He could think of no greater humiliation than being bested by females. Of course, he conceded, these were not the types of females bred within the earth or biospheres. These wenches were like a million Tara Rileys armed to the nines. A comforting presence when on your side. A teeth gritting annoyance when not.

"I take it you've already tried to scale the walls in here?" Xavier muttered.

"Scale? What the kong's to scale?" Kieran's smile evaporated. "Do you see any foot notches within the walls? Smooth as a babe's bottom these walls are." His nostrils flared as he glanced away. "Somewhere out there is my wife. Had I found a way to escape I would have stolen her back and been gone days ago. I ain't hanging around here for fun."

Kerick ignored his brother for the moment and studied Elijah. He realized just by looking at him that his old friend was aware Tara Riley was alive. She might have been the one who put him down here, same as she'd put Xavier and himself here. A fact that would only add to Elijah's anger just as it did Kerick's.

Xavier frowned as he slid to the ground, his back against the earthen wall. "They could at least send a few droids in here," he said under his breath. *Or preferably that virtual program to bring Clara back.* "It would help kill the time if we had some pussy."

Kerick rolled his eyes before turning his attention back to Elijah. "Surely there must be a way out of here," he muttered. "We learned from Kong there is no such thing as an inescapable fortress."

At last Elijah was of a mind to speak, albeit grumpily. "I've tested the walls for weaknesses. There are none." His jaw tightened. "The only chance at escape we stand is through that hole in the ceiling. How we get up to it is beyond me but I'm determined to get up there," he seethed.

Xavier grinned. "Any particular arse you're wanting to spank, amigo?"

"One guess," Elijah gritted out.

Kerick's gaze lifted to the hole in the ceiling. It was at least thirty feet in the air and surrounded on all sides by smooth earthen walls. Impossible? Perhaps.

His steel-gray eyes narrowed. But where there was a will, there was also a way.

* * * * *

Escaping Altun Ha hadn't been nearly as difficult as Nicoletta had expected it would be. She had met with absolutely no resistance as she'd made her way through the air ducts and found herself, as luck would have it, directly on the Outside. The jump from the end of the air duct to the jungle ground floor had been three feet at best. Poor engineering work on the part of biosphere scientists perhaps, but a gift horse she nevertheless chose not to look too closely in the mouth.

She shivered as she glanced around the dark, noisy jungle, momentary fright swamping her senses. Somewhere out here Nellie awaited her. Her daughter — *Sinead's* daughter — had always depended upon her, their bond unbreakable...

Her nostrils flared. It would take more than predatorial insects and sub-humans to keep Nicoletta from aiding the only person in this world Cyrus had given her to love and be loved by. She would find Nellie Kan, she vowed.

A mother could do no less.

* * * * *

Sequestered within the experimental laboratory, Nellie's wide-eyed gaze continually flicked toward the hungry-looking sub-human partitioned off from her and Dr. Riley by an invisible barrier. She had no idea what the wall was made of, for she'd never seen an invisible one, but her thoughts were too overwhelmed to even consider asking. In the grand scheme of things, the barrier was unimportant. The only thing that currently mattered, she decided, was that it worked.

Her heartbeat quickened as a female sub-human growled low in her throat, trying once again to knock the wall down with her brute strength. Eying Nellie up and down, her red-pupil eyes were dilated and her fangs dripped with saliva in anticipation of a meal. Squatting down upon her powerful thighs, she lunged into the air and toward the wall, howling as she again attempted to shoot through the barricade.

She failed. Nellie shivered.

"They are not demons, lass," Tara murmured, her eyes unblinking as she watched the sub-human female stare at Nellie, its head cocking. "They are animals, some of them were once humans like you and me." She turned her head to regard her daughter-in-law. "Try to remember that. It's easier to command your fright and keep your wits intact when confronted by one if you can remember that."

Nellie slowly nodded. She nevertheless felt chilled to the bone but she conceded the point. "For how long have you known they could breed?" she whispered.

"Two, maybe three years." Tara sighed. "When you are virtually alone, removed from everyone that ever mattered to your life, time begins to run together after awhile." Her voice lowered to a hush. "Pretty soon there is little difference between one year and ten years."

Silence.

"Why am I here?" Nellie softly asked. "I recognize you, you know. I've never forgotten the face of the woman who gave me the journal all those years back. It was you. I know that now."

"Yes," Dr. Riley said on a sigh. "Yes, it was."

"But why?" Nellie shook her head before bodily turning in her direction. "Make me understand. What could you possibly have to gain by involving me of all people? If you thought I'd know something you didn't because I was sired of Abdul Kan, you were gravely mistaken. My father keeps his own council, always has."

Tara's gaze absently trailed over Nellie's naked breasts before flicking up to meet her face. "At first I didn't know why I came to you. A hunch, I guess you could call it."

Nellie shook her head, not understanding.

"The disease — the infection — is torture. Painful, unadulterated torture. But it does give a human who has not yet totally succumbed to the full force of it one distinct advantage."

Her eyebrows slowly drew together as she regarded the elder scientist. She stilled as it occurred to her that Tara Riley was, at long last, about to tell her everything. After years of research and questioning Cyrus and whatever other gods lived out beyond this realm, in mere moments she would have her answer as to why — why this terrible thing had come to pass. Why so much suffering.

Why her mother had died.

Nellie's heart was thumping so heavily against her breasts she felt momentarily dizzy. "And that advantage would be…?"

"A heightened sense of awareness. Heightened instincts, superhuman strength — an elevated…*everything*."

Nellie's green eyes rounded in dawning, horrific comprehension. "That's what this is all about, isn't it?" she whispered. The hairs at the nape of her neck were standing on end. "So much death, so much heartbreak, and now the threat of our very extinction…"

"…And all because some fools in the Hierarchy, not satisfied with ruling the whole of the earth, wanted to make sure their power never came to an end." Tara's intense gaze clashed with her daughter-in-law's. "They wanted to become superhumans, Nellie, so they began experimenting on prisoners, a population few in society care little-to-nothing about."

Nellie's hand involuntarily flew up to cover her own mouth. Her father was responsible for the infection of all those prisoners — she was certain of it. No other man within the Hierarchy would have had access to so many voiceless men.

"Only thing is, the experiment broke out of control, and what they ended up with instead was a race of sub-humans—creatures that are more animal than man, creatures more powerful than they could ever hope to be." Her smile was humorless. "Creatures that will wipe them from existence as though they never were. But they are too arrogant and ignorant to realize it."

So many questions sprang to mind, so many horrible questions that needed answers, but all she could do was stand there in the experimental silver-walled laboratory and stare in awe at Tara Riley. Tara Riley who had fought against all odds to not succumb to the infection—the same Tara Riley who had, at least for now, won.

Suddenly she understood just why the elder scientist had faked her own death. Had the Hierarchy known she had managed to live and fight against the perverse disease, she would have become a caged lab rat—tortured through experimentation, then put to death to silence her forever when they had their answers.

The silence seemed interminable, both women lost in their thoughts. But finally, inevitably, Nellie turned to her and quietly asked, "Why me, Tara? Why did you choose *me*?"

Dr. Riley stilled. Her head slowly turned to regard Nellie. "Because," she said, her lilt a whisper, "Because you are the key…"

Ten minutes later, Nellie's jaw felt all but unhinged as she listened to Tara Riley's extremely unbelievable speech. She shook her head a bit as if to clear it. "You want me to…*what*?" she shrieked.

Tara sighed. "I know it sounds unbelievable, but I'm certain to Cyrus it's true. There are very few things in life I am willing to bet my life on, but this happens to be one of them."

Nellie frowned. It wasn't *her* life the scientist wished to gamble with—it was Nellie's. "Dr. Riley," she responded. "There is little I wouldn't do to end this nightmare once and for all, but what you are asking of me is…"

"Frightening?" Tara offered.

She took a deep breath and blew it out. "Yes," Nellie murmured. Her thoughts flicked to Kerick, and of how potentially devastated he would be should she die. They might have only been together a short period of time, but the intensity of the moments they'd spent together more than made up for any shortcomings in time span.

"I understand," Tara assured her as they stood together and stared at the nest of sub-humans separated from them by the invisible partition. "If I am right, we will win, and together we can bring about an end to the madness. But if I am wrong…"

"I will die," Nellie whispered. She swallowed heavily, blinking for the first time in long moments. She took a deep breath and blew it out. "Please give me a day to think it over."

Tara's smile was small but sincere. "Of course," she murmured.

Chapter 42

AND I STOOD UPON THE SAND OF THE SEA, AND SAW A BEAST RISE UP OUT OF THE SEA...AND THEY WORSHIPPED THE BEAST, SAYING, WHO IS LIKE UNTO THE BEAST? WHO IS ABLE TO MAKE WAR WITH HIM?

AND HE CAUSETH ALL, BOTH SMALL AND GREAT, RICH AND POOR, FREE AND BOND, TO RECEIVE A MARK IN THEIR RIGHT HAND, OR IN THEIR FOREHEADS: AND THAT NO MAN MIGHT BUY OR SELL, SAVE HE THAT HAD THE MARK...

HERE IS WISDOM. LET HIM THAT HATH UNDERSTANDING COUNT THE NUMBER OF THE BEAST FOR IT IS THE NUMBER OF A MAN; AND HIS NUMBER IS SIX HUNDRED, THREESCORE, AND SIX.

* * * * *

She had nothing to go on but guts and instinct, no clue as to where her search should begin or where it would take her to in the end. Perhaps she would win. Perhaps she would die. So long as Nellie lived, it no longer mattered…

Nicoletta Kan had no real worth and no value, she decided. Her death would mean little to a husband with so many wives; it would signify absolutely nothing to a society that regarded her as nothing more than mere sexual chattel. She hadn't so much as seen the one and only son she'd given to Abdul in years—Asad had been taken away to attend a real school instead of a virtual one ages ago. And her son, Asad, named for the strength of the Arabic lion, had always identified more with his father than with his mother anyway.

But Nellie? Nicoletta smiled. Nellie had always valued her, had always loved her. It was difficult for a man to understand how a woman could invest so much pure and loyal emotion into one person, but when that one person is all you have to call your own in this realm, the only person left to you who truly loves and values you as a being equal to them, well…it sure as Kalast made sense to Nicoletta that she would even go so far as to die that that one person might live.

"I will find you, bella," she whispered to the jungle trees looming above where she laid in hiding on the ground. She closed her eyes and snuggled as best she could inside a rotted, hollowed-out log, praying to the ancient saints a sub-human wouldn't pick up her scent while she rested. "I don't give a yen how many infected humans stand between you and me," she said tiredly, resignedly. "I will find you."

* * * * *

To say that she felt conflicted would be the understatement of the millennium. If she chose not to carry out Tara's plan through to its fruition, she would be alive to see another day — yet at what cost? Forever, as long as she lived, the words *what if* would be etched into her brain like a mental tattoo. If she did, however, see Tara's plan through to its culmination…

Nellie sighed. She might live. *Or* she might die a very painful, hideously frightening death. The odds, regardless to what Dr. Riley might believe, were about 50/50, if that high. She would be playing a game of chance at which nobody could guess the outcome. The winner-takes-all and the loser-loses-everything. Kerick would be devastated were she to die, yet how could she live with herself if she walked away from the Xibalba a coward?

"Impossible decisions," she muttered to herself as she stared unblinking at the sleeping sub-human female who had given up wanting to make a meal of her long enough to get some rest. Tara Riley had left her alone with her thoughts in the experimental laboratory some time past. Now it was only Nellie, a bunch of sophisticated computers and machinery, an invisible wall partition, and a sleeping nest of infected unfortunates occupying the chamber.

Nellie was so lost in her thoughts she didn't notice when the vacuum-sealed door whisked open. It wasn't until Kora Williams Riley took the vacant seat next to her that she became aware of the fact she was no longer alone on this side of the partition. Both women sat in contemplative silence. It was a long while before either of them spoke.

"How are you?" Kora finally asked, her voice a hush.

Nellie smiled without emotion, without blinking. "I've been better."

She sighed. "I'll just bet. Sweet Kalast, I'm sorry you've been put in so ugly a position."

Nellie's smile this time was genuine as her gaze flicked over to the other scientist's. "Me too."

Kora chuckled, but said nothing else. Both women reverted to the silence that had previously engulfed the chamber.

"You want me to do it, don't you?" Nellie at last whispered.

"Yes," Kora said truthfully, matter-of-factly. She tucked a stray blonde curl behind her ear. "But my reasons are far from altruistic as I think you've already surmised. Therefore, I cannot in good conscience ask you to do it."

"Tara Riley's reasons aren't precisely altruistic either," Nellie pointed out. "That didn't stop her from asking me."

Kora grinned. "It wouldn't. She's a battleaxe through and through."

Nellie smiled, conceding the point.

More silence, though a peaceful one. And then, "Have you made a decision?" Kora quietly asked.

"I have." Nellie inclined her head, her gaze back on the nest of sleeping sub-humans. "I know I can't live with myself if I don't give Tara's plan a try."

Kora closed her eyes briefly as she took a deep breath, the gesture underscoring her relief. "Thank you," she said simply.

"You're welcome." Nellie sighed as she ran a tired hand through her dark red mane of hair. "I will proceed with the plan on the morrow...after my last request has been granted."

"What request is that?"

"Kerick," she whispered. Her smile was nostalgic and a bit sad. "I have to see him one last time."

* * * * *

Nicoletta's forehead wrinkled as she slowly came-to, the unmistakable feeling of arousal knotting in her belly. She had fled from Altun Ha wearing her husband's body décor—the clothes were ill-fitted and ill-suited perhaps, but she'd definitely had them on.

Yet now she felt...naked. Undeniably, achingly naked.

She moaned a little as the cool nighttime jungle breeze hit her exposed nipples, making them plump up on her large breasts. She could feel the air coming into contact with her exposed pussy too, making her wet. "Oh," she whispered, her eyelashes batting open to reveal dark, passion-drunk eyes. "Mmmm…"

She stilled when she saw it. Ice-cold terror lanced through her. She could barely believe it, felt as though she might pass out from shock if she wasn't exterminated first. But there *it* was—

A male…

A sub-human.

Her breathing grew labored, inducing her breasts to heave up and down. She could see the outline of his chiseled, dangerously masculine face from between her two large breasts. His mouth was filled with sharp, dagger-like teeth and was scarce inches from her stiff, aching nipples. His blood-red gaze was heavy-lidded and more aroused than she'd ever seen.

Run! she told herself. *Get up and run!* But the effort was fruitless and she knew it. The male was on top of her—it wanted to mount her…*mount her!* Escape, at least for now, was impossible. *Sweet Cyrus…*

"Please," she panted out, her heart slamming against her chest. "Please do not kill me. I—"

Whatever Nicoletta had been about to say was waylaid as she watched the creature's tongue flick out and curl around one of her jutting nipples. She hissed in the back of her throat, the feeling as frightening as it was pleasurable to nipples so stiff as hers were. "Do not," she gasped, "touch me."

He paid her words no mind at all. She wondered if he even understood them.

The creature's tongue tugged at her nipple and pulled it into the warmth of his mouth. He suckled it vigorously, making her moan before she'd thought better of it. Unthinkingly, she arched her hips— then wished she hadn't. Her eyes widened in horror as she remembered the sub-human male had the look of a creature wanting to impregnate its mate…

Ah gods.

His large hands palmed her breasts as he lifted his head and stared down into her face. Sheer, unadulterated panic engulfed her. He possessed the look of a man and yet he didn't. He was stronger looking than a human male and a thousand times deadlier. His face was slightly contorted, more powerful and chiseled than what it would have been in his former life. His hair was dark, the irises of his eyes an intense, haunting blood red. His serrated teeth were like something out of a virtual horror movie.

Help me! she mentally wailed. *For the love of the ancient saints, Abdul, save me!*

The beast played with her nipples as he watched her, his long, black, vampire-like fingernails scraping against her breasts in a way that forced shimmers of arousal to course down her spine. Why her? she asked herself, sheer terror at war with arousal. Why hadn't it killed her? Why did it wish to mount her? Why—

Nicoletta gasped as his large, thick cock sank into her cunt. His eyes slightly rolled back into his head, a territorial growl rumbling up from his throat. Her heart slammed against her chest, her breathing heavy and shallow. She was in such shock, all she could do was lie there with wide eyes and drag in quick, tiny lungfuls of air.

He began to rock in and out of her, slowly at first, then with more brute force. A warning growl reverberated in the whorl of her ear, letting her know if she tried to deny him what he wanted she was as good as dead.

"Please," Nicoletta gasped, hysteria pounding through her. "Let me go—"

His roar of denial was as deafening as it was frightening. Her heart raced impossibly higher as he sank his thick cock in her pussy to the hilt and fucked her like the animal he was. He took her faster and harder, branding her as his possession with every stroke.

No, she thought, terror overwhelming her. It would kill her when it finished with her. *Sweet Cyrus, Abdul, where are you when I need you?*

Just when Nicoletta was certain she would pass out from the fright of it all, her gaze unthinkingly found the creature's. Staring into his crimson gaze, unable for some bizarre reason to look away, she felt her heart rate begin to come down, felt a curious sense of calm stole over her.

She was being mesmerized, hypnotized. *Ah gods...*

A territorial roar echoed throughout the harsh jungle landscape. Within seconds, both of her large breasts had been palmed and the sub-human male was again fucking her. His fingernails scraped against her breasts, causing her to groan with arousal against her volition. His cock impaled her, sinking in and out of her pussy, over and over, again and again.

Lying on her back, her legs spread open while it fucked her, her tits jiggling with every thrust in the hands that palmed them, she felt like a sexual sacrifice being offered up to an all-powerful beast-god. She could hear their flesh meeting, could hear her pussy sucking his cock back in with every outstroke.

"Why me?" she breathed out. "Why did you not kill me?"

It didn't answer. She hadn't figured it would.

The beast slammed into her cunt, his growl once again piercing the quiet nighttime jungle. He scraped her breasts hard with his vampire-like fingernails, causing Nicoletta to instantaneously gasp and come. Her body shuddered, not understanding what had caused such a reaction on her part, as she felt the creature's entire musculature tense above her.

It was coming. Holy Kalast, it was coming.

For the love of the ancient saints, Abdul, do not let this thing impregnate me! she mentally wailed. *Ah Cyrus, please...noooooo!*

The sub-human male rode her hard, fucking her mercilessly. His growl increased in intensity as he squeezed her breasts and impaled her cunt once, twice, three times more. With a roar that should have deafened her, the beast sank his cock into her sticky pussy a final time, his entire body convulsing as he emptied himself of seed inside her.

Nicoletta lay there, unable to move, unable to blink. She felt as in shock as she was mesmerized. She could be pregnant, she thought, swallowing roughly. Even now a tiny demon could be implanted in her womb.

No! *Nooooooo!*

Chapter 43
February 4, 2250 A.D.

Kerick awoke feeling very groggy and disoriented, wearing the same black leather pants, black tunic, and black boots he'd fallen to sleep in. He moaned a little in the back of his throat as he slowly came to. Realizing that he had been secured in the sitting position to an animal hide chair, his arms chained behind him, his feet manacled to the floor, he frowned, wondering how he'd gotten here.

He blinked. Little by little memories of what had transpired last eve streamed to the forefront of his consciousness. He vaguely recalled he and his men trying to find an escape route. After that, all he could remember was the chamber being showered with a gas that made them all lose consciousness outside of thirty seconds. His last memory was coughing and gagging as he fell to the earthen ground.

Kerick's jaw clenched hotly, anger radiating through him in waves. That his own Cyrus-forsaken mother could allow him to be treated thusly well and truly rankled. He had no idea what would possess her to enchain her own son and ally, but he wanted some answers and he wanted them now.

Somehow, though he knew not how, he understood that Tara Riley wanted his wife as more than a mere daughter-in-law. His mother needed Nellie to accomplish...*something*. The thought that his wife might be in harm's way because of that something caused Kerick to feel desperation the likes of which he'd never before entertained.

A cold, ominous feeling settled in his gut and knotted as he considered the fact that his mother was most likely keeping him chained up so he could not and would not interfere with whatever plans she had concocted for Nellie. In fact, the more he thought on it, the more certain he became. He only wished he knew what those plans were so he could formulate a plan of action. Obviously it someway involved sub-humans and the serum but *how* was the big question.

A door whisked open from behind him, snaring Kerick's undivided attention. He cocked his head and stared over his shoulder to see who the footfalls he heard belonged to. His eyes widened when he saw his wife enter the chamber, the vacuum-sealed airlock shutting behind her.

Kerick was so relieved and elated to see that Nellie was here and okay that he almost—almost—smiled. His good mood was short-lived, however, when it occurred to him that his wife had been clothed, her nipple rings and chain hidden from the world.

His brand on her buttocks hidden from the world.

His nostrils flared. To all who didn't know better, it would appear that Nellie Kan Riley was still claimable. The skin-tight body suit she wore was a camouflaged jungle green and covered her skin from neck to ankle. Every muscle in his body clenched in reaction, the anger and desperateness he felt increasing a thousand fold.

"Nice body décor," Kerick said softly, meaningfully, his eyes narrowing at his wife's approaching form.

Nellie sighed as she came to stand before him. She nervously patted the dark red bun at the nape of her neck into place, skittishly avoiding his gaze all the while. "Kerick," she whispered, "we need to talk..."

His heart began lashing against his chest. Was she here to break things off with him, to tell him she would belong to no man? His stomach tightened at the mere thought. He would never let her go— never. His kong-forsaken mother would have to kill him before he'd give his wife up.

"Yes?" Kerick murmured. "What do you wish to talk about?" His voice turned icy. "I assume whatever you have to say will explain the unwanted body décor?" he barked.

Nellie nodded, confirming his suspicion. Sweet Cyrus, she couldn't be thinking to leave him, he thought, his heart wrenching. He had claimed her, branded her...loved her. Had he been the only one who had felt a special bond growing between them? *No.*

"My last request was that I be permitted to see You," Nellie said quietly, still looking to the ground. Finally her head came up. She met his gaze and peered into his eyes. "I want You to promise me that no matter what happens, You'll be okay—with or without me."

He stilled. Kerick had thought Nellie came into the chamber to inform him of her designs to leave him. Clearly that had not been her intent, a fact that would have made him sigh in relief had his anger and hurt not been abruptly replaced with confusion and dread. Her words had sent a chill down his spine the likes of which nothing else could compete. It was as though she was preparing to die.

"Nellie," Kerick said thickly, his voice kept low. "What are you trying to tell Me?"

Her eyes briefly closed as she concentrated on breathing. "There's a chance I can help end the nightmare," she whispered, her eyes opening as her hands fidgeted to and fro. "And it's a chance I have to take regardless of the potential outcome." She shook her head. "I owe it to my mother." She glanced away, her smile sad. "I owe it to everyone."

"No," Kerick barked, "you do not." He recognized what this was about, of course. He knew she felt guilt at the role her father played within the Hierarchy and of the fact so much death and disease could be placed at his doorstep. But Nellie Kan Riley was not her father. He wanted to strangle his mother for using his wife's misplaced sense of guilt to further her own purposes. "I have no idea what game My mother is playing with your mind, but I—"

"There is no game," Nellie cut in. She sighed. "Tara has spent the last fifteen years of Your imprisonment finding answers. She's certain she at last found the right ones. Hopefully all will be well and this won't lead to my death—"

"This?" Kerick gritted out. He wanted loose. Sweet Cyrus he needed to get loose and protect his wife. "What is *this* precisely?"

"I cannot say," Nellie whispered, glancing up. She threw a hand toward the floating robotic console hovering above them. The robot was a small, silver box-like device that transmitted audio and visual data back to the Command Centre. If she began saying too much, they'd both be immediately gassed or disabled in some manner. "It was the only way I could gain permission to visit You down here. Even now they listen to my every word."

"Nellie—"

"Goodbye, Kerick." She held up a palm to silence him. "I needed to see You," she said softly. "I needed You to know how much I love You before I go."

Something wrenched in the vicinity of his heart. He opened his mouth to command her to obey him and not go wherever it was Tara Riley thought to take her, but before he could get out a single word Nellie threaded her fingers through his dark hair and covered his mouth with her own.

She kissed him long and passionately, her tongue thrusting between his lips and seeking his. He kissed her back with a desperation that bordered on violent, the thought of losing her enough to drive him over the edge. If the mere thought did as much to him, he could only wonder at what would become of him were he to lose Nellie in truth.

By the time she broke away and ended the kiss, both of their breathing had grown labored. Their gazes met and held for an indeterminate amount of time.

"I have to go," Nellie at last whispered. Her eyes gentled as she smiled. "Just know that I love You."

"Nellie," Kerick said anxiously, watching her take long strides away from him. His nostrils flared. "Nellie, come back here! *I order you to come back to Me!*"

The vacuum-sealed door whisked open as he continued to bellow her name. She walked quickly through the portico then turned around to stare at him as the door whizzed shut. Just before it closed he saw a single tear track down her cheek, the sight of which was his undoing.

A guttural sound erupted from Kerick's throat as he thrashed against the chains and manacles that held him bound. He had to get loose—*had to*. He loved her and he refused to lose her.

Nellie. Sweet, selfless Nellie...

Kerick had no clue as to what plan his mother had concocted, but he vowed to himself he would find out.

Preferably before it was too late.

Chapter 44

Nellie quietly and stoically walked at the head of the single-file line of female warrior scientists as they made their way from the protection of the Xibalba and into the heart of the Belizean jungle. She might have appeared calm on the outside, but on the inside she felt like a ball of tightly frayed nerves. Outfitted in camouflaged body décor that plastered her curves like a second skin, she clutched her flash-stick tighter as the group continued its ascent from the cold belly of the earth to the warmer climate of the Outside tropics.

Kora had offered Nellie the use of a weapon she'd called a zapping rod, which worked similarly to a flash-stick in that it contained electrical current that sizzled one's opponent to nothingness outside of a mere second. The zapping rod was, perhaps, more advanced, less bulky, and more efficient a killer than the flash-stick, but because Nellie had never used one before she decided to arm herself with the weapon she did know — now, she decided, was hardly an ideal time to defend herself with a weapon foreign to her.

Dr. Riley knew from observation of sub-human packs that the species tended to hunt, breed, and congregate close to water supplies, so Nellie doubted much in the way of potentially deadly would happen for another few hours or so. And yet her heart continued to pound away in her chest as though death lay in waiting just past the next boulder. She took a deep breath and slowly exhaled, realizing she had to calm down. It was smart to keep her senses on high alert, but too much adrenaline could work against her.

"We'll take a right at that fork," Tara informed the group as she marched up to Nellie's side. She held up a torch, pointing out where the path within the earth would branch off into two disparate routes. "Another five minutes and we'll be on the Outside. Doctors!" she said in that efficient, to-the-point lilt of hers, "ready your weapons for detonation." She frowned. "And for the love of Kalast, do not accidentally detonate them. One woman's accident is another woman's death."

Nellie glanced over to the elder scientist. Her mother-in-law wore the same skin-tight body décor as did she, the green and brown thing a perfect affectation of the jungle environment. Her long raven hair was held secured into a bun at the nape of her neck, the silver streak that ran through one side somehow making her appear wiser, deadlier, and, strangely, more attractive as well. A streak of silver would have made any other woman look old. It made Tara Riley look like what she was: a determined rebel, a fighter who had earned her stripe.

"We're almost there," Kora announced. She was silent for a moment and then, "I can smell them," she murmured.

Nellie's breathing momentarily stilled. "What do you mean?" she whispered. "What can you smell?" She turned her head long enough to meet the gaze of her sister-in-law who walked just behind her.

"Them," Kora reiterated on a sigh. "My kind."

Swallowing roughly, Nellie decided not to question her further. She could pretty much surmise which *them* was being referred to. When she saw the unmistakable color of crimson-red briefly flicker through Kora's eyes, she *knew* which them was being referred to.

"We've reached the fork," Tara threw out to the group. "Dr. Reddy, continue to probe for animal activity with your reading devices just in case my senses don't pick it up."

"Will do."

Nellie's heart began slamming in her chest once more as the group of rebel scientists rounded the fork and continued their upward ascent. It would be but mere moments now before they were spit out into the heart of the deadly jungle. And then, very soon, she would come face to face with destiny. But what, Nellie nervously asked herself again, was her destiny?

Death or victory. It was anyone's guess.

* * * * *

"We are wasting our time," Xavier announced with a frown. His breathing heavy from trying—and failing—to scale the wall again, he swiped at the perspiration soaking his forehead with the back of his arm. "For two hours we have been trying to reach that hole up there and I'm tellin' you we won't be reaching it, amigos. Not today, not tomorrow, not ever. It's time to think up an alternative or we'll be in this pit forever."

Kerick matched his frown with one of his own. "I have been trying to think up alternatives ever since we were thrown into this damn hole. I don't give a yen how we get out," he growled. "I just want out—*now*."

"We still ain't figured out how to get those chains off Elijah," Kieran pointed out. "I don't know where any of us thinks we're going until we get them off him anyway. I mean, we can't hardly leave him here wearing chains that can eat through his flesh. What if he falls asleep wrong and his head touches one of those wrist chains?" His eyebrows shot up. "Can we say 'lobotomy'?"

"Thank you," Elijah sniffed. "I'm glad somebody around here cares," he grumbled.

"I hadn't planned to leave you here in chains," Kerick snapped. "Let me handle one worry at a time. I think that—" His words came to an abrupt halt as the tentative beginnings of an idea struck him. His eyes narrowed thoughtfully. "The chains eat through flesh, you say?" he murmured.

Elijah frowned as he rattled his chains, underscoring the obvious answer that he had no answer. His hands were secured, untouching, at either side of his head. His feet were manacled, untouching, to bolts coming up out of the ground. "The only proof I have they can eat through flesh is the burn on your brother's hand." His eyebrows slowly drew together. "Just what are you thinking, amigo?"

"If they can eat through flesh," Kerick pondered aloud, his mind racing, "then perhaps they can eat through each other."

A hopeful look crossed Xavier's face. "Fuck me! They might even be able to eat through the door."

"It's possible."

"Wait a minute! Wait a minute!" Kieran said, running a hand through his hair. "I hate to be the voice of gloom and doom here but how are we gonna get them to touch? They ain't crossed, obviously for that reason!"

"We make 'em cross!" Xavier shouted back. "I want the fuck out of here!"

"We can't just make 'em cross!" Kieran bellowed. "There ain't no fuckin'—"

"Break my arm," Elijah murmured.

Silence fell over the underground pit as all eyes flew to the man in chains. Kerick slowly shook his head. "Give me a moment to think up something else. I—"

"There is nothing else," Elijah interrupted. His nostrils flared as his gaze snared Kerick's. "Break it, old friend."

"Ah Cyrus, I'm gonna puke," Kieran muttered.

Kerick ignored his brother. His gaze never strayed from Elijah's. "You sure?" he murmured.

"Yes."

Kieran threw up his hands. "I ain't watchin'. I'm here to tell ya, I ain't watchin'!"

"Oh, yes you are," Xavier informed him. "You're going to hold him steady on one side and me on the other so Kerick can make the break as clean and quick as possible."

"You know," Kieran said, wagging a finger at nobody in particular. "Ever since the three of you broke out of Kong, my life's been one 'adventure' after the next. I ain't helpin' to break nobody's arm and that is that." He folded his arms across his chest. "I've got limits," he sniffed.

"You're gonna have my foot up your arse in half a minute," Xavier said, exasperated.

"It'll match the one I put up yours!"

"Ah Cyrus, what a comeback! You talk like the infant you are!"

"Sticks and stones may break my bones but names—"

"Enough," Kerick growled. Irritated, he turned to his brother. "Do you wish to see your wife again?" he asked, coming straight to the point.

Kieran's nostrils flared but he said nothing.

"Well?" Kerick bellowed. "Do you?" His eyes narrowed. "It won't be the first arm you ever broke in your life."

Silence.

"Which side should I hold?" Kieran quietly asked.

Kerick grunted, appeased. A small smile hitched on Elijah's lips. "The right. I want my left arm broke."

Kieran sighed, resigned. "Done."

* * * * *

They'd been walking for four hours, but it felt more like four days. The jungle was humid today, inducing rivulets of perspiration to gather between Nellie's breasts and at her underarms. Worse, the ground was soggy from a recent heavy rain, causing the trek to take double the amount of time it normally would have.

Still, she knew she could manage this. She'd survived the jungles once before with her droid and she could do it again without her droid. It was time to quit reacting to things like a simpering miss, she reminded herself with a frown.

And then it happened. The rains. It fell like buckets from the sky, soaking their entire party within twenty seconds. She sighed, wondering how many more obstacles would beset the group before all was said and done.

"Damn it!" Tara swore, taking the words straight out of Nellie's thoughts. "We will never be able to safely traverse the cavern with muddy slush for a ground!"

Nellie came to a stop next to Drs. Riley and Reddy. "Which cavern are we heading for anyway? I saw tons of them when Cyrus 12 and I ran from Altun Ha."

Her thoughts briefly drifted back to her beloved droid. Cyrus 12 had practically been demolished within that cavern in the Crossroads when the rocks came raining down. Practically, but as luck would have it, not totally. It would take a few more weeks to get her back into working order, but Dr. Reddy had assured her the droid would function normally again.

But Nellie couldn't think on that right now. Cyrus only knew if *she* would be functioning normally in a few weeks. She might not be functioning at all.

"It lays approximately one mile outside the closest entry point to the Altun Ha biosphere," Tara muttered as she gauged readings from some manner of computer Nellie had never seen before. Clearly, the Xibalba scientists were much more radically advanced in terms of technology than their male counterparts within the Hierarchy-controlled biospheres. "I would have preferred taking a hover-craft, but much of the terrain is too shifty and narrow to handle it."

"We lost a pilot a few months back," Patricia Reddy explained under her breath. "We know for a fact if our trained pilot couldn't steer through it, none of us could."

Nellie nodded. "Perhaps we should make camp until the rains cease," she offered. Cyrus's truth, she would have preferred to carry on. She just wanted destiny, whatever form it might rear its omnipotent head in, to be over and done with. "We won't make much time under these conditions anyway."

Tara was quiet as her steel-gray gaze tracked the jungle landscape. She reminded Nellie of a bird of prey intent on capturing its quarry.

"I'm one with Nellie on this," Kora chimed in as she came to stand next to her. "We are accomplishing nothing and darkness will descend soon. The wet conditions do nothing to aid us and much to hinder us. Its safest for us all if we take shelter."

"Agreed," Dr. Reddy concurred, inclining her head. "The insects will be buzzing soon. And then Cyrus only knows what after that. I for one could use the rest."

Dr. Riley's nostrils flared. She wanted to continue on as badly as Nellie did. But, like Nellie, she realized the truth behind Kora and

Patricia's words. "We'll make camp until dawn," she announced. "Get your rest. You'll need it."

Chapter 45
February 5, 2250 A.D.

For two days and nights it kept her a sexual prisoner. Every hour of every day, the sub-human male mounted her, its appetite unquenchable. After their first mating, it had picked her up and dragged her kicking and screaming into a well-concealed cavern—its lair.

From there, the beast's appetite had only increased. Every hole Nicoletta possessed felt sore and well-used. It had taken her everywhere—multiple times. In her pussy, in her mouth, in her arse...

But always it spilled its seed in her womb. It was as if the creature indeed had a mind to breed and it was hell-bent on impregnating *her*.

She was glad at least for the calmness. She had no idea why staring into the sub-human's eyes left her feeling at peace, but it did, so she gazed up at them often. It was either that or be consumed with a terror the likes of which little else could compete.

When she had fled from Altun Ha, Nicoletta had considered many grave possibilities. The bite of a carnivorous insect that would dine upon her after poisoning her to death. Being made a meal of by a hungry sub-human. Even something so "simple" as starvation and dehydration. But this...

She shivered from where she lay stretched out on the cavern floor. Her breasts rose and fell with her labored breathing as she watched it come up on its knees and situate itself in front of her closed, drawn-together legs. The sub-human male growled low in his throat at the perceived insult, expecting perhaps for her to keep her thighs spread wide open at all times so it could use her when he saw fit to.

"Please," she whimpered as its hands found her knees. She gulped as she watched those long, dagger-like black fingernails skim like seductive butterfly wings across the skin there. "I truly can take no more," she panted. Her nostrils flared, anger rekindling. "By Cyrus, kill me and be done with it!" she spat.

It bared its serrated teeth, a hellish growl roaring up from the depths of its throat. Grabbing one of her knees with either hand, the beast wrenched her thighs open, her pussy once again exposed to him.

Nicoletta shivered at the possessive expression permeating the sub-human's face. She wondered with a pang of terror if it would ever let her leave its lair alive—

Alive and without child.

And then it was fucking her again, the sub-human's eyes shuttering with lust as its thick, hungry cock sank into her pussy. It pounded away inside of her, her tits jiggling with every thrust, beckoning attention to them. He lowered his head and sucked on her nipples as he rode her, her breasts palmed within his vampire's hands.

She closed her eyes and gasped as she came for the male against her volition. She had assumed only Abdul could make her come just by stimulating her breasts, yet this creature had done as much from their first mating.

Nicoletta groaned as she came again, the beast atop her slamming into her cunt like mad. *Ah gods*, she thought, hysteria again overwhelming her, *somebody help me!*

* * * * *

Nellie lay in the makeshift tent trying to get some sleep, her alert mind at war with her tired body. Her thoughts drifted first to her birth family. She warily wondered how her stepmother was faring at the hands of so vile a man as her sire. Abdul Kan was evil personified, a demon among men. She could only pray that one day—somehow— Nicoletta would escape him. Her stepmother deserved happiness and such would never be found within the Kan harem.

Abdul Kan—her *father*. Nellie sighed from where she lay, absently staring up at the roof of the animal-hide tent. For as long as she had breath to breathe, she would never understand why Cyrus had seen fit to sire her of that man. So much pain and death, so much grief and heartbreak—all of it could be laid at her father's doorstep. And yet...

Her nostrils flared. And yet her foolish female heart still loved him.

Nellie frowned as she admitted to herself that she had never *stopped* loving him. Even from a very young age, she had always— *always*—prayed to Cyrus he would change and become the father she wanted him to be.

Her prayers were never answered. She supposed it was little wonder.

Cyrus was revered as though it were a god when in reality it was but a concept, an invention of men and therefore as limited in its omnipotent abilities as the Hierarchy leaders who created it. In the old days, the people believed in an all-powerful God. In this age they believed in the concept of a male muse, in the spirit of invention, technology, and alleged progress. There was no higher purpose in the world men created, just drifting empty souls who do what they could until death claims them. Cyrus was as empty and devoid of meaning as the society that revered it.

And yet Nellie had continued to hope in a world with no hope. Eve after eve she had fallen to her knees and prayed like a faithful little girl to the only god she'd ever known. She had begged Cyrus to change her father's vile ways, to heal her infected mother, and repair their shattered family.

Always she had loved Abdul Kan. Never had Abdul Kan loved her.

But, Nellie thought, a small, contented smile forming on her lips, there was a man who did love her. He was gruff and he was grim and he wasn't given to smiling or laughing, but he did love her.

Kerick.

Ah, Kerick. I can only pray that if I die on the morrow You will carry on and find happiness. You deserve it. You have suffered enough in this realm, my love.

Nellie knew in her heart Tara's plan to separate them had been for the best. Her son never would have permitted his wife to do what needed to be done were he not chained up in a pit within the Xibalba, unable to intercede. Kerick would have insisted upon being the one who entered the devil's lair rather than Nellie. But according to Dr. Riley, only Nellie stood a chance of surviving it…

Nellie worried her bottom lip as she considered just how angry her husband probably was at this moment. He did not take well to orders, let alone being held hostage in an underground pit by female warriors.

She grinned just a bit at the visual image her mind conjured up, conceding she would probably not find the situation amusing if she were in the same chamber as him, feeling the force of his wrath. She winced, for once grateful Tara had separated them.

No, Kerick would definitely not be laughing. And Nellie definitely didn't want to know how angry he was at her for disobeying him and walking away.

He didn't understand. And, unfortunately, he wouldn't have the answers until it was all over.

* * * * *

"Talk," Kerick raged, his nostrils flaring as he pinned the female guard up against the nearest wall. His hand was clenched around her throat as if preparing to strangle her, though in truth he doubted he could kill her. But frighten her? Certainly.

"Never!" the guard spat, her nostrils flaring back.

"I said," he hissed, his hold on her neck tightening until her eyes widened with fear, "talk."

Their plan had worked. Elijah's chains had eaten through the doors and they were free. Armed to the teeth and free. That knowledge would have elated him were it not for the fact he had no clue as to where his mother and Nellie had gone off to. He didn't even know if his wife was still alive. The realization he might already be too late made his stomach muscles clench and twist. He felt sick inside. Worried, more frightened than he'd ever been before, and just plain sick.

"Never! I will not betray mine own race!"

Had he doubted he could kill her? His teeth gritted as he pondered the possibility. "That is my mother and my wife out there, wench. No harm will come to them at my hands." No permanent harm, he mentally qualified, getting angrier by the moment. "I do not make that claim where you are concerned. Talk or die. *Now*."

Her breathing was heavy as her gaze flicked back and forth from Kerick to his men and back to Kerick. "Your mother doesn't wish for your involvement."

He tightened his hold. She gasped.

"They've gone to a cavern deep in the jungle," she said quickly. "I don't know which one. Cyrus's truth!" she added when Kerick's eyes narrowed.

"Why? What do they seek there?" Elijah barked from where he stood a pace behind Kerick.

"The serum," the guard breathed out. "Dr. Riley believes the serum has existed from the very beginning, that it's been concealed all these years within a cavern so overrun with sub-humans not even the Hierarchy scouts dared venture back inside to obtain it."

Kerick stilled. He was feeling more ill at ease with each word the wench spoke. "What does my wife have to do with this?" he quietly asked.

She sighed as his hold on her throat weakened. "I do not know," she murmured. "Your mother holds her own council, revealing things only to those she feels must know. Certainly you are aware of that facet to her personality."

He said nothing. But then there was no need to. The guard was correct and they both knew it.

"They headed northeast, toward Altun Ha. This is all I know. I vow it."

Kerick nodded, itching to move at once on the little that they knew. "Tie her up," he muttered to Xavier as he briskly walked away. "I'll gather more weapons and join you in a minute."

* * * * *

Nicoletta's breathing hitched when she realized her captor had finally — *finally!* — fallen to sleep. Its breathing was relaxed and even, its eyes definitely closed.

Her gaze widened as she sat up and studied him, immediately noting that the sleep was quite deep. She wasn't surprised. She didn't know how any creature could have enough energy to copulate over and over, again and again. At long last its body wore out and slumber claimed it whether the male wanted that to happen or not.

Run! Now could be your only chance to escape. Get off your arse and run!

Taking a deep, calming breath, Nicoletta slowly drew herself up to shaky feet and inched her way toward the mouth of the cavern. She never once looked back at the predator for fear she would lose her nerve.

She had so many questions she realized would never be answered. Why had the creature stolen her? Why had it attempted to breed her? Surely it knew by her scent alone she was not of its species...

Upon reaching the mouth of the cavern, she ran as fast as her feet would carry her. Naked, her breasts bobbing up and down, her nipple chain jingling, Nicoletta thrust herself out into the encroaching night where the rains had recently began to cede and an all-encompassing mist shrouded the muddy ground. Her breathing was so shallow she felt near to fainting.

So many questions...

But the answers, she realized, would remain shrouded in a mystery that was as thick as the fog encapsulating the jungle. It was either that or return to the possessive man-beast with the haunting stare.

Chills raced down her spine. That she would never do.

Chapter 46

Nellie slept fretfully that eve, tossing and turning within the animal hide pelts that covered her. Her thoughts kept drifting to Kerick and to the pit within the deepest recesses of the Xibalba. She hoped her husband was doing well and not worrying too greatly over what was yet to come. Cyrus's truth, she was worrying enough for both of them.

She sighed, willing herself to fall asleep. Willing didn't work, so she then tried counting cyber-sheep. She tossed and turned. She meditated, breathing deeply and attempting self-hypnosis. Yet still deep sleep eluded her.

Nellie laid in the tent, her mind in chaos, for the better part of an hour. Finally, blessedly, her body gave out and her mind went along for the ride. Her eyelids fluttered closed and at long last the blackness overtook her.

* * * * *

Abdul Kan's eyes narrowed in thought as he came to a standstill in the thickest area of the jungle and considered which way his wife might have run. When she fled from Altun Ha she'd headed west. It would make sense then for Nicoletta to continue due west.

Unless, he thought with a frown, she had fled from the biosphere without a course in mind. Perhaps even she didn't know where she was going. Such would make anticipating her future movements all the more difficult.

But it could be done. Where there was a will there was also a way.

"Where have you gone, Nica?" he murmured, his acute gaze scanning the horizon. He stepped over what was left of the carcass of a dead animal, the beast having been made a meal of by a larger predator.

"I will find you," he vowed. His jaw tensed. "I will find you."

* * * * *

It was a small sound, barely audible to the human ear, and yet it was enough to semi-rouse Nellie from the world of dreams. What was that sound? she tiredly asked herself, her face scrunching up as her eyelashes batted open. An animal of sorts? A —

She stilled, her breathing hitching as she recalled her whereabouts. Recalled too that any manner of predator could be out lurking just beyond the tent, hunting for food. Thin animal-hide pelts hardly made for impenetrable protection.

That realization jarred her senses enough to make her feel less groggy and more alert. Coming up on all fours, she quietly scooted toward the end of the tent and peered through a hole near the flap.

Nothing.

Ever the cautious type, she looked left, then right, then back and forth again. Still, nothing.

She released a pent-up breath. "Silly wench," Nellie muttered as she scooted back into the makeshift bed and plopped down. She closed her eyes and sighed. "You really need a vacation."

"You really need your arse spanked," a masculine voice growled.

Nellie's eyes flew open. She jolted upright into a sitting position. *Kerick.* Ah Cyrus...

"Well," he drawled, sarcasm and ice tinting his voice. "Have you forgotten how to greet your Husband already, Nellie? Did not your droid schoolmarm teach you anything of use at Deportment school?"

Her nostrils flared. Given the enormity of what his presence here meant—arguing with him over what was to happen on the morrow, feeling the brunt of his anger for leaving the Xibalba without him—she supposed his comments shouldn't have signified, yet they did. If he poked fun at her education even one more time she was liable to slap him.

"Not all of us were bred with the manners of a pig let loose at a techno-opera," she sniffed. A ridiculous argument to be having when she was so elated to see her husband she could have cried, but insult was insult. Her teeth gritted. "I'll have You know I earned the highest marks all throughout my schooling!"

He grinned—actually grinned. Nellie swallowed against the lump of emotion in her throat. She was so taken by the masculine beauty of the gesture she forgot what it was she'd been angered about.

"I've missed You," she breathed out, her eyes searching his face.

He was silent as his gaze drank in her features, memorized them. And then, "I've missed you too," he rasped.

Kerick looked away, as though the weakness in his voice was an embarrassment to him. Nellie's heart thumped pleasurably in her chest.

"It's okay, You know," she whispered, coming up to her knees. "Loving me, I mean." Her smile was warm, her eyes gentle. "Because I love You, too."

He breathed in deeply and exhaled before craning his neck to gaze upon her. "Then don't do it," he said thickly. "We don't even know that this serum exists."

Her eyes briefly closed, flicking back open after she took a calming breath. "I have to try," Nellie said softly. "I could never forgive myself if I didn't. I could never forgive You either if You try to stop me. Please understand, Ker—"

"No," Kerick ground out, his jaw tensing, "I won't allow it."

"You have fought for this chance the whole of Your life! Tara weaned You for this moment. This is about more than You or me. It is about our entire world, the survival of our species."

His nostrils flared. "I don't give a yen if you *can* save the whole wretched world. If the price of salvation is your death than I rather our species stay damned."

Her expression grew intense as if willing him to side with her. "And what of our children? And our children's children?" She pressed on when he glanced away, knowing he was unable to say anything to counter that. They could run from fate, but they could never hide. Someway, someday, it would find them. "Please—*please*—understand. Stand by me in this. I will face the dawn unafraid if I know You are with me always."

"Nellie," he choked out, his sense of duty and honor at war with his heart. "I—"

"I know," she whispered. "I'm afraid too." Her smile was tender. "Never in my most secret dreams did I ever think to find a love like Yours. I want it to last for eternity and beyond." Her breathing hitched. "I love You."

Their gazes clashed and held. They studied each other for a long, tense moment.

"I will stand beside you," Kerick murmured.

Nellie breathed a sigh of relief. "Thank You," she whispered.

He said nothing to that, only stared at her. "Have you removed My chains?" Kerick asked thickly, his gray gaze roaming over the camouflage body décor she wore until arriving at her breasts.

Her cheeks tinted pink like a blushing virgin. "No."

"Show Me."

She stood up, unable to meet his gaze. Ridiculous given that they'd mated dozens of times before this night, but there it was.

Nellie unzipped the body décor slowly, her large breasts popping out as soon as she zipped past them. She could see his breathing grow heavier as he stared at her nipple rings and chain, the knowledge that he desired her increasing her own arousal.

His large, callused hands palmed her breasts, his thumbs running over her distended nipples. Her breathing hitched as her swollen nipples grew impossibly stiffer.

Kerick took her hand and firmly pressed it against his thick erection. "It's time to put your schooling to use," he murmured.

Nellie blew out a breath, having never been so aroused. She immediately complied, removing the rest of her bodysuit and discarding it on the floor of the tent. That accomplished, she went down to her knees and got on all fours. Pressing her face close to the ground, she lifted her buttocks, waiting as she'd been taught for the Master to take her.

Discarding his own body décor, Kerick stared at the brand on her right buttock, the proof of his ownership. As he undressed his gaze repeatedly flicked back and forth to her exposed, swollen pussy, to the submissive arch of her hips, but always his eyes came back to the brand.

She was his. She would always belong to him.

Nellie didn't know it yet, but on the morrow he would give up his life to protect her did it come to that. His life, he decided, mattered very little to this realm. But Nellie Kan Riley mattered a lot. Cyrus dwelled within her in the form of a scientific mind, giving her the ability to affect lives and future generations. Were brute force removed from the equation, there was little Kerick had to offer.

And yet, he realized as he came down to his knees and ran a hand over the proof of his ownership, his desire to be with her always could not be dampened. He wanted to leave a part of himself behind, something tangible Nellie could love and cherish, and each time she gazed upon it, she would know in her heart she was loved through infinity.

If Nellie was not yet with child, she would be before the dawn.

Spreading her buttocks wide apart, Kerick ran his tongue from her tight asshole down to her puffy pussy. She hissed, pressing her flesh into his mouth as best she could manage. He licked the lips, then ran his tongue down the length of her slit.

"Oh," Nellie breathed out, her back arching and eyes closing.

Taking her to the ground he laid down on his back, his face between her legs. Drawing her tiny, erect clit into his mouth, he growled appreciatively in the back of his throat as he suckled it.

"*Kerick — yes.*"

He sucked on the piece of flesh harder, making her gasp and moan.

"Yes...oh...*please.*"

Nellie began riding his face as though she were fucking him, groaning as she rubbed her hands all over her big jiggling tits. "Suck it harder," she breathed out, her eyes closed tightly in concentration. "Oh yes — *oh Kerick yes.*"

She rode his face faster, grinding her wet, sticky pussy against his mouth. He worked her flesh hard, slurping and sucking sounds filling the tent. Her stomach muscles clenched and knotted as she prepared to climax.

"Here I come," she gasped, her cat-green eyes opening as she rode his face faster and harder and — "*Oooohhhh!*"

She moaned long and loud as a violent orgasm ripped through her belly. "*Kerick — yes, Kerick.*" Blood rushed to her face, to her nipples and cunt. The climax seemed to go on and on and...

A long, thick cock sank into her soaked pussy, making her groan.

"You are Mine," Nellie heard her husband growl as his fingers dug into the flesh of her hips. "You will always be Mine."

"Yes," she breathed out, arching her hips as he began to stroke in and out of her. "Always."

He took her slowly, savoring every stroke. Over and over again Kerick sank his cock in her to the hilt, his breathing growing increasingly labored with each thrust. Nellie moaned in response, groaning louder when he palmed her breasts and began massaging her stiff nipples while he made slow love to her. It felt to her like the most exquisite torture.

"Fuck Your pussy faster," she breathed out. "*Please.*"

Kerick's nostrils flared. "That's a good girl, remembering *My* pussy belongs to Me."

She said nothing to that, but showed him instead. Rotating her hips, she threw her cunt back at him — hard — making him hiss.

Kerick's jaw steeled as he drove his cock in her to the hilt. "Mine," he said thickly, his fingers clamping down on her nipples. "Mine," he ground out as he picked up the pace and fucked her faster. Her moans made his erection impossibly stiffer. "Forever *Mine.*"

Perspiration soaked skin slapped against perspiration soaked skin. Nellie's pussy clamped around Kerick's cock in a series of small contractions, indicating she'd climaxed again. The sounds her flesh made as it sucked him back in, refusing to let go, made his teeth grit. He rode her cunt hard, possessively, slamming in and out of her in fast, deep strokes.

"Kerick," she groaned. *"Faster."*

He rode her cunt mercilessly, letting go of her nipples and digging his fingers into the flesh of her hips. He held her steady as he sank his cock into her, over and over, again and again. He growled as he fucked her, holding on as long as he could, wanting the moment to last forever.

Flesh slapped against flesh. The sound of her sticky pussy sucking him back in with every outstroke reached his ears.

"Kerick!"

His jaw clenched hotly as he pounded her pussy in fast, violent strokes. "I'm coming," he rasped, his eyes squeezing tightly shut, his teeth gritting. "I'm — *ah Nellie."*

He came on a roar, his entire body shuddering and convulsing. He continued to pound away inside of her as he spurted out the largest, fiercest orgasm he'd ever before had.

"Nellie," he said thickly, slowing down his thrusts. "Nellie…"

When it was over, when their breathing had calmed to an acceptable level and they were able to move again, they fell as one to the animal hides. Nellie turned over on her side and snuggled up against Kerick. They laid there in the dwindling hours before dawn, holding on to the other, never wishing to let go.

"I will always be Yours," Nellie whispered, pressing her face close against the beat of his heart. "And You will always be mine."

Kerick stilled. He'd never heard her say anything in the way of possessive to him before. Six simple words and tears began stinging the backs of his eyes. Tears he would never let fall.

It was all he had ever longed for — to love another with his entire being and be loved by her in return. A simple thing, perhaps, yet something that had eluded him the whole of his life. And now, when at long last he had seized his impossible dream, it could all end.

"Yes," Kerick murmured, pressing his lips against the top of her wine-red hair. "I will always be yours, Nellie Kan Riley." He closed his eyes. "Forever."

Chapter 47

"This is ridiculous!" Tara snapped. "Your left arm is broken and You've chained me to Your right. We'll be sub-human food for certain!"

Elijah frowned down at the decidedly short woman who thought to gainsay him — again. "Be grateful I have not forced that hideous body décor from your sly skin," he hissed. "I would prefer it, did My nipple chain show at all times."

Nellie hid a smile as she watched the newly wedded couple bicker back and forth. Or, more to the point, as the bride bickered and the groom all but ignored her.

Tara rolled her eyes. "Ah gods, as if the sub-humans care," she muttered. "You are testing my patience!" she snapped. Her nostrils flared. "Unchain me this moment before I turn here and now and eat You for dinner!"

That seemed to irritate him just a bit. "If you desire another spanking on the arse then by all means — "

"Enough," Kerick cut in, frowning. "By Cyrus I've never had the displeasure of hearing a more asinine argument." He turned his steel gaze to his mother. "I side with Elijah," he said, earning him a harrumph. "If he unchains you then kong only knows what trouble will be underfoot."

Tara's teeth gritted, but she said nothing.

Nellie glanced away, her gaze honing in on the tent where Kieran and Kora were to remain. Dr. Riley had decided Kora was too far gone, too close to turning, to accompany their party into the cavern. Nellie couldn't help but to agree with her husband's mother. She'd seen Kora's eyes shift one too many times for her peace of mind. If the serum was not within the cavern, she would be lost to their species within days.

"Those chains are hardly restrictive at all," Kerick growled, drawing Nellie's attention back to the argument he was having with his mother. "You are fortunate it is Elijah you answer to now for I would have gagged you an hour past."

"Mine own son. Sweet Kalast, I feel the love."

"Ah, that must be the same love I felt within the pit. Or the same love your husband felt while I was breaking his arm that we might be freed!" His nostrils flared. "I will hear no more. It is time to begin the trek up to the cavern."

"Ready your flash-stick," Dr. Reddy muttered to Nellie. "It doesn't look engaged."

Nellie winced. "So it isn't." She flashed a smile at the other scientist. "Thanks."

"Let us go," Xavier growled, walking off to scout for their party. "The sooner we end this, the better."

Nellie took a deep breath and exhaled slowly, her gaze scanning the foggy horizon. She agreed with Xavier—the sooner it was over with, the better for all involved. She could only pray Dr. Riley had been right.

She could only hope she was the key.

* * * * *

She was so damned tired. Naked, hungry, sore, and tired.

Nicoletta winced as she stepped on the edge of a jagged rock she'd failed to notice. She hissed as fire shot through her foot, the cut semi-deep.

The jungle was so foggy this morning it was difficult to anticipate much of anything. Realizing she needed to rest, she took to the first large boulder she happened across and plopped down.

It was hunting her.

She didn't know how she knew as much, yet she did. It wanted her back but it couldn't find her. Goosebumps formed on the flesh of her arms as she silently vowed to keep it that way.

Nellie, she reminded herself, exhaustion at war with desperation to reach her daughter. *I must carry on. I must find my bella Nellie…*

She allowed herself five minutes more of precious rest, then bodily forced herself up from the boulder. She was lost, she conceded, glancing around—terribly lost and had no clue which way she should go.

Nicoletta had fled from Altun Ha following a mother's intuition, yet even instinct could bring a woman but so far. "Please," she whispered to the winds. "Show me the way. Give me a sign. Give me any—"

Her breathing stilled as a faraway sound reached her ears, a sound that somehow felt foreign to the foggy jungle environment surrounding her. She didn't know that it would lead her to Nellie, but admitted to herself that anything was worth a try at this point.

"East," Nicoletta murmured, dragging herself toward the sound. "Due east."

* * * * *

It took them three hours and one lost life before they made their way through the narrow ledges and into the heart of sub-human breeding ground. A Xibalba scientist named Claris had lost her footing and, unable to regain it, fell to her death in the ravine below that was pitted with jagged rocks. Both Xavier and Kerick had tried to reach her in time; both men failed. Kerick would not soon forget the blood-curdling sound of the scientist's death scream or the look of horror on her face when she realized she was about to die.

Their party was down to six: Drs. Reddy and Riley, Elijah, Xavier, Nellie, and himself. The footing had gotten so tricky that Elijah had eventually relented and unchained his wife from his good arm. Kerick's mother was free now, though he noticed the rebel scientist never ventured far from her husband's side. Elijah had given her a choice and she had quietly made it. Now, in the final hour, she was committed for a lifetime to the man who had always loved her...however long or short that lifetime would turn out to be.

They made camp long enough to rest and to eat. There was a piece of the puzzle still missing and one he had let go of until this moment. But now that fate was upon them he needed to know. He wanted to understand. "Why?" Kerick asked softly, staring at his wife. "Why you?"

Nellie's eyes widened. She quickly glanced away, her lack of desire to answer him obvious.

Kerick sighed. He had realized something was bothering her. He had also rightly assumed the answer to this question would explain what that something was. "Tell Me," he murmured.

"It makes no difference," she whispered. She cleared her throat, dismissing the subject. "All that matters now is I have to go into that cavern." She shot up to her feet, her meal forgotten as her gaze lifted upward to the cavern in question. "They will wake up soon and they will be hungry. We best get this over with."

He watched her walk away and ready her weapons before he stood up and prepared to follow. He cocked his head, his eyes narrowing at his mother, his patience for being kept in the dark wearing thin. "Why?" he barked.

Tara sighed, her eyes so much like Kerick's staring unblinkingly at Nellie. "Because if I'm right the serum is within the heart of the sub-human infested cavern..." She blinked, then looked to her firstborn. "And if I am right twice, the creatures within that lair will not kill her."

Kerick stilled, his stomach muscles clenching. "What are you saying?" he murmured.

"I'm saying her blood runs through their veins. I'm saying that all species have a starting point." Her eyebrows rose. "All species have a Mother Eve."

Elijah looked as horrified as Kerick felt. "Are you saying she's infected?" he asked his wife.

"No." She shook her head slowly, her eyes lifting to meet first Elijah's and then finally Kerick's. "That child's own father allowed Hierarchy scientists to base their genetic experiments off her DNA. I'm certain of it."

"No," Kerick muttered, his blood chilling. He wanted to kill Abdul Kan with his bare hands. He wanted to strangle the life right out of him, and what's more, he'd enjoy every moment of it. "This is unbelievable."

"How can you know this?" Elijah countered, asking the question Kerick had been too dumbstruck to put to her. "That can only be conjecture—"

"No." Tara firmly shook her head. "I have spent the last fifteen years studying sub-humans and comparing them to non-infected individuals. I know of what I speak!"

"But how can you know with all certainty?"

"Eli," she sighed, "You know as well as I there is no such thing as certainty. But when the facts all point heavily in one direction..."

"What facts?" Kerick inquired. Nellie was right—dusk would be upon them in a few short hours and with it the creatures would begin to stir. They needed to get in, retrieve the serum, and be well away from this place before nighttime descended. If they were to do this thing, it needed to be now, yet he would not permit his wife to enter that cavern without probable justification. "Tell me and hurry."

"All infected humans share a similar genetic breakdown," she said quickly. "It's difficult to explain without tutoring you in the sciences, however, suffice it to say they carry a DNA pattern no Xibalba scientist has ever found within the blood of *any* non-infected human."

"Until Nellie?" Kerick muttered.

Tara nodded. "Until Nellie," she whispered.

His eyes briefly closed as he pinched the bridge of his nose. "I see," he sighed.

Kerick's head came up and his gaze found Nellie's. She was a few feet away standing with Xavier and Patricia Reddy, but he could see it in her eyes...she knew that he now knew the truth too. He also understood why she felt the burden of the entire species rested on her narrow shoulders even if he didn't agree with her. He hadn't thought it was possible for him to love her more. He had been wrong.

She looked vulnerable, as though she was worried that somehow he would fault her for the wrong that had been done by her sire. His gaze gentled, telling her without words of his love for her. She visibly relaxed, even offered him a small smile, before returning to the work of readying her weaponry.

"My son," Tara said gently, placing her hand over his heart. "I would not be here were I not certain. She will be fine. And we will win."

He frowned. "We cannot know that. I—"

"Yes we can," she cut in. "I tested my theory in the lab on a hungry sub-human female." She sighed at his frown. "We would have sizzled her had she gotten overly close to your wife."

Kerick grunted. "And?"

"The barrier between the female and Nellie was removed, the female readied herself to pounce..." She shook her head. "She retreated. I damn near fell to my knees in gratitude to Cyrus to see my supposition affirmed, but, yes, she retreated."

Kerick blew out a breath. This was so much to take in, yet he didn't have the time to ponder it. He was quiet for a moment and then, "Let us go," he murmured to his mother and Elijah. "We've a lot of work left to us and not much time to finish it in."

Chapter 48

And I looked, and behold a pale horse: and his name that sat on him was Death, and Hell followed with him. And power was given unto them over the fourth part of the earth, to kill with sword, and with hunger, and with death...

And with the beasts of the earth.

* * * * *

In sharp contrast to the humid, foggy jungle outside, the cavern was chilly, almost cold. Nellie shivered, grateful for the camouflaged body décor that offered at least minimal protection from the elements. She trained her gaze on the cavern wall as it curled eastward and forced them to turn. Her senses stayed on high alert, her ears scanning for sounds.

"Their sleep is deep," Tara murmured, her acute senses picking up much more information than the others were capable of. "We've still got a couple of hours left to us, but only a couple of hours. Patricia," she whispered to her friend, "are you registering any activity on your tracking device?"

"No," Dr. Reddy murmured back, careful to keep her voice to a hush. "The readings are showing the same thing you are sensing. They sleep...deeply."

Nellie released a pent-up breath. "Why haven't we run across any sleeping sub-humans yet? We've been inside close to ten minutes and we haven't seen anything."

"They congregate in the darkest, coldest part of the cavern's belly," Tara whispered back. "It's always the way of it."

Nellie nodded, but said nothing. This was the most intense and tense moment of her entire life and her body was reacting accordingly. Beads of perspiration dotted her forehead. Her heartbeat was rapid, but thankfully not so bad that it pounded in her ears. She followed quietly behind the elder scientists, her flash-stick trained and prepared for detonation at a moment's notice.

"We're here," Tara said quietly, coming to a halt and turning to face the group. She took a deep breath and blew it out. "Chances are the belly is through there," she said, pointing over her shoulder without looking back. "I haven't turned, so I'm as likely to be made a meal of as the rest of you. Well, save Nellie," she reminded the group.

"It's time to switch to infrared," Dr. Reddy announced. "Put on your goggles and let's do it."

"Wait!" Tara said quickly, though quietly. "Eli, how's the armor holding up?" She had earlier covered her husband's left, defenseless side with spiked armor so if he was attacked from that angle, the sub-human would be impaled. "It guards You well?"

"You made it so you know it does," he affirmed, amusement in his eyes. "You're the most efficient killer I've ever known, in Kong or out of it."

She blushed. "Why thank You," she muttered, patting the bun at her neck into place.

Kerick rolled his eyes. "Woo my mother later. We need to move and we need to move now."

Nellie's heart slammed against her chest. She took a deep, calming breath before putting her goggles on. The last thing she needed was for her ears to be ringing with too much adrenaline. It would dull her hearing and, if Tara was wrong about her being the key, such a situation would make her easy pickings should any of the creatures unexpectedly awake.

But that sub-human in the lab, she reminded herself, had not harmed her. It had not even *tried* to harm her. Which meant one of two things: she was the key or the experiment had been a fluke.

The horrible thing about destiny, Nellie thought as she switched to infrared, is you never know what it will be until it's too late, until it's already happened. One thing was certain: no matter what happened in the belly of the cavern, it would change all of their lives.

Forever.

* * * * *

Nellie worked on steadying her breathing as their party quietly meandered past yet another sleeping sub-human. Their breathing was very heavy, very noticeable. They dragged as much air into their lungs as possible and exhaled just as deeply.

Already they had come into contact with at least twenty-five of the things. It didn't bear dwelling upon what sort of Armageddon would occur did these creatures awake. Their group might have been armed to the teeth, but they could only shoot one to two predators at a time.

A bloodbath. If these things began to stir, the only image that came to mind was that of a bloodbath.

The sub-humans slept within body-sized grooves that had been dug into the cavern walls by them. Nellie was grateful for that because it made inching past them a bit easier. She only wished it made the ordeal less terrifying too.

"There it is," Tara breathed out, coming to a halt. Her eyes were round, hopeful. "The inner lair." She turned to Nellie. "The rest of us need to remain out here where we at least stand a chance. Odds are the inner sanctuary is infested with dozens of the creatures."

Nellie closed her eyes briefly as she took a breath deep enough to rival that of a sleeping predator. "Okay," she whispered. Sweet Kalast, but she needed a drink. Or ten. "I'm ready."

"I'm going with you," Kerick murmured, inducing Nellie's breathing to still. "The rest of you can remain out here."

Her eyes widened from behind the goggles. "But—"

"I will go all the way in with you," he firmly reiterated. "*All* the way." His jaw tensed. "We live together or we die together."

There would be no swaying him, Nellie realized. And what's more, this was hardly the time or place conducive to a loud argument. She relented with a nod, albeit a hesitant one. Besides, she understood precisely how he felt. She didn't want left behind either.

Should death claim Kerick, Nellie would follow.

* * * * *

The sounds had come from the east, yet now they were no more. Nicoletta came to a halt near the steep cliff and glanced around, uncertain which way she should go. She turned around and glanced over to the cavern carved into the earth, the big, ominous thing jutting upwards and making the hairs on the nape of her neck stand on end for reasons she could not name.

Someone was in there. Some*one* or some*thing*.

She swallowed heavily, her instincts screaming for her to retreat. She quickly glanced around, noting for the first time a very narrow ledge that wound down the side of the mountain. It would be tricky, but it was doable.

A sound reached her ears. That of a growl. A very possessive and all too familiar warning growl. Her heart pounded against her breasts, ringing in her ears. She was afraid to turn back around and look at it. She was afraid, yet conversely, she knew that she must.

"Please do not hurt me," Nicoletta whispered, her breathing catching as she slowly turned on her heel to face him. Her eyes widened when she saw the man-beast. Ah gods, it was the same one. She would recognize him anywhere. How could she not when it had mated with her for two straight days? "I'm sorry I ran," she lied, her eyes wild with fear. "Please do not hurt me," she breathed out.

His territorial snarl was perhaps the most frightening reaction imaginable. She knew it would drag her back to its den now and Cyrus only knew if she'd ever again escape it again. It would mate her until she died.

Unless she forced it to kill her first.

The creature began moving towards her, its powerful gray-skinned body stalking her. She shivered as she backed up a step, wondering how merciless their next mating would be if she didn't find a way to escape it.

Then it was there, standing before her, looking as mighty and ferocious as a conquering god. She closed her eyes as its vampire-like fingernails inched their way down her breasts. The warning growl issued low in his throat told her she better not even dare to run from him. *Ah gods – think! Think!* And then…

Nothing.

Nicoletta's forehead wrinkled as the man-beast's hands retreated. Her eyes flew open.

It was…

Listening.

Her breathing grew heavy as she watched the beast stand there, its gaze trained on the cavern. It was so focused on whatever it was it saw or heard – or both – that it was as if Nicoletta no longer existed.

And then it was gone. Nicoletta blinked. As quickly as it had found her, it departed, surging into the cavern at top speed.

She couldn't seem to move, only to stare. There was something about that man-beast, something hauntingly familiar…

Snapping out of the daze that had ensorcelled her, she told herself it didn't matter. Turning on her heel, her heart still pounding in her chest, Nicoletta quickly made her way toward the ledge.

* * * * *

Sweet Kalast, Nellie thought, trying not to lose her wits. When Tara had predicted the inner sanctuary would be infested with sub-humans, she couldn't have possibly known just how on the mark her words would turn out to be.

Sleeping, predatorial bodies were *everywhere*. Groove after groove after groove of infected creatures lined the walls of the inner chamber like vampires without coffins. If these things woke up…

She gulped. It didn't bear dwelling upon.

"I always thought sub-humans could operate in the daylight," Nellie whispered, her eyes searching for she didn't know what — anything that appeared unusual.

"They can," Kerick confirmed. "They tend to reserve their slumber for daylight hours rather than the eves as humans do, but they have no trouble at all carrying on in daylight."

Nellie stilled. That wasn't what she'd wanted to hear.

"Be calm," Kerick murmured. "Their sleep is so deep, so drugging, it resembles a hibernating creature."

She blew out a breath. "Right."

"Look," Kerick whispered into the whorl of her ear. "Up that incline."

Nellie did as he'd bade, her eyes covered with goggles that permitted her to see in the dark, honing in on the structure that must have caught his attention. There it was, she thought, her heartbeat accelerating. A crate — a small, singular crate crafted from a black diamond structure.

If indeed a serum had been housed here, the Hierarchy mistakenly thinking they could retrieve it at a later date should the need arise, it had to be in that weathered crate situated up the incline. It *had* to be. It was the only man-made creation in the whole of the cavern.

"I'm scared," Nellie breathed out.

Kerick squeezed her hand. "Just take it slow and steady like we've been doing. If we find no serum in that crate we are leaving here without one."

Nellie nodded, agreeing. If there was no serum in that crate, it didn't exist. The odds of it being anywhere else and having remained intact throughout the years without protection from the elements by the black diamond exterior was so minimal as to not be worth the effort of continuing the search.

They began ascending the incline, making their way toward the black diamond crate inch by slow inch. The climb felt as though it was taking hours since they were being cognizant to go slowly and remain quiet. They crept past groove after groove filled with sleeping sub-humans, creatures that when awake were more powerful than any human could ever hope to be.

Don't wake up, Nellie silently willed them. The sweat of stark fear soaked her hairline. *Please don't wake up…*

Nellie scanned the area visually, noting their location. When they reached the apex she could clearly register with the infrared goggles that the right side of the incline dropped off into nothingness. It could be a hundred foot drop or only ten. There was no way to tell. The goggles were not so powerful as to be able to see that far down.

"There is but one sub-human nest up here," Kerick muttered. "Look to the upper left of the crate."

Nellie's eyes widened. Yes, there was only one nest. Unfortunately, unlike the other grooves which contained one body apiece, the large groove dug out directly above and to the left of the crate contained five sub-humans—a sleeping female and two males slumbering at either of her sides.

Her scientific mind began to hypothesize. "She must be the Queen," Nellie murmured. "The alpha female."

"That would be a good guess."

Nellie stilled. She knew—*knew*—this Queen would present the greatest danger to her should she awaken. Unlike with the other sub-humans, the fact Nellie carried the alpha female's scent, or shared DNA with her, would only make the female want to kill Nellie more, not less. In the animal kingdom, there could be but one ruler. Even amongst bees, when two Queens are born, they fight to the death over who will rule and who will die.

No, this Queen would not take to her scent well at all. The female could only continue her role as Mother Eve if she disposed of the original one.

"We're almost there," Kerick said in a reassuring whisper as if he'd guessed her thoughts. "Stay steady and keep moving."

She just wanted it over and done with. This was like a nightmare from which there was no awakening. The only way to end it was to leave this place before the creatures began to stir. And sweet Kalast they would all be hungry when they woke up.

Finally—*finally*—they arrived at the crate. Nellie kept her gaze trained on the Queen, her heart drumming like mad, while Kerick fiddled with the black diamond lid, prying it open. The lock had long since popped, but the top was no longer a perfect fit to the bottom.

Someone or something had damaged it, the result being it was difficult to open.

"I don't believe it," Kerick muttered.

"What?" Nellie asked quickly. If her heart beat any faster it would beat right out of her chest, she decided. "What is it?" she breathed out.

"She was right," he murmured. The pride she could hear in her husband's voice was unmistakable. He picked up something—a vial?—out of the black diamond shell then turned to Nellie with a semi-smile. "My mother was right."

Her eyes widened. It *was* a vial. A black vial made of tough Kalastian diamonds. Sweet Cyrus, they'd found it! They'd really found it! Elation overwhelmed her. She offered Kerick a small smile before insisting they get out of there—now.

He pocketed the serum then nodded. "Let's go," he whispered, raising the flash-stick he carried. "I know the need to run is overwhelming, but go slow and steady down same as we came up."

"Yes," she agreed on a whisper. "I think that—"

Nellie gasped, her expression shocked, as the alpha female struck at Kerick without warning. One second he had been standing there next to her and the next he had been picked up and bodily flung against a wall.

Oh Cyrus, He isn't moving! He isn't moving! No! No! No!

She had thought the Queen was sleeping—she had been wrong. The alpha female had been but preparing…

Nellie raised her flash-stick. The female batted it out of her hand with a blood-curdling growl.

"Shit," Nellie muttered, her heart pounding in her ears as she began backing away. The other creatures still slept, their breathing heavy. It came down to Nellie and the alpha female—two Mother Eves and the physically weaker one was weaponless.

It was Nellie the Queen wanted. Kerick mattered nothing to her. She had flung him against the sanctuary wall merely to get him out of her way.

The female crouched down low on her thighs, her sickly snarl revealing razor-sharp, serrated teeth. She was preparing to pounce, Nellie thought, terrified. *Help me! Help me!*

The Queen made her move, lunging toward Nellie with a powerful jump. It was all over, Nellie realized, the look of horror on her face surely to be the one she wore to her death. *Ah Cyrus—*

The Queen cried out with a howl, the sound jarring. Nellie blinked, the fact the alpha female had been attacked slowly registering.

She felt numb. Too shocked to move. What was happening? *What was happening!*

And then she saw it—two sub-humans fighting to the death. But the opposing creature was not another Queen...it was a male.

The male and female lunged at each other, chilling growls filling the inner sanctuary. The female reached for the male's heart as they wrestled for control, apparently trying to pull it from his chest still beating. The male roared and backhanded her, sending the Queen sailing near to the ledge. He was on her again within seconds and this time it was the male reaching for the female's heart.

Nellie could scarcely think, let alone move. She felt frozen in place, the numbing words "this isn't happening" pounding in her head like a deafening song. It wasn't until she heard a third growl that she snapped out of it and whirled around.

Ah Cyrus not another one! One of the Queen's males had awoken and it was Nellie he was eyeing. Did her scent not matter to it? she hysterically wondered. Was she too far away for him to pick it up? Perhaps it would not realize what she was until after the deathblow. The only thing it understood at this moment was its Queen was being attacked and she was standing there.

It growled low in its throat as it prepared to spring, the horrific serrated teeth clearly visible. The male lunged low on its thighs, its gaze snagging hers, as it let loose and whipped up into the air with a roar.

It was sizzled in mid-air.

Kerick.

Yes! Yes! Yes! Yes!

Nellie ran to him, her heart slamming against her chest. "You are alive!" she exclaimed, the words ripped from her throat with a guttural sound. She had thought the impact had broken his spine but it hadn't. She quickly looked him over, ascertaining that he was injured but would be okay. He looked to have suffered only minor abrasions.

His gaze, still a bit foggy from the knock to the head he'd taken, flicked over to where the two sub-humans still fought. The male had wrested control and was preparing to deal the Queen a deathblow. "Let's go, Nellie," he panted as he forced himself up to his feet. "This flash-stick is out of juice and the winner will turn on us in a moment's notice."

The situation reversed itself and now it was the alpha female on top once again. The two ultra-powerful bodies clashed over and over, first one seizing control and then the other. Their roars were numbing, their fight merciless. Winner takes all and the loser dies.

Nellie took a step closer, fascinated, ignoring Kerick's order to step back. There was nothing in science to explain this. There was no reason for the male to turn on his Queen.

And then the man-beast looked at her, at Nellie. Their gazes locked. His eyes shifted for one brief moment, the only evidence of what the male had once been there between them. It lasted for only the blink of an eye, then his gaze shifted back. Incredibly, unpredictably, and defying all scientific explanation, the male picked up the female, his gaze still locked on Nellie, and threw both himself and the Queen over the ledge, plummeting with a roar toward certain death.

She gasped.

"Holy gods," Kerick murmured, taking the words she was too shocked to speak out of her mouth. He gathered himself together quickly. "Let's go," he barked. "Now." He shook her. "Nellie!" he said forcefully, snapping her back to reality. "Do you hear Me?" His gaze was gentle but forceful. "Come back to Me. We must leave this place — *now.*"

"Yes," she breathed out, still stunned but thinking rationally again. "Yes, let's go."

Chapter 49

They had the vial and they'd managed to get away from the cavern a good thirty minutes before darkness began to descend. It was over. They had won. Nellie could hardly credit it. Tara had been right—about everything.

The journey back to the camp was a quiet, reflective one. Nellie and Kerick walked hand-in-hand in silence, both of them realizing now was not the time to reflect on the odd events that had transpired within the Queen's lair. There would be plenty of time for that after returning to the Xibalba, a female safe-haven that now boasted four male residents.

Nellie stilled, causing Kerick to halt beside her and look quizzically down at her. Her gaze was zeroed in on a naked woman resting on a boulder. The wench was cut, her feet looking slightly injured, but she was okay. Nellie's heart soared, a laugh of happiness escaping from her. She let go of her husband's hand and ran to the woman as fast as her feet would carry her.

The last person on Federated Earth Nellie had expected to see after crossing the ledge was her stepmother. She screamed out her name to get her attention, her legs moving quickly, her arms outstretched. Nicoletta gasped when recognition dawned. She shot up off of the boulder and wobbled towards Nellie.

Their bodies clashed. Nellie hugged Nicoletta tightly while tears of happiness burned the backs of her eyes. "What are you doing here? How did you ever find me?" she choked out, half crying and half laughing.

"A mother's intuition," Nicoletta answered, hugging the child of her heart just as firmly. "I feared that you needed me." She chuckled, her warm brown eyes filled with tears. "I should have known better."

Nellie pulled back far enough to meet her gaze. "I'll always need you. Always."

Nicoletta smiled.

Later, when they were alone together within the safety of the Xibalba, Nellie went to her stepmother's chamber and told her about what had happened in the cavern. Nicoletta's eyes had gone wide when she'd spoken to her of the man-beast, an emotion Nellie couldn't name in their brown, haunted-looking depths.

"It is dead then?" Nicoletta whispered, looking away.

"Yes." Nellie's forehead wrinkled. "Nica, are you well?"

"Of course," she said quickly, a smile that somehow seemed forced coming to her lips. She hugged Nellie again before insisting she leave her chamber and go spend time with her husband. "I'll see you on the morrow."

Nellie eyed her curiously before giving in. She inclined her head. "On the morrow, then. And Nica?"

Nicoletta's head snapped up. "Yes?"

Nellie smiled. "I love you," she murmured.

Nicoletta smiled back. "I love you too, my bella."

* * * * *

"I never thought we'd be alone," Nellie said on a grin as her husband undressed her and admired his nipple chain. "The Xibalbians certainly throw a long party."

He grunted. "I was glad to be gone from it," he growled, pushing her down onto the pillow-bed and settling himself between her thighs. "I'm of the mind to perform various wicked sexual acts upon My wife's body."

She giggled. Lucky her, she decided.

Nellie's teasing mood turned serious as soon as Kerick sank his cock inside of her. "Thank You," she whispered.

He stilled. "For what?" he asked, looking down at her.

"For loving me enough to go in that sanctuary with me. I never would have made it out alive without You."

He kissed the tip of her nose. "Save your thanks for the man-beast."

"I'm serious," she said, her gaze finding his. She was thanking him for more than a single act and they both knew it. She was thanking him for everything, but most especially for a love that she didn't doubt would endure and grow deeper over the coming years. She would never fear abandonment at this man's hands. He loved her and she could trust in that love. It was more than she could have ever hoped for.

Her smile was warm as her eyes searched his. "Thank You," Nellie whispered again.

"You are welcome." He smiled. "And thank you, too."

Words were no longer necessary so their bodies took over from there. Kerick Riley, the Grim Reaper, made slow love to his wife, his cock sinking into her welcoming flesh over and over, again and again.

And when it was over, Nellie Kan Riley, once his captive and now his wife, clung to her beloved Kerick as he had prayed she one day would.

Epilogue
A sennight later

AND THE GREAT DRAGON WAS CAST OUT, THAT OLD SERPENT, CALLED THE DEVIL, AND SATAN, WHICH DECEIVETH THE WHOLE WORLD: HE WAS CAST OUT INTO THE EARTH, AND HIS ANGELS WERE CAST OUT WITH HIM.

* * * * *

It was over. For now.

They had collected the serum and escaped with their lives — barely, but they'd done it. Unfortunately, the Xibalba scientists had quickly discovered that the antidote had its limits. It could kill the infection within a human that had not yet succumbed to disease, but it could not regress the disease in sub-humans. At least for now, that part of humanity was still lost to them. Tara was cured, as was Kora. For now they would celebrate that as the victory it was.

Nellie, Tara, and Patricia would continue their work with the serum in the hopes of being able to find a cure to make regression a reality. Kerick and Elijah would continue their work, too, formulating and eventually executing plans to end the Hierarchy's stronghold over Federated Earth. It would take years before they could amass a strong army, but they would do it. And as it turned out, they would do it without Xavier.

"You'll see me again, old friend," Xavier murmured to Kerick who was escorting him as far as the Crossroads. His wink was jovial, but masking a great deal of pain. "You have found your place in this world, you have found your destiny in Nellie. Now I need to figure out what mine is."

Kerick couldn't pretend he didn't understand. Xavier had lived most of his life as an Outlaw and the rest of it as a death row slave laborer in Kong. Nothing could erase the horror of those years, but maybe, just maybe, something or someone out there could make it all seem worthwhile. "I hope you find whatever it is you seek, amigo." He came to a halt as the Underground Crossroads came within sight. "And I hope one day you return to us."

Xavier held his stare. "I make no promises," he said truthfully. At Kerick's nod, he qualified that statement a bit. "The only vow I make is that if you need me, I will find you."

Kerick sighed, sadness at watching his lifelong friend walk away mingled with hope that Xavier would find his happy ending. "I guess this is it." He grunted. "If you get yourself killed I'll dig up your bones and kill you twice."

Xavier snorted at that.

Kerick smiled. "Be safe, old friend," he murmured.

They embraced in that awkward way men do. In all of the years they had known each other, it was the first outward gesture of affection they'd ever shown.

Kerick pulled back and watched Xavier walk away. When his comrade veered left at a corner and disappeared, he turned on his heel and went back to the Xibalba and to Nellie…

He went back to his life.

* * * * *

Nellie awoke in the middle of the night, Kerick's body draped over hers. She briefly closed her eyes and sighed with deep contentment, deciding then and there never to spend another eve apart from her husband. Not that he'd permit her to, she conceded as her eyes flicked open. She'd be surprised if Kerick Riley ever let her venture further than three feet away from him again. If she didn't love him so much, Nellie mused on a small smile, she'd no doubt find him exasperating in the extreme to deal with.

She shifted slightly on the pillow-bed where they lay. He reacted as though he could sense she was awake. His arm tightened in a possessive manner around her, making sure even in his slumber that she didn't leave him. She turned her neck that she might kiss him on the forehead. "I'll never leave You," she murmured. "Sleep well, my beloved."

Snuggling in closer to Kerick's warmth, her back to his front, Nellie's mind began to drift toward the eve she had almost been erased from existence. And, inevitably, to the sub-human male who had, for reasons she would never comprehend, died that she might live.

There had been something about him, that creature. Something almost…familiar. Something about his haunting eyes and the way they had shifted just before death claimed him.

His eyes, she thought, her forehead crinkling as she concentrated on the memory. They had been crimson-red just like every other sub-human's, but for one brief flicker in time they had been—

"Green," she whispered, her heartbeat accelerating. Her eyes widened. "Green," she breathed out.

And not just any green. A familiar green. The eyes of a jungle cat, eyes that made her feel as though she was staring at her own gaze in an image map.

"No," she rasped out, jolting upright into a sitting position on the pillow-bed. Her breathing grew increasingly labored, blood pounding in her ears, as she came to terms with the grave possibility that—

No.

"Nellie," Kerick said sleepily, sitting upright next to her on the pillow-bed. He ran a soothing, callused hand down the silk of her back. "Nellie, what is it?"

Her thoughts were so far away and in so much turmoil she hadn't felt her husband's touch nor heard his voice. Had her father, the man whom she had always loved, but whom she had thought didn't return that love...

Had he died to save her life?

"Oh no," she choked out, tears welling in her eyes.

"Nellie," Kerick said, more forcefully this time. "Speak to Me."

She turned to look at her husband, tears now flowing freely down her cheeks. What could she say to him? How could she make him understand? She herself did not understand.

Abdul Kan had never showed a care for his daughter. Every overture of love on Nellie's behalf had been scorned, shunned, and rebuffed. But when all was said and done, when the Hierarchy's most powerful male could have walked away unscathed and continued about his business with none the wiser...

On a cold, dreary night, in the deepest recesses of a lonely, haunting jungle, a father committed the ultimate sacrifice and gave up his life that his daughter might live.

Cyrus had answered her prayers. Too late.

"Please just hold me," Nellie gasped as Kerick's arms came around her. "Never let me go."

"I won't," Kerick murmured, his grasp tightening. "We'll be together always."

* * * * *

She knew that she must leave this place. Nellie and Kerick deserved time alone together. And Nicoletta, well, she deserved time to herself too. Time to think and time to heal.

She had always wanted to see Kalast and so to planet Kalast she would go. Kora had already booked her tickets under a false name and all was ready. Nicoletta felt guilty leaving without telling her daughter, but she knew Nellie would only try to talk her into staying when she realized she needed to leave. At least for now. At least until she figured some things out.

Perversely, inevitably, her thoughts strayed to her husband. She wondered if Abdul missed her at all, then chastised herself for even caring. Would he look for her? she wondered. Did he want her back? Her teeth gritted, knowing as she did that the answers simply didn't matter.

All the yen in Federated Earth could not entice her into returning to the harem. She deserved to be mastered by a man who would take no wench to wife but her. She wore Abdul's brand, but she was pretty enough that other males would overlook it to have her. But did she want another man? She sighed. She just didn't know.

Her beloved Sinead had once said to her that destiny can never be defeated. You can battle, you can rage against it, but in the end it always wins.

But what, Nicoletta asked herself as she gathered together a few meager possessions and prepared to exit the chamber, what *was* her destiny? Throwing open the doors and breathing in deeply, she closed her eyes and dragged in a long, cathartic breath.

Her brown, searching eyes slowly opened. Somewhere out there was Nicoletta's destiny.

She would find it.

* * * * *

Nicoletta's story:
"Death Row: The Mastering"
In the anthology *Enchained*
ISBN # 1-84360-522-8

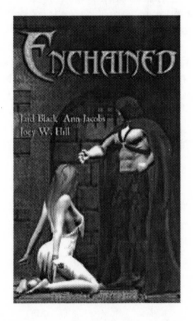

An erotic bondage romance anthology
By Jaid Black, Ann Jacobs, & Joey W. Hill

Xavier's story:

Death Row: The Conqueror

COMING IN 2005

About the author:

Critically acclaimed and highly prolific, Jaid Black is the best-selling author of numerous erotic romance and erotic suspense tales. Her first full-length title, *The Empress' New Clothes*, was recognized as a readers' favorite in women's erotica by Romantic Times magazine. A full-time writer, Jaid lives in a cozy little village in the northeastern United States with her two children. In her spare time, she enjoys traveling, horseback riding, and furthering her collection of African and Egyptian art.

She welcomes mail from readers. You can write to her at P.O. Box 362, Munroe Falls, OH 44262.

Why an electronic book?

We live in the Information Age—an exciting time in the history of human civilization in which technology rules supreme and continues to progress in leaps and bounds every minute of every hour of every day. For a multitude of reasons, more and more avid literary fans are opting to purchase e-books instead of paperbacks. The question to those not yet initiated to the world of electronic reading is simply: why?

1. *Price.* An electronic title at Ellora's Cave Publishing runs anywhere from 40-75% less than the cover price of the <u>exact same title</u> in paperback format. Why? Cold mathematics. It is less expensive to publish an e-book than it is to publish a paperback, so the savings are passed along to the consumer.

2. *Space.* Running out of room to house your paperback books? That is one worry you will never have with electronic novels. For a low one-time cost, you can purchase a handheld computer designed specifically for e-reading purposes. Many e-readers are larger than the average handheld, giving you plenty of screen room. Better yet, hundreds of titles can be stored within your new library—a single microchip. (Please note that EC does not endorse any specific brands. You can check our website for customer recommendations we make available to new consumers.)

3. *Mobility.* Because your new library now consists of only a microchip, your entire cache of books can be taken with you wherever you go.

4. *Personal preferences are accounted for.* Are the words you are currently reading too small? Too large? Too...**ANNOYING**? Paperback books cannot be modified according to personal preferences, but e-books can.
5. *Innovation.* The way you read a book is not the only advancement the Information Age has gifted the literary community with. There is also the factor of what you can read. Ellora's Cave Publishing will be introducing a new line of interactive titles that are available in e-book format only.
6. *Instant gratification.* Is it the middle of the night and all the bookstores are closed? Are you tired of waiting days — sometimes weeks — for online and offline bookstores to ship the novels you bought? Ellora's Cave Publishing sells instantaneous downloads 24 hours a day, 7 days a week, 365 days a year. Our e-book delivery system is 100% automated, meaning your order is filled as soon as you pay for it.

Those are a few of the top reasons why electronic novels are displacing paperbacks for many an avid reader. As always, Ellora's Cave Publishing welcomes your questions and comments. We invite you to email us at service@ellorascave.com or write to us directly at 1337 Commerce Dr. #13, Stow, OH 44224.

Welcome to the Information Age!

Printed in the United States
58596LVS00001B/64-99